One Lie

For Mum and Dad.

About the author

JON RANCE writes novels about love, family, relationship, and all the messy bits in-between. His novels have been described as hilarious, romantic, heart-warming, and perfect for fans of *Mike Gayle* and *Beth O'Leary*. His first book *This Thirtysomething Life* was a self-published Amazon top-ten bestseller and subsequently published by Hodder and Stoughton. Since then, he has written numerous novels including, *Sunday Dinners*, *About Us*, *Dan And Nat Got Married*, and *The Notecard*.

Jon grew up in England and studied English Literature at Middlesex University, London, before travelling the world and meeting his American wife in Australia. He now lives in California with his wife, two kids, and a dog called Pickle, where he writes full-time and drinks far too much tea.

Also by Jon Rance

This Thirtysomething Life
Happy Endings
This Family Life
A Notting Hill Christmas
Sunday Dinners
Dan And Nat Got Married
About Us
The Summer Holidays Survival Guide
Good Grief
The Notecard

All it took to destroy their lives was … one lie

Alexander Burke opened his car door and got in. The sky was overcast with leaden clouds and spots of rain had begun to fall. He closed the door and then put his satchel on the seat next to him. He put the keys in the ignition, turned the car on, and sat there for a moment. A horrible sickness sat in his stomach. He felt the weight of history on his shoulders. He put his hands on the wheel and felt his grip tighten immediately. Nervousness. Tension. This was it. Home or Sara's flat? The decision. Perhaps the biggest decision of his life. He pulled the sun visor down and looked at himself in the little mirror. Could he really cheat on the woman he loved so much? It seemed impossible, but that was the plan. It's all he had thought about for the past few weeks. Every waking second and she had been on his mind. Sara Coupland. That body. The things she would do. Alexander wasn't the sort to cheat, but how could he turn her down?

He checked his mirrors, lifted the handbrake, and started to drive. He backed out of his parking spot, drove out of school, and onto the main road. There were still lots of pupils milling around, and cars parked on both sides of the street. He used the wipers to wipe away the rain that had covered his windscreen in a thin layer, and then he was off. In about half-a-mile was the turning. Left to home or right to Sara's flat. A literal fork in the road. Two pathways that might define the rest of his life, or perhaps not. It was only one night. Not even a night. Maybe an hour or two. And then he could move on. Get back to normal. Be his old self again. Olivia would never find out. He drove. The decision was getting closer and closer.

Part One

1.

The past

Alexander Burke loved having dinner with his family. It was his favourite time of the day. Alexander was forty-three-years old and lived in a four-bedroom Edwardian house in Richmond with his wife, Olivia, and his sixteen-year-old daughter, Laura. Today Olivia had made spaghetti Bolognese with garlic bread and a salad. It was one of his favourite meals. As always, Alexander was sitting next to his wife, and his daughter was opposite. Laura was his pride and joy. At sixteen, she was in her last year of secondary school and then it was off to sixth form to do her A levels. After that it was hopefully Oxford university. That was Alexander's dream for her. The dream that hadn't quite happened for him. Laura was going to be the first Oxbridge Burke. She spoke with such steadfast certainty about studying law and becoming a barrister, it was hard to believe it wouldn't happen.

'Could you pass the pepper?' Alexander said to his daughter.

She passed it over, and Alexander took the big wooden pepper grinder and ground pepper all over his spaghetti. Black flakes like ash dropped onto the bright red of the tomato sauce. Alexander and Olivia had a glass of wine each. Laura had orange juice.

They were in the dining room at the back of the house. They had extended into the garden a few years ago, adding a gourmet kitchen with an attached dining room, and bi-fold doors that opened up the entire back of the house to the large garden beyond. Alexander loved that room, especially when the sun shone like a giant torch, illuminating them with its warmth. Alexander and Olivia had spent an age choosing the Victorian floor tiles, the kitchen countertop, and the new appliances. It had cost a fortune, but it had been worth it. It had transformed their house and made Alexander happy. He always had visions and aspirations of things he wanted to achieve, and a perfect house was on that list. Next he wanted to renovate the family bathroom. He wanted to give it a complete makeover within the next year. He wanted Laura to enjoy it before she went off to university because there was always the possibility that she might not come back again. A dreadfully painful thought, but it was possible.

'How was your day?' Alexander said to Laura.

'Fine, yeah, the usual,' said Laura casually. She gave her father a token smile before she expertly twisted spaghetti onto her fork.

She was too engaged in thoughts of Tom Chance. Tom was Laura's secret boyfriend. Her parents didn't want her to have a boyfriend yet. The next year was 'too important', and she wasn't going to 'mess up her life for a boy'. She was about to sit her GCSE's and then it was the start of her A levels, and if she did as well as hoped, she might squeeze into Oxford. Laura wanted to go to Oxford more than anything. It was her dream. She loved the idea of it at least, but she could still have a boyfriend and do that. She didn't see them as mutually exclusive.

'I heard there was an issue in English today?' said Alexander.

Alexander taught history at Laura's school. Alexander loved history. It was etched deep within his soul. He lived for history and loved his job because it meant he got to impart some of his knowledge into the spongy minds of his pupils. He had long ago dreamt of teaching at university, and perhaps publishing a history book, but he had settled into secondary education. It was fine and he still got to submerge himself in the subject he loved so much.

'Oh, it was nothing. Stupid boys.'

'I heard they were being disrespectful to Miss Coupland,' said Alexander.

'A bit, yeah. I wasn't involved.'

'I didn't think you were,' said Alexander with a warm, proud smile.

Olivia glanced at her husband. At his face and the deep darkness of his eyes. She had loved his eyes when they met. He was a handsome man then. He still was, and his Scottish accent made him even sexier to her. They were students then. Now he had a thin layer of stubble on his face, and his dark hair was shorter than it was. She knew, had always known, she had married a handsome man. She looked at him and wondered at the thoughts that crept secretly through his mind when he thought she wasn't paying attention. Olivia was a relationship counsellor. A couple's therapist. She spent her days listening to the complex lies of failed relationships, and she continually thought about her own marriage. They were happy. Content. At least they were no less happy and no less content than other married people she knew. They lived in a lovely house in an expensive suburb of London, far enough away from the hustle and bustle of central London to feel like they lived near the country, but close enough to pop in for an evening meal or to watch a play if the mood took them. A house they had only been able to afford after her mother had died and left them a considerable amount of money, and before London house prices had gone through the roof. That had been fifteen years ago. A lifetime ago, it seemed to her.

They tucked into their spaghetti Bolognese. No more mention of school. They ate in relative silence. The house was quiet. Laura, like most teenagers, spent most of her time in her bedroom or out. The place that was spoken of as if it meant something, although it was never clarified. *Where are you going, Laura? Out. Right, well, don't be late.* Alexander liked to read. He had his reading chair. The expensive chair he'd bought from Habitat and placed near the fireplace in the living room. Comfortable with wooden legs and lemon-yellow velvet upholstery. He read dense, heavy, hardback books about history. Books that looked as old as the history he was reading about. He lived half of his life in the past, Olivia joked.

Olivia kept herself busy with work. She had three or four clients a day, each one lasting an hour. In addition, she cooked and cleaned the house, although they had recently hired a woman to come in and do the cleaning to give Olivia more time for work. The cleaning lady was from Bulgaria and very nice. She somehow got things so much cleaner than Olivia ever could, and she had no idea how. It was a magical Bulgarian secret. Olivia imagined Bulgaria as a country with a difficult cultural and political history, but with pristinely clean houses. Olivia took a sip of her wine and looked across at her daughter. So much like her father. The same ink-dark eyes and hair. The same intensity to her work.

They ate and spoke about their days until they were finished. Laura had some studying to do, and so went upstairs to her bedroom. Alexander loaded the dishwasher while Olivia sat in the living room. She switched the television on. It was just after six o'clock. She could hear Alexander pottering about in the kitchen, stacking the dishwasher and turning the kettle on for after dinner tea. *The routine.* She flicked between a few channels before settling on BBC One. The news was on and then it was The One Show. She loved The One Show. It was the foundation on which the rest of the evening sat. She took the last sip of her wine and put the glass down on the coffee table. Life was good. They were happy. Slightly ordinary, perhaps, but good. Middle-class and middle-aged, with all the connotations that came with that.

Olivia thought about the couple she had seen that morning. Olivia worked out of her house in a purpose-built office at the bottom of their garden. It was a luxury shed with electricity, a wooden floor with rugs, and a small kitchen for coffee and snacks. It was like one of those small rooms in IKEA. It had been the couple's first session with her. David and Lydia Branch. Mid-forties with three children. He worked in the financial sector, and she did something in design. They were so much like Olivia and Alexander. Happily married, contentedly middle-aged and middle-class. Then he had an affair. It was totally out of character, completely unexpected, but it was over, and they wanted to work on their marriage. Olivia saw the love that still existed between them, and how it had been split down the middle and the space that lived there now. They spoke about their lives and their marriage, Lydia cried, and David tried to hold her hand and she brushed him off. Olivia looked at them and she saw her and Alexander. It could so easily be them. Perhaps it was because of her job, or that Alexander was a handsome man, but the voice in her head had been getting louder recently. Be careful, it said. Watch out. Take nothing for granted.

Upstairs in her bedroom, Laura sat on her bed and scrolled through her phone. She looked at the photos that Tom had sent her. Funny faces. Sexy faces. A few of him shirtless. God, if her parents ever saw them, she'd be grounded for a year. There had been the slightly risqué photos she had sent him. A few of her in just a bra. One looking down at her legs with just the very bottom of her underwear on show. White, lacy, nearly see-through knickers. She wasn't sure if she should send them because what if they broke up and he showed his mates? But she trusted him, and they weren't going to break up. And it wasn't like she'd sent topless photos. They were tasteful. She sent Tom a message. *Thinking about u.* A message quickly came back. *Me 2. My parents won't b here on Friday.* She replied with a smiley face. He messaged back. *They won't b home till 9.* Laura smiled to herself. She knew what it meant. She replied with a love heart.

In the kitchen, Alexander took out his mobile phone. He turned it on, went straight to messages, and clicked on the one that said School. He looked down at the last message he had received. It was four minutes ago. Luckily, but not luckily because he did it on purpose, his phone was on silent.

The message just said: *Friday*.

Alexander looked down at the single word on his phone. *Friday*. One word. A day of the week. It had so many meanings. If anyone had seen the message apart from him, it would mean nothing. *Friday*. What was happening on Friday? Was it an answer or a question? Alexander knew exactly what it meant because it was the answer to a question from an earlier conversation. It meant everything in his world. He wasn't going to reply. He looked at the word and then he pressed delete. The word vanished. Friday was gone. He wouldn't have to lie to his wife. He got back to cleaning up before he put tea bags in mugs, and then he joined his wife in the living room. She smiled at him when he walked in, and he smiled back. He sat next to her on the sofa. She had her legs pulled up next to him, and he put a hand on her leg. She was wearing a pair of thin cotton trousers, and he liked how they felt.

'All right?' said Olivia.

'Yeah,' said Alexander. 'I'll get the tea in a minute.'

'I got some of those biscuits you like from Waitrose.'

'Oh good. Do you want one?'

'Sure.'

She smiled at her husband, and then looked back towards the television, and they sat like that for a few minutes until he got up to finish making the tea.

2.

The present

Alexander thought a lot about home. The home he used to have. He still lived in the same house, but it wasn't the same home. It looked similar, but that was about it. If you looked closely enough there was something missing. It was a house that looked lost in a moment in time. It was tidy enough in the sense that only one man lived there, and he didn't move enough or buy enough to create any sort of mess, but it lacked something. If you inspected it closely, you'd see a thin layer of dust over everything. You'd notice that the bathroom hadn't been cleaned properly and the carpet needed a vacuum. If it wasn't for Alexander himself, you might think it had been left like one of those ships you heard about, found floating and empty, abandoned at sea.

Alexander looked at himself in the bathroom mirror, took his razor, and started shaving. It was just past seven o'clock in the morning. He would have to leave for school soon. He would shave and then go downstairs, have a cup of tea, some toast, sit in silence, then brush his teeth, get his things ready, and leave the house. The same thing he did every weekday morning. The routine. The house was so quiet you could hear a pin drop. The only noise was the distant rumble of life outside that infiltrated the windows. Alexander looked at himself in the mirror. He didn't look good. Too thin. Some might say gaunt. His eyes were lifeless. He used to have great eyes, women said. Deep, mysterious, even sexy, had been words used in the past. Now they stared back at him, and they were hollow. Empty pools. He finished shaving, rinsed his face with cold water, and then dried it with a towel. He applied a little aftershave, and it stung his skin.

Alexander sat in the kitchen and stared out into the

garden. He had a cup of tea, and a piece of toast with some butter, and a thin layer of marmalade. He used to love the garden. When they had bought the house, one of the things that had attracted them to it had been the garden. It was unusually large for the area. It was slightly wider than all the other gardens, and it went on for what seemed like forever. At the bottom of the garden was her office, and a fence that led to the lane behind and more houses. Down the sides of the garden, mature bushes and plants sat against the fence, and in the middle of the lawn was the tree. Alexander loved the tree. Olivia had drawn it once. A doodle, she had said. Black ink on white paper. It was in a drawer somewhere.

The tree stood like a sculpture. It twisted and turned like a dancer, its branches shooting up and out, and the leaves covering it until autumn when they'd fall and scatter across the grass. A vision of Laura kicking the leaves and running through them giggling. They had made a swing over the course of a weekend one summer. He'd built the swing, and then Olivia and Laura had painted it yellow and blue. He remembered Laura's screams of delight as they pushed her for the first time. Photos and videos remained somewhere. A moment captured forever lost on a hard drive. He looked outside now, and the swing was still there. It sat unused and still; the paint chipped away, and like him, it looked forlorn. Swings were only important, only worthwhile if they were loved, but otherwise they were just there. Something, but nothing. It's how Alexander felt. He existed. He was going through the motions of life without really living. A ghost.

He finished his tea and toast, washed up, and got ready for work. He brushed his teeth, slipped his jacket on, and grabbed his work bag. The leather satchel that had been a present many years before. It was fairly warm outside for the time of year, but he grabbed a jacket anyway, just in case. He had an umbrella in the car too. He walked outside, closing the front door behind him, got into his car and sat for a moment. He took a deep breath, checked the mirrors, and then started his car. The radio came on automatically.

BBC Radio 4.

Alexander pulled out of his driveway and onto the road. It was only a fifteen-minute drive to school. It should be less, but with morning traffic, it was around fifteen minutes depending on lights. He left at almost the same time each morning and would get to school thirty minutes before his first class. Time to make a cup of coffee in the staff room and use the toilet. It was a bright cloudless morning and Alexander listened to The Today show. A mixture of news, current affairs, sport and weather. Alexander liked to listen to it because it reminded him that despite everything, life was still going on. He liked that Radio 4 was sort of quiet and dignified. There was something slightly old-fashioned, stuffy, and comforting about it.

He drove the same route each morning. He could almost do it blindfolded. The same turns, lights, and often the same cars. He would see the same people on the streets, the same children as he got nearer to school, running, laughing, pushing each other, and the girls in their uniforms talking quickly in small groups. Life felt like a conveyor belt to Alexander. He was just going along, moving with everything else, without a chance of getting off. The breaks when they came weren't anything to look forward to either. They happened and then they were over, and life continued. Nothing out of the ordinary ever happened to Alexander Burke.

Alexander slowed down as traffic built up and then stopped. He sat in his car listening to the morning headlines. He looked around, and that's when he saw her. He hadn't seen her before. She was a new face in an otherwise sea of familiarity. She looked as though she had been sleeping rough. Mid to late twenties, although it was hard to tell. Red hair that went down to her waist. One of the first things that Alexander noticed was that she wasn't wearing any shoes. Bare feet on the slab of grey concrete. She had on a long skirt that looked as though it had been nice once, and a brown t-shirt. She looked as though she barely had any life left inside of her. It was this he not only saw but recognised. She had bracelets around her wrists, and a tattoo on her ankle. He couldn't make out what it was. A word, he thought. He couldn't stop watching her. She was walking slowly, but purposely. Alexander was stopped on a railway bridge, and she was facing away from him. Alexander thought for a moment of opening his window and asking if she was all right, but he didn't. It was probably nothing.

A long line of cars had pulled up behind Alexander. He watched the woman. She wasn't moving. There was something about her. Something so sad and final. As if he was watching death itself. Slow. Steady. She was about the same age as his own daughter. She stood and stared out towards the train tracks below. The cars in front of Alexander slowly began to move. The train was due soon. Alexander didn't move, and then a car behind him beeped their horn. They were in a rush. Alexander slowly pulled away, but as he did, he saw the woman take a step towards the bridge. Alexander drove a short way, and then he pulled over to the side. A car drove past, and an angry commuter stared at him. Alexander took a moment. He took a breath and then looked in his mirror. The woman was standing closer than ever to the bridge. He could forget all about her and drive to work. It was probably nothing. She was just looking out towards the train tracks that ran into the distance towards London. But there was something about her. Something in his mind said, don't drive away. Nothing extraordinary ever happened to Alexander.

He opened his door and got out. In his dark suit, white shirt, blue tie and black shoes, Alexander looked like any other commuter. He was slightly overdressed for teaching, but he liked the formality of it. He walked towards the bridge. She stood there, staring away into the distance. Her red hair needed a wash, and she needed some new clothes. Her feet were dark from the dirt and her teeth were yellow from not being brushed in months.

'Hello there,' said Alexander as he got nearer.

His voice sounded weak and far away. Almost as if he hadn't really said it. She turned and looked at him, and for the first time he saw she had tears in her eyes. He stopped about ten feet away from her and they just looked at each other. Cars passed and people passed, and no-one seemed to notice either of them. It was as if they were the only two people left in the world. Alexander didn't know what to do or what to say. She looked at him, tears rolled down her cheeks, and then she mouthed the word, 'sorry'. Alexander didn't know what she was sorry for. The next moment, and she clambered up onto the bridge. Alexander could hear the train coming. The distant shock of the train hit him. She was going to jump. At that moment, Alexander realised. She was going to kill herself.

3.

The past

Olivia made herself a cup of coffee. She was in her office waiting for her first client of the day. She had recently bought herself a new Nespresso coffee machine. She put in the pod, closed the lid, and soon had a coffee in her favourite mug. It was the mug she'd bought from a little shop in Cornwall. It was four years earlier during the school summer holidays, and they had rented a small house in St Ives for the week. The weather had been glorious, and it was just before Laura had started secondary school. It felt like a big moment, as if life was about to change irreversibly forever. Ten days in Cornwall, and they had been from Land's End to Tintagel and everywhere in-between. They spent days relaxing on the golden sandy beaches, others wandering across desolate moorland, and strolling along the beautiful coastal pathways. Cream teas and Cornish pasties were eaten daily. One day, they had wandered into a little tourist shop and Olivia had found the mug. It had a drawing of St Ives by a local artist, and St Ives in blue writing underneath. It was simple, but it reminded her of a wonderful time before Laura got big, and when she and Alexander seemed so much younger. She didn't know why, but life seemed so much easier then.

Olivia sat down in her chair and waited for her client. It was a woman by the name of Susan Farringdon. She had been seeing Susan on and off for the best part of a year. Susan was sure her husband was cheating on her. She also had no plans to confront or leave him. Susan was caught between wanting to know the truth and being too afraid of what might happen when she did. Olivia saw far too many people like that. People that were more afraid of the truth and prepared to live with the unhappiness of not knowing than finding out and potentially being alone. Olivia understood how women like Susan felt. She also knew it wasn't something she could do. She had been there the day her mother had finally confronted her father. The day of the shouting, tears, and the day he had moved out for good. The day Olivia had watched her mum crying at the bottom of the stairs and had held her for what felt like forever until she finally stopped.

Susan eventually arrived and sat down on the sofa opposite Olivia's chair. She was attractive and dressed in a dark grey business suit. It was quite ironic, thought Olivia, because she was so afraid of being alone and yet she was beautiful and successful, and wouldn't have a problem finding someone else. Olivia imagined that at work, Susan was confident and strong, and people looked up to her. They probably thought she had everything. She was the HR manager at an accountancy firm in the city. Professionally she was everything she wanted to be, but personally she was a mess.

'How are you?' said Olivia.

Susan sat with her legs crossed. Olivia took a sip of her coffee. It was hot and smooth.

'Pete's going out with work tonight,' said Susan, a tense expression on her face.

Susan chewed on her lip. A nervous tick she often did before she'd start crying. Her hand was on her knee that bounced repeatedly up and down.

'And how does that make you feel, Susan?'

'Nervous, and worried. I think she might be there. You know the girl from his work I'm sure he's sleeping with.' She left a brief pause, then said, 'I'm thinking about following him.'

'I don't think that's a good idea.'

'Why? Maybe I'll finally see it for myself. Catch him in the act,' said Susan, who paused and then looked at Olivia. 'I've seen her before. She's got an Instagram account. God, she's young. Mid-twenties, I think. All boobs and confidence. It's no wonder he can't resist her. She's like me before everything went south.'

'I don't think it's a good idea to follow him on a night out. I know it's difficult for you, but I really think you need to talk to him. Calmly. At home.'

Olivia emphasised 'calmly' and 'at home'.

'That's easier said than done.'

'I'm not saying it's easy, but it's what needs to happen. Can I ask you a question?' Susan nodded. 'Say you follow him tonight, and you see him and this woman together, they're flirting, perhaps they kiss. What would you do?'

Susan looked at Olivia. Her knee bounced up and down faster, her whole body was full of tension. Her eyes suddenly glassed over, and a tear leaked out and down her face.

'I don't know. Nothing, probably,' said Susan. The anger she felt moments before turned to weakness and self-loathing. 'I just don't know what to do, you know.'

Olivia handed Susan a tissue. Susan blew her nose and said sorry for crying. Susan cried most visits. Olivia didn't mind the tears. It was all a part of her job. People needed to open up, and crying was a part of it. Emotions were good. Olivia let her stop crying before she spoke.

'Susan, we've spoken about your ex-husband before. He cheated on you, and you had the courage to leave him. If Pete is doing the same, then you can deal with that too. You're a strong, successful woman. You're the master of your own life. Not fear. Not the constant anxiety that Pete is cheating on you. You deserve to be happy. You deserve to be with someone you can trust, and who loves and respects you.'

'I know,' said Susan, crying again. 'I know, it's just …'

Susan looked towards the window and outside into the garden. She envied Olivia. She had an incredible house in Richmond, and a wonderful garden. She had seen her husband, and he was handsome. Olivia was beautiful too. Susan wanted what Olivia had. Instead, she had a small two-bedroom house with barely any garden, and a husband she couldn't trust. Why did some women get all the luck? She looked towards the tree and the swing. She imagined Olivia's daughter out there. Susan had wanted children once, but it hadn't happened for her. She was approaching forty, and that window was almost closed. Susan looked across at Olivia, at her trendy earrings, at her nice clothes, and at the Scandinavian inspired office at the bottom of her beautiful garden. Susan had never seen inside her house, but she imagined it was gorgeous too. A magazine article house.

'It's just what?' said Olivia.

Susan noticed the plant in the corner of the room. A tall, green, leafy plant in a simple white plant pot. It was the sort of thing that Susan tried at her house, but it never quite worked out.

'If I find out the truth, I'll have to make a decision. I'm thirty-eight, and I can't face the thought of turning forty single and alone. I just can't.'

'But is that better than facing it in an unhappy marriage?'

Susan took a moment, and Olivia had another sip of coffee. Was it better? The truth was that Susan didn't know. She knew she loved Pete and didn't want to lose him. She hated the idea of him sleeping with someone else but didn't think she was strong enough to face life without him. Unhappiness or loneliness? What sort of choice was that?

'What would you do?' Susan said to Olivia.

Olivia, she noticed, moved uncomfortably in her seat for a moment. Her face gave a quick glimmer of something else other than her usual expression of calmness. For a second, Susan saw through the facade of Olivia. The door was slightly ajar. But Olivia quickly closed it again.

'This isn't about me, Susan, this is about you. You need to decide what sort of life you want. Whether you can live not trusting your husband or whether it's something you need to face. Either way, I am here for you. You have me, and my advice is to be honest with yourself and with Pete. Perhaps speaking about it, maybe together, might help. You could come here, and we could discuss it together if you'd like?'

It wasn't the first time that Olivia had suggested it and like before Susan shook her head. Pete wouldn't do it. He didn't get therapy. He didn't see the point. He was old school. He didn't even know she was going there and if he did, my God, the argument it would cause.

The rest of the session went much the same way. Olivia tried to get Susan to open up and really think about her life. It seemed to Olivia that Susan was holding things back from her. Perhaps she was holding things back from herself. Olivia knew there was more to the story than she knew, and she always tried to push the idea of Pete coming in too. She wanted to hear his side of things. Maybe then they could really get somewhere. Susan left after an hour, and Olivia had thirty minutes before the next couple. They had been married for thirty years, and they had lost the spark. They were still together, no one had cheated, but they needed help to reconnect.

Olivia made herself another coffee and took a protein bar out of the fridge. She sat in her chair and opened up the book she was reading. It was a tense psychological drama. She loved how they took her away from herself. She set an alarm, which would go off five minutes before her next clients were due to arrive. When it went off, she set her book down and waited.

She thought about Susan's question. What would she do if she thought her husband was cheating on her? Olivia knew she would do something. She couldn't live her life like Susan, forever wondering, always questioning where her husband was and what he was doing. Olivia had spent far too long watching her own mother go through it with her father.

Olivia had her suspicions. Actually, it was more than that. She was sure that something had happened. Two weeks ago, Alexander had come from school and when he leaned in and gave her a kiss, she smelled it on him. A perfume. Sweet, floral, and sophisticated. He kissed her cheek, and the scent drifted up her nose, and she thought then that perhaps something wasn't right. But it was more than just the perfume. Alexander had been acting differently. Whether he knew it, he wore his emotions on his face, and she could read him as easily as a book. She knew him the same way she knew her daughter. It was one of Olivia's skills and perhaps why she went into the profession she did. She had a sixth sense for lies and for seeing things in people they didn't always know themselves. The fact that Alexander knew this and thought he could hide something from her made her so annoyed with him. Then a few days after the perfume, she had been in the hallway, about to put his jacket on the hook when she saw a single blonde hair on it. A long blonde hair on the shoulder of his jacket. She might have thought nothing of it, but that along with the perfume and his recent behaviour had made Olivia think that something had happened. Olivia wasn't a jealous person by nature, but she knew how to see the signs of trouble in a marriage. Perfume. A stray blonde hair. Guilty behaviour. All that was left was the sudden arrival of flowers or a surprise weekend away.

By the time her next clients arrived, Olivia had finished her coffee, and was sitting calmly waiting, all thoughts of Alexander pushed from her mind. She was ready to help the Daglish family recover whatever it was they had lost. She started as she started each session with a clear mind. Relaxed. Calm. Ready. The seed of doubt about her own marriage, stored away for later.

4.

The present

Louise Bailey leaned down and picked up her daughter. She was getting so big. She remembered when she hardly weighed anything at all. A watermelon. Now she was four years old, and the size and weight of her was something else entirely. It seemed impossible she would start school in the autumn. She looked into her eyes. She loved her so much. Despite this love, there was the thought in her mind which made her think about the life she could have had. The other life. Everything stemmed from that one moment. That blinding flash of light that had created an alternate universe which she now inhabited with Ella and Jim.

Louise thought her life was like a tree. Childhood and adolescence were very much the trunk. They supported everything else. Solid, stable, and reliable. The trunk had done its job. But then, after the trunk, the branches had gone off in all directions. Some branches were big and strong, while others quickly withered away to nothing and died. Some had a myriad of branches going off of them, creating different pathways and routes to the top, where the leaves took over and covered everything like a heavy umbrella. Her life was a tree, and it had all changed when the trunk stopped, the first branch took off, and she with it.

Louise looked at her daughter. She had her mother's soft blue eyes and her father's sturdy chin. She looked at her smile and how happy she was, and she thought about the moment when the trunk had become the branch, and how she wished she could go back and change what had happened. A tear leaked out and down Louise's cheek. Ella gave her mum a strange, inquisitive look, and said,

'Why are you crying, Mummy?'

Louise wiped the tear from her cheek and smiled at her

little girl.

'It's something that happened a long time ago. Before you were born, baby girl.'

Then Louise put Ella down on the bed, lifted her shirt, and planted her lips on her soft, creamy belly, and blew. Ella laughed so loudly that Louise never wanted to stop. She only wanted to hear her daughter's laughter because it drowned out the noise of her own terrible sadness.

Louise sat on the bottom of her stairs and took a deep breath. Ella was upstairs in her room playing Lego, and Louise needed a moment. She had washing to get done. She still needed to clean up breakfast, and it wouldn't be long before Ella would come trotting downstairs asking to go to the park. It was a warm day, and the lure of the park was too much for Ella. She loved the park. Louise loved it too. On a nice day, she would bring a book, maybe get a coffee from Costa. It made her feel sort of normal. It made her feel like the other park mums. Louise always took Ella to the big park, which was a good thirty-minute walk away, but it was so much nicer than the park near their house with rubbish littered everywhere, graffiti, and broken beer bottles and the occasional syringe. The park they went to was surrounded by nice semi-detached houses, and the mums she saw were the sort of mums she had imagined that one day she might be herself. Dressed impeccably with expensive buggies and even more expensive shoes. Hair done, makeup, and husbands who worked in finance, medicine, or the media.

Louise had a hard time admitting this was her life. A cramped, rented, ex-council two-bedroom house in one of the worst parts of Croydon. It felt like a million miles away from where she had grown up. Her boyfriend Jim worked all the hours he could to keep them going. Jim was a plumber. He had left school at sixteen with no qualifications and had started working with his father. Jim still worked alongside his dad, although with his dad getting older, Jim did most of the work. He said he was going to make the business better. His dad had never had the work ethic or knowledge to improve things. They had zero online presence and only got work from word of mouth. Jim was going to change all of that. He was usually out of the house before seven, and he wouldn't be home until six in the evening. This left Louise at home with Ella for most of the day. A day in which she kept Ella busy with Lego, books, and television, attempted to do all the housework while trying to fit in some reading for herself. She still dreamed about going to university. It had always been her plan. Louise had a sharp mind. It was quick-witted, absorbed knowledge in a way that most people couldn't, and she loved to learn and to think. She enjoyed debates and ideas, and when she read a book, she could lose herself and pretend for a moment that she was still in her old life. That all the possibilities she had were still there. It was easy to forget when all you were surrounded by was poverty and people barely getting by that they were in London, and anything was possible. Louise still dreamed.

'Mummy, I'm bored,' said Ella, trudging into the kitchen twenty minutes later with a very dramatic 'I'm bored!' face. Louise had just made herself a cup of coffee and was trying to clean the oven. It wasn't good coffee because they couldn't afford good coffee, and the oven needed more than just a good clean. It needed throwing out and a new oven installed, but there was more chance of them winning the lottery than the landlord agreeing to buy them a new oven.

'And what would you like to do, baby girl?' said Louise.

'Park,' said Ella with a bright, beautiful smile.

'How about a snack first?'

Ella looked at her mum. She had teddy in her hand. She always had teddy in her hand. He was a small brown bear called Floyd and had been a present from Jim's parents. They'd brought it to the hospital when Ella was born. Her first present. Ella had slept with Floyd ever since, had tea parties with Floyd, and spent most of her time with him. They discussed all manner of things together, and when Ella put on plays, Floyd always had a starring role.

'Okay. Then park,' said Ella after a moment. 'Floyd wants to go on the slide.'

'Very well. If that's what Floyd wants.'

'It is,' said Ella resolutely, and Louise looked at her daughter and smiled.

Relieved that Ella had agreed to a snack first so she could sit down and finish her coffee, and have a biscuit, Louise cut up an apple and put it on a plate with some peanut butter. It was one of Ella's favourite snacks. They sat down together. Ella asked Louise why dragons didn't exist anymore, and that she thought Floyd needed a new friend, and then Louise made her do her numbers. She was starting school in the autumn, and Louise wanted Ella to be ahead of the game. She was a smart little girl, and Louise wanted her to do well. By age three, she could count to twenty. By age four, it was fifty, and she was aiming for one hundred by the start of school. She could write her own name. She knew all the shapes, even the really hard ones, and she could easily recite the alphabet. Jim thought it was amazing how intelligent his little girl was. Jim's parents thought she was going to be a genius. It reminded Louise of her own potential.

They eventually got ready and headed to the park, where Ella met a couple of other kids, and they ran around for well over an hour. Louise brought along her book, and she sat down on a bench and read while the other mums stood around talking. Most had their heads down, looking at their phones. Louise liked the feeling of a proper book in her hands. She loved the smell of the pages. She couldn't afford to buy new books anymore, and so she got all of her books second hand or from the library. It didn't matter, and most were in decent condition. A few dog-eared pages, and some had notes scribbled by previous owners, but otherwise they were fine. The main thing was that she was still learning. She wanted to be ready when the time came. She watched Ella running around with the other little children, Floyd flying through the air with her. They sat and ate another snack before Ella was off playing again.

That night, Ella watched CBeebies while Louise made dinner. They didn't have much in the fridge, but she had cobbled together fish fingers, chips, and peas, with a few slices of buttered white bread. Jim got home just before six o'clock. It was always so strange when he came in. His presence, after an entire day of just the two of them, seemed like a shock. As if they had both forgotten that a man also lived in the house.

'Hello, love, all right?' said Jim briskly, walking into the kitchen.

'Yeah, good day?'

'All right, yeah, the usual. What's for dinner?'

Louise told him, and Jim mumbled something about being starving and a fish finger sandwich, washed his hands, and said he was going to see Ella. He gave her a quick kiss on the cheek, and she could smell the day on him. It clung to him. The smell of work. She didn't like it.

Jim Smith was a big man, tall and strong, with a shaved head and easy to please. He didn't need much. He was generally happy, content with a normal life, or at least what he thought of as normal. He had grown up in a small house on an estate in East London. A mum, dad, and three kids in a tiny three-bedroom house. Not much money to go around. His dad was always working, and his mum stayed at home and did her best. They supported West Ham, and the kids all grew up to be much like Jim. They were good people. Salt of the earth. Jim was a wonderful dad to Ella, and he loved her to bits. He had a slightly old-fashioned view of the world. He knew Louise was cleverer than him and could do something incredible with her life, but he was happier with her at home raising Ella. He dreaded Ella starting school because it would give Louise the time to do something else. Jim was afraid of losing Louise and the life they had created. It wasn't much, he knew that, but it was something.

After Louise had put Ella to bed, she sat downstairs in

the lounge with Jim. She made tea, and they watched television. Eastenders, and then an American sitcom. Jim laughed hysterically at the comedy. He loved a good laugh. Louise did too, but it had been years since she had properly laughed. Since she had really lost herself in it. Emotions didn't come easily to Louise after everything that had happened. She had stuffed them all so far down she had lost them almost entirely. Memories and feelings locked away in vaults.

When Louise met Jim, she was twenty years old. Living on the sofa of a friend's flat and working in a coffee shop. She had lost her way. She was drinking too much and trying to heal the wounds of the past. She liked being numb. Then she met Jim, and he was this huge man, this fun-loving thing who liked her. They started going out, and having sex, and then she fell pregnant with Ella. From easy and fun, it quickly became something serious, and without really thinking about it, she let him talk her into a life with him. It would be all right. Jim, Louise, and Ella. They could make it work. She had told him she was an orphan and that her name was Louise Bailey. It was a good name. She had taken Louise from a girl she liked at school. She had seen the surname Bailey in a magazine article. One day she would have to legally change her name if she and Jim were to get married. She didn't want him to find out the awful truth. It had been so long since Louise had thought of herself as Laura Burke. In her mind, Laura Burke was dead. She was Louise Bailey, and this was Louise's life. But she wanted better. She wanted more. Her version of normal wasn't the same as Jim's. It wouldn't ever be the same.

5.

The past

Laura was in her bedroom getting ready for school. Her parents were downstairs having breakfast and doing whatever it was her parents did. Laura was looking at herself in her full-length mirror. Ever since she had started going out with Tom, things had changed. She had changed. She thought about things differently. It was like for her entire life she had thought in two dimensions and suddenly there were four. She felt alive. Grown up.

Tom Chance was just so lovely, and he was hers. He could have chosen so many girls at school to ask out, but he had picked her. Tom was one of those boys destined to do something great. He was good at everything. He was in the school football team, cricket team, athletics team, and in the top sets for everything. Like Laura, Tom had ambitions to go to Oxford. They had talked about it together. Perhaps if they kept going out during sixth form, then maybe they'd go to Oxford together. Two young lovers on the cusp of everything.

Laura looked at herself in her mirror. She adjusted her shirt, put on her tie, and felt slightly giddy about seeing Tom at school. It was happening on Friday. His parents were away until late in the evening. Apparently, they liked ballroom dancing and were going to an event in London. They were really into Dancing with the Stars, which Laura thought was funny but whatever. Her father only read history books and her mum talked to other married people about sex. At least, that's what she assumed. Laura had heard fragments of conversations between her parents, and when her mum had mentioned work, she talked about sexual things. It grossed Laura out to imagine her parents and other people of their age having sex.

The plan for Friday was all set. Laura was going to tell her parents she was going to Charlotte's house after school, and then she was going to sneak off to Tom's instead. Laura was going to lose her virginity. It was a moment she had thought long and hard about for the last year. When would it happen, and with whom? Tom was a virgin too, and they had done other things together. They had done everything else except sex, and it was time. She was ready. Laura's best friend, Charlotte, had already lost her virginity, and she'd told her all about it. It was all Laura could think about. It consumed her mind that morning as she got ready for school. What underwear was she going to wear? Not that it probably mattered that much, but she wanted to look nice. She had recently gone shopping with her mother and bought a pack of new underwear that had frilly lace on top. She thought a pair of those in black with a matching black bra would be nice. Just the thought of it sent shivers of nerves and excitement through her young body. It was one of the seminal moments of growing up. She was standing on the edge of childhood and peering across at the vast space ahead of her that was adulthood. Sex with Tom was one of the first steps.

Downstairs, Alexander was having breakfast with Olivia. Alexander was sitting at the kitchen island drinking his tea and nibbling on a slice of toast. Butter with a thin layer of dark, sticky Marmite. Olivia had a small bowl of Muesli with a few blueberries on top. She didn't eat much in the morning. She wanted to speak to Alexander about something, but she wasn't sure how to broach the subject. Its origins were based on her fears about them drifting apart. About them not being happy in the way they used to be, and perhaps the blonde hair on his jacket and the perfume. She felt like they were on a small boat, and they were drifting, and if one of them didn't start rowing back to shore soon, they might be too far out and they might never make it back. She worried that their marriage, like so many, was beginning to fall apart and so slowly that by the time either of them noticed it might be too late to save it.

'I was thinking,' said Olivia.

'A dangerous thing, thinking,' said Alexander with a smile.

'Oh, stop it,' said Olivia. 'I thought we should go on a date.'

She looked at him. He looked at her. Slightly astonished, it seemed.

'A date?' said Alexander, who stopped eating.

'Yes, a date. Remember when two people who quite like each other go out for a meal, talk, drink wine, maybe go for a walk afterwards, before they go home and have sex.'

'That does sound familiar.'

Olivia laughed.

'A date would be fun, and it's been so long.'

It had been too long, and they didn't really have an excuse. Laura was fine at home by herself. They could go on dates whenever they wanted these days. They just didn't. When Laura was young and it was hard to go out, they would forever be complaining that they never got to go out anymore. It was too difficult with a young child. When they didn't have sex for weeks, or occasionally months, they would blame it on being tired or having a child. Life, they said with disappointed tuts, but they didn't have that excuse anymore. They were drifting and Olivia didn't know why or what had happened. She needed to get them back on course again. She needed to take control of the rudder because she knew Alexander would just let them drift.

'Okay, let's go on a date,' said Alexander.

Alexander wondered where this had come from. A sudden request for a date and the mention of sex. God, it had been an age since they'd had sex. It had been even longer since they'd had good sex. Sex that he remembered with a wistful smile and thought about long after it had happened. The sort of sex they used to have all the time. Wild, passionate, orgasmic sex that left them both sweaty and breathless in a beautiful agony. Now she was talking about a date with dinner and sex, and it made him think that something was going on. Something was on her mind. Perhaps it had been jolted by listening to one of her clients. Alexander had always been slightly uncomfortable with her choice of career subject matter. When they had met and she was studying psychology, he never imagined she'd end up as a relationship counsellor at the bottom of their garden. It was physically and metaphorically too close for comfort.

'How about Friday?' said Olivia suddenly.

She looked at him, almost as if she knew. But she couldn't know. It was impossible. She hadn't seen any of the messages between them. He had been careful to delete them all. Alexander felt a heat rise up inside of him. A warmth that covered his body and stretched to his face. Guilt. He felt it soak his entire body. He immediately stood up, trying to draw any attention away from his sudden redness. Alexander knew he had never been good at hiding his feelings. He also knew that Olivia was good at reading people. They used to play a game when they were younger, and before they had Laura. When they were at a restaurant, Alexander would get Olivia to watch another couple and make guesses about their situation, just from their body language. They never knew whether she was right, but she always seemed confident in what she said. She knew how to read people. A slight alteration of a facial expression, a sudden movement of a hand or a touch to the face. All of it meant something.

'I can't on Friday,' said Alexander. He put his plate and mug in the sink, purposely facing away from his wife. 'I have a work thing.'

'A work thing? You never mentioned it.'

'It's someone's birthday and they're having drinks at the pub. I said I'd go. Sorry.'

He knew he couldn't turn around and face her. She would know. He started washing up. He had thought about excuses when he was going to sleep the night before. Going to the pub had been one of them. It was plausible. It could be last minute. Olivia had no reason to question it. Alexander turned and looked at his wife. He smiled.

'Maybe Saturday?'

'Yes, Saturday,' said Olivia, returning his smile, while inside her heart sank because she knew deep within herself that her husband was lying. She didn't know why. She couldn't imagine why he would lie to her about going to the pub, but he was. She could tell. It was easy to see the lie written across his face. His eyes always gave him away. When Alexander was uncomfortable, he would blink. It was a nervous reaction. If he was stressed or nervous, he blinked. Olivia smiled at Alexander as he got his things together for work. Saturday. A date and sex. She hoped he wasn't lying to her. She hoped he wasn't cheating on her. Olivia hoped, and she smiled, and as her husband walked out of the kitchen and went upstairs to get ready for work, she tried to think of all the reasons why he might have lied to her. She tried to rationalise why he would need to say he was going for drinks with work when he wasn't. But as much as she tried, she could only think of one thing. One horrible, devastating, insidious thing. But it couldn't be true. It was Alexander. He was many things, but not a cheater, and they were fine. They were happy. They had been drifting, she knew that, but it wasn't that bad, was it?

Laura caught up with Charlotte, and they walked the last few hundred feet to school together. Laura had been friends with Charlotte since primary school.

'Someone is looking hot,' said Charlotte. 'Any reason?'

Laura giggled. Charlotte already knew the answer.

'It's happening on Friday,' said Laura, looking at her friend with a slightly bashful smile.

'Oh my god,' said Charlotte with an excited squeal.

'I'm going to tell my parents I'm at your house after school, so you need to cover for me.'

'Totally,' said Charlotte.

'I mean, it's not going to come up. It's just in case.'

'Yeah, yeah, of course. Wow, you and Tom Chance,

getting it on.'

'Shut up,' said Laura playfully.

The girls walked towards school. It was a sunny morning, and they talked, joked, and laughed about things. Charlotte wanted all the gossip about Tom. What was he really like? Was he a good kisser? Did she love him? They spoke briefly about their upcoming exams. Charlotte wasn't as gifted or as clever as Laura. Charlotte wanted to go to sixth form, and then probably get a job, maybe go travelling or something. She had no idea what she wanted to do with her life. Her older cousin Jess worked in an office in London, and she seemed happy. Charlotte might do something like that. She liked the idea of working and earning money. She knew she wasn't like Laura, who was destined for something much weightier. Charlotte knew Laura wanted to be a lawyer or something, and she would probably do it. Charlotte was a little jealous of her best friend, and truth be told, she had always quite fancied Tom Chance herself.

Once they got to the school and walked through the playground, Laura spotted Tom waiting for her. Laura had a quick look around just in case her dad was skulking around near the playground. He would most likely be in his classroom getting ready, but better safe than sorry.

'I'll leave you to it,' said Charlotte with a wink.

'See you later,' said Laura, as Charlotte bounced off towards a few of their other friends who were huddled together, talking loudly. Laura didn't care. All she could think about was Tom and Friday. Just seeing him gave her goosebumps, and her heart started beating quickly. She felt her body flush with excitement. Sixteen-years-old, and she felt for the first time in her life like something incredible was happening just to her. Tom was her thing. It had nothing to do with her family or friends. It was like she had glimpsed over some invisible barrier and seen something clear, true, and forbidden.

'Hi,' said Tom.

'Hi,' said Laura.

They both blushed. Tom wanted to hold her hand, but he knew he couldn't. She wanted to hold his hand but knew that if her father found out, then she and Tom would be over. Friday was only a few days away. The day everything was going to change, thought Laura. The day her life wouldn't ever be the same again.

6.

The present

Alexander's father was an unremarkable man in that he had a fairly ordinary job he hated, worked at for nearly forty years, and then he died of lung cancer a few months shy of his sixtieth birthday. Alexander's memories of his father were all much the same. A man who spent most of his time away from his family at the pub. He was a man of a certain generation. Strong. Silent. A heavy drinker. Working class. Distant. He suffered with the changing world. He didn't understand it. He didn't understand his son, who had ideas about university and life away from Glasgow. A boy who loved history and learning. He thought something must have been wrong with Alexander.

Alexander's sister was two years older than him. She was a spitting image of their father, right down to his dour disposition and contempt for everything that Alexander deemed important. Alexander got his mother's dark hair and eyes. When his father died, Alexander returned to Scotland for the funeral. It was the first time he'd been back in a few years. He hated returning home because it reminded him of all the reasons he couldn't wait to leave. It wasn't Scotland itself. He loved the countryside of Scotland. The rolling hills, lochs, and the constant foggy greyness of it. He loved the history of the country of his birth. He loved Edinburgh with the castle on the hill like something from a fantasy film, the narrow alleyways, and sandstone houses. He loved sitting in parks and listening to the voices. The Scottish accents that sounded so familiar to him. The accent he had tried so hard to lose when he was young; shed like unwanted skin. It wasn't Scotland he couldn't stand, but his family. The only thing he knew he never wanted to be was his own father. It loomed large over him, greater than anything else. A dark cloud that had followed him for most of his life.

She was going to kill herself. This was the thought that went through Alexander's mind in a flash. She was going to jump in front of that train, and she was going to die, and the only person who could stop her was him. She had clambered up on top of the bridge. Other cars stopped as they realised what was going on. A scene was unfolding. Someone dialled 999.

'Don't do this,' said Alexander. He walked a step nearer. She didn't move. She was crouched down on top of the bridge. Tears dripped down her face. Her bare feet on the hard, cold brick of the bridge. 'Please.'

She looked towards him.

'There's nothing left,' she said in an Irish accent.

'You think that,' said Alexander. He wasn't thinking, he was just talking. His heart raced. He felt truly alive for the first time in years. 'But there's always something to live for.'

'No. There's nothing.'

Alexander heard the train in the distance. The track clicked and fizzed below them, warning them it was close. Alexander didn't know how long he had. Minutes? Seconds? Not long. He took another step closer.

'Just come down and we can talk. I'll buy you a coffee. We can have breakfast, whatever you want, and we can just talk.'

His accent somehow sounded more Scottish. More like the man he used to be. He thought about walking through the hills and highlands of Scotland. The beauty of it. Miles from there. Miles from anywhere. He was aware of other people nearby. People were watching. The police were on their way. Alexander took a step closer.

'My name's Alexander. I'm a teacher.' She looked at him. 'What's your name?'

'Belinda,' she said between tears.

'Belinda. Irish, by the sound of it. I love the Irish accent. Why don't you get down, Belinda, and we can talk, eh?

Come on. You don't need to do this. You don't. I promise.'

The train was getting closer. Alexander looked out over the bridge and at the train track. There was no train coming. Then he realised it was coming from the other side. Belinda had obviously thought about this. The train driver wouldn't see her up there. They wouldn't know until it was too late. Someone shouted from the nearby crowd that the police were coming. Help was on the way. Belinda barely heard them. The noises in her head were too loud.

'You don't have to do this,' said Alexander.

'I do.'

'I want to help you, Belinda. I can help you. Please.'

'No-one can help me,' she said, the tears subsiding. She sniffed. She wiped her face. The train was getting closer. Alexander was getting desperate. A minute or less.

'How about this? Don't do it now, eh. Let's talk, and if you still want to do it tomorrow or the day after that, I'll drive you back here myself.'

She looked at him. She almost wanted to laugh. He'd drive her back. What was his deal? Alexander noticed her face changing. Maybe he was getting through to her.

'I'll push you off myself. Just give me a day. Please, Belinda. Please. One day.'

The train was approaching. It had left the station, and it was gathering speed as it headed towards London. It was filled with commuters heading to work. The driver, unaware of the drama that was unfolding ahead of him. Alexander reached out a hand.

'Take my hand. I can help you. Please, Belinda. Take it.'

Belinda didn't know what to do. When she had woken up that morning, she had been certain it was her last day on earth. She had woken up in a doorway on the high street underneath an old sleeping bag covered in cardboard boxes. She had been living rough for months, and she'd had enough. There was no way back. Sometimes in life you had to accept it was the end. You had done all you could, but due to bad luck, an awful start in life, and some truly horrible people, you couldn't win. And so she had decided to kill herself. It was the only way out. She couldn't spend her life living rough on the streets. She would rather be dead. It was only a matter of time before she was raped or killed, anyway. At least if she was going to die, she wanted to take matters into her own hands. For perhaps the first time in her short, depressing life, she was going to take charge of it. So much of her life had happened without her consent. The least she could do was end it on her own terms. All she had to do was jump and the pain would be gone. But then this Scottish man had come along and ruined it. There was just something about him. Something in his eyes. She trusted him.

She took his hand as the train flashed by underneath the bridge. The speed of it took her breath away, and she fell into him. She cried, and Alexander pressed her into him. He held her, and a collective sigh of relief spread through the waiting crowd as the police finally arrived. Belinda hadn't wanted to live. She still didn't. But at least for a moment she was alive, and this man, Alexander, had saved her.

Belinda sat in the back of the police squad car. A woman was talking to her, while she sat staring aimlessly out of the window, a vacant expression on her face. Alexander was speaking to a policeman. He had already spoken to school and told them what had happened. He wouldn't be in today. It was the Friday before half-term, anyway. After he let Belinda go, and into the arms of a policewoman called Cath, he felt his knees buckle, and he sank to the ground. All the adrenalin and life he had felt coursing through his veins while he talked her down was gone, and he was suddenly in shock. A woman had almost died. Belinda. Twenty-six from Dublin.

'She wants to speak to you,' said the woman, who had been speaking to Belinda.

Alexander walked over and got into the back of the police car next to Belinda. He looked at her, and she suddenly looked so much younger. She was just a kid. He felt a wave of emotions take him over. He thought of his own daughter. This could be her. He looked at Belinda. Her face was weathered. Chapped, cracked lips, and dirty skin. Her eyes were so green and yet they contained so much sadness that it hung in them souring all the colour. She had the smell of someone who hadn't bathed in weeks, and her clothes stuck to her thin frame like a sack. She was a shapeless mass of sadness and poverty. The whites of her eyes were yellow and yet, despite all of that, she was pretty. There was a beauty inside of her that had been crushed and pushed down under a scowl of fear and anxiety. Something terrible had happened to her.

'Thank you,' said Belinda finally.

'You're welcome. What happened today? Why …'

She looked at him.

'They said I should talk to someone. A doctor. There's a place—'

'That's probably a good …'

'I don't want to,' said Belinda quickly. 'I want to get that coffee with you. Like you said.'

Alexander looked at Belinda. He didn't know what he had said up there. He had just spoken. He was desperate. He wasn't a trained counsellor. He couldn't help someone like Belinda. He had just been there at the right time. That's all. How could he help her? They sat for a moment in the back of the police car. It wasn't his first time in the back of a police car. It brought him back to that moment for a second. That awful moment. He thought of her face and felt a sadness rip through his body. He snapped himself out of it. He couldn't. Belinda needed him. He wondered whether it was Belinda's first time in a police car. It was then that he realised he knew nothing about her. She could be a drug addict or a criminal. She could be anything, and yet here he was with her, and his instinct told him to help her. His gut said she needed him. And anyway, what did he have to lose? The answer was as dreadfully sad as it was obvious. Nothing.

'Let me talk to the police and see if we can go somewhere.'

He didn't even know what the police would say to him. Did she have to go with them? Was she in trouble? Was he able to get a cup of coffee with her? He had no idea. He just knew that for the first time in a long time someone needed him. He walked across to the policewoman, who had been talking to Belinda. She was fairly short with mousy brown hair.

'She said she wants to get a cup of coffee with me,' said Alexander.

'How do you feel about that, sir?' she said. Her accent was all London. Thick and heavy.

'I, umm, don't mind if it's okay with you.'

'I said she should probably get some professional help. I think it's best, sir.'

'Right. I agree. But maybe right now she just needs a coffee and chat.'

'If you're okay with that, sir. Technically, she hasn't broken the law. We can't force her to do anything, but I would strongly recommend that she see a mental health professional.'

'I'll do my best to make sure she sees someone,' said Alexander.

The policewoman gave him an uncertain smile, and then she walked away. The other cars and passing people had left, and soon it was just Alexander and Belinda. The drama was over. They stood on the pavement for a moment, before they walked towards his car, and he took her to get a cup of coffee. Alexander had woken up that morning, sure it would be another dull, mundane day. Nothing exciting ever happened to Alexander Burke. Then he met Belinda, and he didn't know it at that exact moment, but she was going to change his life. She would fill that gap that had existed for such a long time. The space where his life had once fitted so perfectly. The space that had once been so full of love.

7.

The past

They met in the Bristol University student union. It was 1986, and they were both twenty-years-old. The Buzzcocks, Ever Fallen in Love (With Someone You Shouldn't've) was playing. Olivia was dancing with a couple of friends, and Alexander was next to her on the dance floor. He had a Marlboro cigarette in one hand and a bottle of Red Stripe beer in the other.

'Well?' said Alexander, leaning across and speaking to Olivia.

'Sorry?' said Olivia, who had never seen this tall, thin Scottish boy before with the dark eyes and mop of unruly black hair.

'Have you ever fallen in love with someone you shouldn't have?'

Olivia smiled at him. A ridiculously crap chat up line, but when he smiled at her something inside of her knew she would talk to him, and maybe even let him buy her a drink.

'Maybe. What about you?'

'Me?' he said in his broad Scottish accent. 'Nah, I don't fall in love.'

'Never?'

He smiled again.

'Not until now, anyway,' he said, and she laughed so hard she had to stop dancing.

They sat at the bar as her friends danced to Heart of Glass by Blondie. They talked, and despite his awful chat up line, there was something about Alexander Burke that Olivia knew she liked and would keep liking. Within weeks, they were officially going out, and they would never look back. Olivia had always felt lucky she had met Alexander so early in life, and she had been so sure. Falling in love had been so

39

easy for them. A good song, a crap chat-up line, and a couple of drinks were all they needed.

Olivia was sitting outside a coffee shop on the Sheen Road in Richmond. It was one of the newer, trendier coffee shops that served excellent coffee and a decent selection of cakes. It was a warm day with a cloudless cerulean sky and barely any breeze. She was ten minutes early, and so she sat with her cappuccino. She watched people walk past and listened to a couple having a conversation at a nearby table. The woman seemed annoyed about something, and the man was eager to explain himself. A little too eager, Olivia thought to herself. Olivia had been lost in her own thoughts of Alexander. What was she thinking? He wouldn't have an affair. It was Alexander. Her husband. The love of her life. They had been together for twenty-three years. They had been happy for most of it. Even now things weren't bad. They weren't arguing regularly. There wasn't any tension between them. She knew it had been better. When they were younger, the sex had been frequent and mind-blowingly good. Even the last few years it had still been good. Less frequent but that happened. They were in their early forties. Their priorities had changed. But their relationship was so much more than just sex. It was about supporting each other, taking care of Laura, and creating a life where they could do the things they wanted. Sex was a small part of it. He wouldn't toss a grenade into their life, potentially blow it all up, for a quick shag with someone else.

Olivia saw Jenny walking towards her. Jenny was wearing black trousers and a white blouse. She was a GP and on her lunch break. Olivia and Jenny had been friends for years. Olivia had first met Jenny just after they had moved to their house. Jenny was a junior doctor then, and Olivia had just started out as a therapist. Olivia had been introduced to Jenny through a mutual friend, and they soon started spending time together. They had a lot in common and living so close, it just made sense. Since then Jenny had got married, had two boys, started her own practice, and their friendship had blossomed.

'Sorry I'm late,' said Jenny quickly.

She was always in a rush.

'You aren't. I was early,' said Olivia. 'Coffee?'

'Oh, let me get it and cake. Do you want some cake?'

Olivia had been watching her weight. Her lunch for the past few weeks had been Ryvita crackers with low-fat cottage cheese and an apple. She had been trying to drink more water and had cut out biscuits during the week, but the lure of cake with Jenny was too much to turn down.

'Oh, go on then. Something chocolatey.'

Jenny went inside, and then reappeared a few minutes later with a coffee for her, and two slices of cake. A carrot cake for herself and something gooey and chocolatey for Olivia. The two friends sat together, sipped their coffees, and took small bites of their cakes.

'How are you?' said Olivia.

'Good, yeah, okay,' said Jenny. 'The boys are driving me mad as always, and Greg's away this week.'

'Oh, where is he?'

'A boy's trip. A friend's fortieth in Ireland. A castle, cigars, shooting, and whisky. Lucky bastard. I can't remember the last time I had a week away on my own.'

'Me either. We should do it. Perhaps one of those country spas.'

'Oh god, it sounds heavenly.'

The friends smiled, laughed, and talked about other things. About work and life, and they promised they would definitely do something soon. A weekend away. They both needed it. Jenny talked about her surgery, and how she was trying to find a new receptionist as the old one had left to follow a man to Manchester. Before lunch was over, Olivia circled the conversation back to Jenny's husband going away. Greg was a gregarious person and was, by his own admission, a terrible flirt. Despite convincing herself that Alexander definitely wasn't cheating, the thought like a cancer just wouldn't go away, no matter how much she wanted it to.

'Do you worry about Greg, away on a boy's trip?' said Olivia, searching her friend's face for any small fragment of doubt or uncertainty.

The empty coffees and plates with smears of cream and chocolate remained on the table between them.

'Greg? God, no. He's all mouth and no trousers. He loves to flirt, but he wouldn't do anything about it. I think he'd actually run a mile if a pretty, young girl came onto him.'

'That's good,' said Olivia, slightly stiffly.

Jenny noticed a slight change in her friend's expression. It was hardly noticeable, but Jenny knew Olivia. The change was ever so subtle, but it was there. There was a flicker of something in her eyes, and she fidgeted uncomfortably in her chair.

'Is everything all right with you and Alexander?' said Jenny inquisitively.

For a second, Olivia thought about unpacking all of her worries about him potentially having an affair, but she knew it would sound ridiculous and it wasn't true. She didn't want to put the thought out there in the world. She didn't want it in Jenny's mind. It wasn't fair to Alexander, who had done nothing wrong. Best keep it inside. But then another part of her wanted to share it with Jenny. She wanted Jenny to tell her it was crazy, and that there was nothing to worry about. A problem shared is a problem halved. This wasn't always true but keeping it inside was killing her. Before she even realised it was pouring out of her.

'I think Alexander's having an affair,' she said quickly.

'What?' said Jenny incredulously. 'Why do you think that?'

'I just have a feeling. He's been off recently, and things between us have been weird.'

'But that doesn't mean he's cheating on you, Liv.'

'I know, but it's more than that,' said Olivia, before she took a breath. 'A few weeks ago he came home from school, and I could smell perfume on him.'

'But that could be from anywhere.'

'And I found a blonde hair on his jacket, and yes, I know, it could have come from anywhere too, but I just have this feeling. I suggested we go on a date on Friday night, and he suddenly has plans to go to the pub with school. I don't know, it's …' said Olivia, and a tear leaked out suddenly and slid down her face.

Jenny reached across and put a hand over Olivia's.

'Olivia. I know you and I know Alexander. I really don't think he's the sort of man to have an affair. You need to be sure before you accuse him of doing something.'

'I know, I know,' said Olivia. 'It's just … I've told myself over and over that he wouldn't do it. He's Alexander. It's not in him.'

'Then why do you still think he is?'

Olivia left a pause, and then she looked at her friend.

'Because most of the couples I see start off by saying they didn't think they were capable of it. It came out of the blue. It's how it always starts, Jenny. It's how lies are believed because not believing them means your marriage is probably over.'

'Gosh,' said Jenny, squeezing Olivia's hand. 'But you must realise that just because you see it at work, it doesn't mean it's true of Alexander.'

'I realise, of course.'

'Then make sure you know before you confront him because once it's out there, once he thinks you don't trust him, you can't take that back again.'

Olivia smiled at her friend, and then they both said they had to get back. Jenny told her not to do anything rash without calling her first. They hugged and promised to start planning their spa weekend soon. They walked their separate ways back towards their work. Olivia realised that seeing Jenny, having a chat and a catch-up, had grounded her a little. Perhaps she had been too much in her own headspace. Jenny didn't believe for a moment that

Alexander would cheat on her. He was a good man. It had eased her worries somewhat. It didn't explain the perfume, the hair, or the sudden drink on Friday, but it made Olivia slightly less worried. Perhaps she had been looking for things that just weren't there. She relaxed slightly as she walked back to her car. It was only a five-minute drive back to her house. She could have walked the twenty minutes, but she had an afternoon client, and didn't want to be all sweaty. It had been good talking to Jenny. She had needed it. Her mind felt clearer and slightly emptier than it had. Everything would be all right. It was nothing, just the silly worries of a middle-aged woman.

Alexander was having lunch in his classroom when the door opened, and Sara Coupland walked in. Sara had started working at Alexander's school that year. She had moved from Brighton, where she had been teaching. She had wanted a change, wanted to be nearer to London, and that was the first job that had come up. She was twenty-eight, pretty with light blonde hair, large blue eyes, and a body that was moulded in the gym. She worked out every morning before school, and at least three times on the weekend. She was young and beautiful, and when Alexander met her, shook her hand in the staff room, he would never have imagined that she would have kissed him that one time a few weeks ago, completely changing and altering the fabric of his life.

It had happened after school on a Friday. Alexander was tidying up and getting ready to go home when she came into his room. They had spoken a few times, and Alexander thought her quite easy to talk to. She laughed easily and touched him often. An arm here or a shoulder there. He assumed it was her age. So much more tactile than Alexander's generation. She'd had a tough day and needed a chat. Alexander offered her some words of comfort, encouraged her to not let the little shits get to her, and when it was done, she gave him a hug. A simple hug was all it took. Feeling her perfect young body pressed momentarily against his. He had stiffened up immediately, and he had felt something. Something raw and passionate within himself that he hadn't felt in years. When she pulled away, they both for a second clung onto each other. Their eyes locked. Alexander would never have done it. He wouldn't have considered kissing her, but she leaned in and kissed him. Their mouths met and something seismic happened to Alexander.

She walked into his classroom during lunch and sat on a desk in front of him. Alexander felt his entire body change. All of his senses heightened, and he became aroused without even thinking about it. Something else that hadn't happened to him in years.

'Mr Burke,' said Sara with a salacious smile.

It was a game they played.

'Miss Coupland.'

She was wearing a knee-length skirt and a soft pink top. She sat back on the table, her legs slowly easing apart until Alexander could see enough of her legs to send his brain into a complete meltdown. The merest hint of a pair of white knickers in the darkness. His arousal only grew, and he could barely contain his need for her. She elicited a physical reaction in him he hadn't felt since his early twenties when he had first met Olivia. It was partly from the fact he couldn't believe that someone as young and as beautiful as her would find him attractive.

'Friday,' she said.

'Friday,' said Alexander.

He felt his voice wobble. He couldn't believe this was happening. He felt awful for what he was doing. The guilt was attacking his insides, causing him physical pain, and the idea of cheating on Olivia made him feel sick to his stomach. But he also couldn't stop thinking about it. About her. Her supple, smooth legs, and the way her breasts moved when she walked. She had worn a shirt a few days ago, with the shirt unbuttoned a few buttons less than she'd had in class. She stood next to him, and he'd looked down at her breasts. So young, perky, and full. He couldn't stop himself. A glimpse of her bra. A momentary glance at her knickers. If only she didn't tease him like that. If only she hadn't kissed him. Her tongue in his mouth and with such passion, it made him feel young again. She was complex and dangerous. He knew it was sad, the last hurrah of a middle-aged man. She was toying with him, but it was as if there was nothing he could do about it.

'I can't wait,' said Sara, who closed her legs and stood up straight.

She walked right up to him until she was close enough to kiss him. Alexander could barely stop himself from grabbing her there and then and having sex on his desk. He fantasised about it. She was a few inches from him. Her perfume aroused him further still. She reached a hand down and slowly traced a finger around the top of his trousers, where his penis was hard and straining at the fabric. She ran a finger along it. It was unbearable. She looked at him, smiled, ran her tongue slowly along her top lip, and then she turned around and walked out. Friday. A simple word with a lifetime of consequences. It wasn't about Olivia. It wasn't about his marriage. It was just a desire for Sara Coupland. How could any man resist her? It wasn't his fault. And anyway, Olivia would never know. It was just once, and then it would never happen again. He had told himself that. Just once. That was the rule. He just had to know what it was like to touch a body like that. To have her touch him. He had to know. He wished it wasn't so, but it was.

8.

The present

Alexander put their coffees down on the table and sat opposite Belinda. They were outside a small cafe, and Belinda had a blank, lost expression on her face. After the initial adrenalin caused by her attempted suicide, Belinda quickly sunk back into herself again. The depression that had ravaged her last few months returned. The nightmares that had haunted her were still there, and she didn't want to be sitting with Alexander having a coffee. She couldn't even enjoy the coffee. It tasted strange and bitter. People walked past and saw them together, and Belinda knew what they were thinking. Why was this smartly dressed man with this homeless woman? What could he possibly have to do with someone like her? What they didn't know, didn't imagine for a moment, is that she could so easily have been one of them and they could so easily have been her. A couple of different decisions, a bit of bad luck, and it was so easy to fall between the cracks.

Alexander looked across at her. He saw what everyone else saw. A homeless woman who had been living rough on the streets for months. No shoes, dirt squashed underneath her bitten fingernails, and hair that was so matted together it barely looked like hair at all. It was her eyes that were the most difficult to look at. They were empty. The life that had lived in them was long gone. If you passed Belinda on the streets, you might not look at her. Too afraid that by engaging with her, admitting her existence, you would question your own. Belinda was a reminder that we are all at the mercy of luck and choices. One wrong decision, one piece of bad luck, one unwanted biological trait from the family gene pool, and any of us could end up like her.

Alexander didn't know what to say. She sipped her

coffee. He wondered when she had last had a hot drink or a decent meal. He wanted to take care of her. He felt an overwhelming desire to make sure she didn't try to kill herself again. He wanted to know her story and how this had happened to her. What takes someone from being a child, a teenager, to trying to kill themselves at such a young age? What misfortunes had she had to endure? Alexander was curious because he knew how it had happened to him. One moment. One lie. And everything can fall apart.

'How's the coffee?' he said, eventually.

She looked across at him. She sort of smiled. A stale smile that barely registered on any other part of her face. Alexander wanted to know everything about her, but he quickly realised it wasn't the time. She wasn't going to suddenly tell him everything. He needed time. She needed help. They weren't going to fix everything over one cup of coffee. It's when the idea came to him. It was perhaps a ridiculous idea, but when it came to Alexander in the cafe, he thought it was the only workable solution. He looked across the table at Belinda.

'Do you want to come and stay with me? Just until you get yourself sorted.'

Belinda looked across the table at Alexander. What was his deal? Maybe he was some sort of weird pervert, and he was going to get her back to his house, lock her up and use her for sex. Maybe he was genuinely nice and just wanted to help, or maybe it was somewhere in-between. The thing was it didn't really matter. Obviously, she hoped he wasn't a deviant sexual predator, but if she said no and left, where would she go? Back on the streets? And perhaps she would wake up tomorrow and feel like killing herself again. At least if she went with Alexander, she could sleep in a bed again. She could eat, wash, and feel like a human being. Perhaps after all the bad luck she had had in her life, Alexander was finally a bit of good.

'You sure?' said Belinda.

He looked uncertain. Perhaps he was already second

guessing his decision.

'Of course. It's half-term next week, so I'm off anyway.'

He smiled at her. She took a sip of her coffee. Alexander did the same.

Life was so unexpected, thought Belinda. She fully expected to be dead that day. Hit by a train, her lifeless body tossed onto the tracks. A small news story on a local radio station. Perhaps a few lines in a newspaper because that's all her life was worth. She had thought about it that morning. How she wanted to go. It had to be quick. She wanted to die, but she didn't want to suffer. The trouble when you're living rough is that there's only so many ways you can do it. She thought about jumping off a tall building. It's going to sound silly, but Belinda was afraid of heights. The thought of standing on the edge of a tall building made her feel sick. It would also take a few seconds to fall, and what if in those few seconds she changed her mind? She didn't want time to think. That's when she heard the train in the distance and the idea came to her. Getting hit by a train would be fast. Hit and then you're dead. Perhaps a second of excruciating pain. No time to change your mind. She momentarily felt bad for the poor driver, and even the passengers, but they weren't her problem. She just wanted the pain to stop. But then Alexander turned up, and now she was going back to his house until she got herself sorted. She didn't know what that meant, and truth be told, neither did Alexander.

'Okay,' said Belinda. 'Just for a bit.'

'Good. That's settled then.'

They finished their coffees in silence. He asked if she had any stuff she needed to get, and she sort of laughed, and said no. What did he think she had back in the high street doorway? A priceless family heirloom? They got in his car, and he started to drive. He said it wasn't far. Belinda had no idea what sort of house he lived in, or what sort of life he had. He had to be in his late forties or maybe fifties. He wasn't wearing a wedding ring, and so she assumed he wasn't married. They drove in silence. It had been ages since she'd been in a car before that morning. Memories of being in a car as a child came back to her. Sat in the front next to her da' in silence. Belinda staring out of the window at the world, her da' driving too fast as he always did, and Belinda wishing she could get away. She had dreams then.

She watched suburbia go by until they arrived at Alexander's house. Belinda was shocked because it was larger and much nicer than she had imagined. It was on a tree-lined road full of beautiful houses. It was classic Richmond. An old house with plenty of character. It was the sort of house she had imagined living in one day when she had dreams. When she thought about the life she wanted. Alexander parked the car on the small gravel driveway in front of the house.

'Here we are,' he said, turning the engine off.

She sat in the car next to him for a moment. She was trying to catch her thoughts. She took a deep breath, and they both got out. The large house had a small front garden that looked like it needed a bit of work. The grass was long, the flowers and plants needed cutting back, and even the wall needed a few bricks replacing. Alexander opened the front door. It was a large, green door with a heavy brass knocker. He walked inside, and Belinda followed him.

'I'll give you the tour,' said Alexander, slightly nervously. He tried to laugh at his own silly joke, but it was half-hearted, and his face quickly dissolved back into an expression of someone who didn't quite know what they were doing. Belinda momentarily felt bad for him. It was obvious he was doing his best, but he wasn't used to this. To people. The house had a stuffy smell, as if it had been closed up for a long time. They walked along the hallway and into the living room. It was nice. Two sofas, a television, and a yellow armchair. A rug on a wooden floor, and an old fireplace. She noticed some photos on the mantelpiece. A girl of about sixteen or seventeen. A young couple getting married a long time ago. A family holiday. A school sports day.

Alexander took her through into the large room at the back of the house. It was nice, and beyond the large back door, she noticed the garden. It was wide and long, and in the middle of the lawn was a tree, and on the tree was a swing. A wooden swing that had been painted blue and yellow. It made Belinda smile for a moment because it reminded her of a swing from her own childhood. A wooden swing tied to a tree over a small stream. Kids shouting. Belinda wondered if Alexander had any children. Maybe the girl from the photo. They walked upstairs where Alexander showed her a bathroom, and then her room. A sizable room that looked like it had been decorated for a teenage girl. Light pink walls, flowery curtains, a pink fuzzy rug, a bed with a white duvet that looked like it hadn't been slept in in years. Belinda thought about asking Alexander who the room belonged to but decided against it.

'Would you like a shower or a bath?' said Alexander. 'I have spare towels, and I can probably find you some clothes.'

Alexander was nervous because he didn't know what Belinda needed. The idea for her to come and stay with him had been a spontaneous one. What he hadn't thought about was the practicality of having another human in the house. Another body, and a female one at that. It had been a long time since someone else had been in the house. Belinda said she would like a shower, and Alexander wandered off to find a towel and some extra clothes. He went into his bedroom. Her wardrobe stood in the corner of the room. The white wooden wardrobe with some of her clothes still inside. Alexander hadn't been able to get rid of all of them. He just couldn't. The wardrobe stood against the wall and hadn't been opened in years. He opened the door. They were probably about the same size. He had a quick look through and found a dress, some underwear, a cardigan, and a pair of socks. He didn't know what she liked, and so he grabbed a few other things too. A pair of jeans, a jumper, and then he got a spare towel from the airing cupboard. He walked back into the room where Belinda was sitting on the bed. It was a strange sensation walking into her bedroom again and seeing a woman there.

'Here you go. I hope they're okay. It's all I could find,' said Alexander. He laid the clothes neatly in a pile next to her. 'There's shampoo and body wash in the shower. I think there's a spare toothbrush in the drawer too. I can go shopping later and get anything else you need.'

Belinda looked up at Alexander. She had as many questions for him as he had for her. Who did these clothes belong to? Who lived in this bedroom? Why was he living by himself, and why did he look so sad? So terribly sad and lost. Belinda knew she would have to talk to Alexander at some point. Maybe she would tell him her story. How she had ended up living rough on the streets and why she had wanted to die. But it would have to wait. It would all have to wait. At that moment, she wanted to take a shower and then sleep. She hadn't slept properly in months. You couldn't sleep on the streets. People, noises, and the fear of what might happen to you kept you awake. It was why most people drank or took drugs, because it was the only way. But Belinda didn't drink or do drugs. She didn't want to lose herself completely. For the longest time, she wanted to keep fighting, keep dreaming, and hoping that things would get better.

Belinda turned the water on and then peeled her clothes off. They were disgusting. She knew it and hated herself for becoming that version of herself. She put them in a pile on the floor. They would all have to go in the bin. She had a fresh pile of clothes next to them. She stood under the water and let it run over her naked body. Over the dirt and the scars of her life. She stood there and let the tears stream down her face and join the water on the shower floor and get washed away. She couldn't help crying, and once she started, she found it hard to stop. The water ran down her legs and past her ankle where the tattoo was. The tattoo she'd had done when life had been so different. When she couldn't have imagined how bad things would get. The tattoo in black ink that just said, Rachel.

9.

The past

'I'm home,' said Alexander as he hurriedly walked in, closing the front door behind him. He was late back from school and knew dinner would almost be ready.

'In the kitchen,' Olivia replied.

Alexander put his satchel against the wall and his coat over the banister. He had a quick look at himself in the hallway mirror. Did he look different? Did he look as guilty as he felt? Did the searing, burning fire inside of him show on his face? Surely it had to, but when he looked in the mirror, all he saw was his usual old self.

'Hello, Dad,' said Laura, walking down the stairs.

'All right, love. Good day?'

'Yeah, okay, s'pose.'

She had changed out of her school uniform, and was wearing a pair of dark blue jeans, a white t-shirt, and the necklace they had bought her for her last birthday. A silver love heart pendant she wore over her t-shirt. She had opened it at Pizza Express. Her choice for a birthday meal. Pizza, dough balls, and cheesecake for dessert. Her sweet sixteen, she had called it. Everything was getting more and more American, and Alexander hated it. Why did kids' love America so much? Couldn't they see what an awful country it was? Why didn't they revere Sweden or New Zealand instead? Countries with better infrastructure, better quality healthcare, education, and kinder societies? Alexander and Laura walked into the kitchen where Olivia was serving dinner. Steak, chips, and steamed broccoli. She had a bottle of wine for her and Alexander, and a loaf of crusty bread for the table.

'This looks great,' said Alexander, kissing Olivia on the cheek.

He could still feel Sara's finger on his trousers. He could still smell her perfume. It was as if when he was at school with Sara, he could almost forget about Olivia. He could compartmentalise the two different worlds. In one world, he was a happily married man with a daughter, and a lovely house, and everything was just as it should be. Content. Middle-aged. Middle-class. In the other he was with a sexy young teacher who teased him, wanted him, and made him feel alive. He had to keep the two worlds separate in his mind or he couldn't cope. He couldn't look into his wife's eyes or talk to his daughter if he was thinking about Sara. At that moment he was at home, and so he put all thoughts of Sara Coupland away. Locked up in a vault at the very back of his mind. He was going to relax with his wife and daughter. He was the happily married version of himself. The other man didn't exist.

'It's almost ready,' said Olivia. 'Could you lay the table, Laura?'

'Sure,' said Laura.

Laura walked over and started getting the table ready for dinner. She wanted to get dinner over with as soon as possible because she was going to see Tom. She was going to tell her parents she was going out for a walk, and then she was going to meet up with him in secret. How had this happened? Tom was all she could think about. She had gone from quite liking him a few weeks ago, to now being all she could think about. She had seen him at school, but she wanted to see him properly. She wanted to kiss him. Hold him. Hug him. There was a park nearby, and they were going to meet there. It was risky because they might be spotted, but she didn't feel like she had a choice. She yearned to be with him. Every fibre in her body called out his name. Tom. Tom. Tom.

'How was your day?' Alexander said to Olivia.

'I met Jenny for a coffee,' said Olivia, putting food onto the plates.

'Oh, how is she?'

'Good. It was nice catching up. I think we're going to have a spa weekend soon.'

'You should,' said Alexander. 'You deserve it.'

Olivia looked across and smiled at her husband. She was lucky. She really was. He smiled back as he filled up two glasses of wine for dinner. The idea he was having an affair seemed silly at that moment. She had no reason to believe he was cheating on her except a hunch that something wasn't quite right, and a couple of very explainable coincidences. She had always put so much weight behind her hunches, but perhaps now she was wrong. There could have been a million reasons why Alexander was acting strangely. The perfume was easily explained, as was the strand of hair, and Friday night was probably just what he said it was. The only reason her mind went to the possibility of an affair was because of her work. But it was nothing. She knew that now.

'I'll take the wine to the table,' said Alexander, before he gave her a kiss on the cheek.

Laura had finished laying the table, and everything was ready. Olivia brought the plates across, and they started eating. Laura and Alexander both said how good the steaks were. Perfectly medium rare. Olivia looked across at her daughter. She was so big now. So grown up. Olivia knew she was seeing a boy. She didn't know the details, but she could tell that something had changed, and a boy was the most likely reason. A mother's intuition. Olivia hadn't meant to find out. She wasn't snooping, but she overheard a phone call and sensed something in the way that Laura was behaving. Olivia put two and two together and she was sure it made four. The thing was, she didn't mind. Alexander had been the one putting his foot down about her having a boyfriend. After her exams, he had said. She needed to focus. Olivia understood his position, but she hadn't wholeheartedly agreed. Laura was a young woman, and she was going to have boyfriends, and things were going to happen. They had to trust that she would make the right decisions when the moment arose. Olivia trusted her. She was a good girl, and she was as ambitious as Alexander was for her. Her bloody single mindedness had always surprised Olivia. Her daughter was going to succeed, and she didn't think a boy was going to get in the way.

'So, when are you and Jenny going away for your spa weekend?' said Alexander.

Olivia took a sip of her wine. Laura was chewing on a piece of steak.

'Oh, I don't know. We always say we will, but then it never happens.'

'Then make sure it does this time,' said Alexander.

'You really should, Mum,' said Laura.

Alexander looked at Olivia, smiled, and then rested a hand on her leg. He gave it a soft squeeze. She liked it when he did things like that. He used to do it a lot when they were younger. He had been so much more tactile then. She longed for it again. To be touched.

'I'd love to go away for a spa weekend,' said Laura. 'I need to relax with all the studying.'

'We'll do something for you after your exams,' said Alexander. 'Promise.'

'Like a spa weekend with a friend?' said Laura.

'As long as I'm your friend,' said Olivia, and Laura made a face at her mum, and then they both laughed.

Alexander was so proud of Laura. It was like a light that glowed from within him. It started deep within his soul and then got stronger and stronger until it came out of him like a giant beacon that shone so brightly. She was his pride and joy. She would do everything he hadn't been able to.

'I'm going for a walk after dinner before I start studying again,' said Laura casually. 'I need to get some fresh air, or I'll go mad.'

Olivia looked across at her daughter and immediately wondered if she was going to meet her boyfriend or whatever it was she called him. The boy she was seeing. Hooking up with. She wondered if they were having sex.

She hoped not. She needed to have a talk with Laura. Make sure she was being careful. She would talk to her later that night.

'Just don't be too long,' said Alexander. 'There isn't much time left before your exams.'

'I know, Dad,' said Laura, slightly annoyed.

'I'm just saying,' said Alexander.

'I think she knows,' said Olivia to her husband.

This time she reached a hand down and softly squeezed his leg, before she had a sip of her wine, and Alexander did the same.

They finished their dinner in relative silence. Alexander gave them the brief bullet points of his dad, leaving out any mention of Sara Coupland. Laura spoke about some drama with one of her friends at school. Her parents were separating, and her friend just cried all the time. They were soon finished, and Olivia told Laura she could go on her walk while they tidied up. Laura quickly dashed upstairs, put on some lipstick, a spray of perfume, grabbed her coat, and headed out to meet Tom. They were meeting at the park by their tree. The tree where they had their first kiss. The tree that meant so much to them. He had carved their initials into it with a penknife. TC Loves LB. She ached to feel his body in hers. To feel his lips on her lips. She had never known a feeling like it. When it had started, she was so sure of herself. So sure that she could control it, be in charge of it because she knew what boys were like, but now as she hurried off to meet Tom, she felt giddy and completely out of control.

Alexander told Olivia to sit down. He would tidy up and make them a cup of tea.

'Thanks. Love you,' said Olivia, before she planted a kiss on his lips. Maybe they could have sex that night. She wanted to have sex. Alexander had a way about him sometimes that made her want to sleep with him. It was like she forgot how attractive he was, or that he had such a sexy accent, and then in a moment she would remember. It was in those moments when she really wanted him. Needed him. She knew they were too infrequent for Alexander's liking, but she did her best. The kiss was slightly more passionate than she had intended, and when she pulled away, she found herself smiling at him.

'What?' he said.

'Nothing,' said Olivia with a coquettish grin.

She felt silly, like a schoolgirl with a crush. Yes, they would definitely have sex that night. She might even put on some nice underwear for him. One of the newer sets at the back of her wardrobe that hardly ever got put to use. She felt herself getting slightly aroused just thinking about it. She left Alexander and headed towards the living room. She would put on the television, have a cup of tea, and watch the news. She was feeling quite happy and relaxed, but as she passed Alexander's satchel in the hallway, she heard it rumbling. He must have got a message. She thought about leaving it for a moment. It probably wasn't important. But then she thought perhaps it was, and she decided to retrieve it and give it to him. She reached into his satchel and took out his phone. The screen was still on with a message from a contact that just said School. She knew she probably shouldn't, but she was curious. She opened his phone. She knew the passcode. She had set his passcode when they had bought the phones. She opened his phone, went to messages, and opened the message from School. There was only one message.

FYI No knickers tomorrow xxx

Olivia felt a chill go through her body. She didn't understand what the message meant, and who it was from. Who was School? No knickers tomorrow and then three kisses. The thought of what that meant shot through her mind like scenes from a film trailer. Short shots cut together and edited down to form a slightly coherent story. A woman who wasn't going to wear knickers to school, and she was telling her husband. Why? Olivia's head went numb and a noise like a distant scream reverberated around her head. A heat rose inside her body. Her suspicions were right. Something was going on. Olivia's first thought was to march into the kitchen, show Alexander the phone, and get him to explain himself. If she confronted him, perhaps he would come clean and confess everything. Maybe nothing had happened. Perhaps he had a crazy stalker. But she couldn't. She was too angry, too confused, and nothing good came from reacting with pure emotion. If she confronted him at that moment, it would be a disaster. Instead, Olivia deleted the message and slipped his phone back into his satchel. She went into the living room, sat down, turned the television on, and waited for Alexander.

'Tea will be ready in a minute,' said Alexander.

He sat down next to her on the sofa, a hand on her leg. She let it stay there. The news was on. Alexander made a comment about one of the news stories. Another stabbing of another teenage boy in London. What *a ridiculous waste of life*. But all Olivia could think about was the message, and who had sent it. Why would Alexander cheat on her? Were things that bad? And then she thought about Friday. He had said he was going for drinks after work. A last-minute thing. Perhaps it was true, but maybe it wasn't. Alexander got up to make the tea, and Olivia knew she wasn't like her client, Susan Farringdon. She would do something. She wouldn't suffer in silence. The truth, however painful, was better than living a lie. As soon as he was gone, she felt a tear slide down her face, but she wiped it away quickly. A vision of her own mother doing the same thing shot through her mind.

Alexander got up and walked back towards the kitchen. He realised that he'd forgotten to take his phone out of his satchel. He reached into his bag and felt for his phone. He found it, opened it, and checked for messages. For a terrifying moment he imagined Olivia finding a message from Sara, but there was nothing. He had told her not to message him unless she really had to, but she seemed to have a penchant for danger. Alexander put his phone in his pocket and walked into the kitchen to finish making the tea.

10.

The present

Louise left Ella's bedroom. She crept out quietly and closed the door carefully behind her. It was dark, and Ella was finally asleep. Sometimes she fell asleep quickly, but today it had been nearly an hour. Louise was tired. It had been a long day. A day of rain and dark, heavy clouds that had painted everything with a dullness. A day of keeping Ella occupied, making food, cleaning up, and trying without success to have some time to herself. It had been one of those days. Ella was annoyed, fussy, and wanted her mummy. Louise didn't want to wish away the years, but she longed for the day when Ella finally went to school, and she could focus on herself again.

Downstairs, Jim sat on the sofa, scrolling through channels without settling on anything, and drinking from a can of cheap lager. Louise sat next to him. She wanted to do some reading. It had been her plan all day, but she was too tired. Her eyes were heavy, and she wouldn't be able to focus. Instead, she would watch TV with Jim and let her mind be absorbed by that instead.

'All right, love? She finally asleep?' said Jim.

'Finally.'

She sat down next to Jim. She immediately pulled her legs onto the sofa. She sat back and put her feet up on Jim's lap. If she was lucky, he might give her a foot rub. He gave her the occasional food rub if he was in the mood. He was watching a reality show she didn't care about.

'Is there anything decent on?' she said.

'It depends on what you mean by decent?'

Louise and Jim had different tastes in television. Jim liked American sitcoms, reality shows, Eastenders, and sport. Louise liked tightly plotted psychological thrillers and period dramas. Jim started scrolling through the channels again. It was one of the many things that annoyed her about Jim. She often thought about the day when she had agreed to all of this. Agreed to have Ella, get a house with Jim, and be in a relationship. If she hadn't fallen pregnant with Ella, there's no way they would still be together. They were just a fling. A one-night stand that had escalated. She would have stopped seeing him and gone for someone else. Someone with more of a brain, with money, a decent career at least. Not that she was that superficial, but if you were going to start a life with a random man, he might as well be able to offer you something. The condom had split. That was the official prognosis. That's what must have happened. They were a bit drunk. There was brief talk of an abortion, but it soon fell away to the realisation that they were having a baby together, whether or not they wanted to. Once Ella was on the scene, Jim started talking about getting somewhere together, settling down, being a couple, and she had gone along with it. Mainly because the alternative was raising a baby alone with no money and no help. On the sofa, with Jim half-heartedly rubbing her feet and searching through channels trying to find something to watch, and with Ella asleep upstairs, Louise wished she had made a different choice. This wasn't the life she wanted. Jim suddenly switched the television off and turned to Louise.

'Fancy going to bed?' he said with a smile. He downed the last dregs of his beer.

It was a smile she knew only too well. It had been a couple of weeks since they'd had sex, and she knew it was due. She felt bad for Jim because he worked hard, did his best with Ella, and he treated her well. It was why they were still together and why she occasionally still had sex with him. Not because she really wanted to, but because she felt guilty if she didn't. She was quite tired, but what else were they going to do? It was only eight o'clock.

'Come on then,' she said, getting up and taking him by the hand.

Jim was happy to go along with her. Deep down, he knew she wasn't really into it, but maybe if they kept going and had another kid together, she would finally be okay with him. Jim really believed that. He had asked her about having another baby before, but she had said no. A categorical no. But with Ella off to school in the autumn, it made sense. Jim had also been planning a little surprise for Louise. His parents had given him some money. Not much, but enough to go away for a little holiday. He was going to take Louise and Ella to a caravan in Devon. Five days away, and he was going to ask her to marry him. They had spoken about it before, but nothing had been decided or finalised. Instead, it sat at the back of Jim's mind, slowly gathering pace. If they got married, had another kid, and he worked hard, maybe they could get their own place and be a proper family. It's all Jim wanted. He didn't need much to be happy. Just Louise, a couple of kids, a house, and maybe a better car. Yeah, thought Jim, one day.

Louise turned the light off, and they got into bed. They had to be careful because the walls of their house were paper thin. It was an ex-council terraced house, and you could hear everything the neighbours were doing. Louise knew the intricate details of their lives just from the conversations she overheard through the walls. The shouting matches she heard every Friday night after he'd been out drinking. Friday was payday. Louise dreaded Friday nights. She could hear them, and so she knew they could hear her. It meant sex had to be done as quietly as possible. Not that she had much reason to scream in ecstasy. Sex with Jim, she thought, was a bit like painting with numbers. He started at one and went through all the numbers, checking them off the list. The list he had once read in a copy of a Cosmopolitan magazine that had been left lying around. Kissing. Breasts. Vagina. Then when he heard her make any sort of noise, he'd stop, they would get fully undressed, and then they'd have sex. It lasted no longer than two minutes, and Louise would orgasm roughly twenty per cent of the time. It was a numbers-based game. This time she didn't orgasm. Too tired and not really in the mood. Jim, who had been starved of sex for the past two weeks, orgasmed in record time before he laid back on the bed, a sweaty, exhausted mess. Louise had to focus her mind to orgasm with Jim. After a minute, she went to the bathroom to get cleaned up. The word that came to her while she was sitting on the toilet was perfunctory.

Afterwards, Jim did his usual pee, brushed his teeth, and then spent time on his phone reading about the biggest love of his life, West Ham United. He could spend hours reading football reports and watching videos. Louise said she needed a drink and went downstairs. Jim would probably fall asleep before she went back upstairs again. The upshot of having sex was that Louise had a second wind. She wasn't so tired, and so she decided to have a read. She got a glass of water and headed into the lounge. She had two books she'd got out from the library she was trying to read before they were due back. She turned the light on, put her glass of water on the coffee table, and opened the thickest of the books. She submerged her mind into the world of law, and it felt good. It made her happy. It reminded her of the girl she used to be.

After everything that had happened, Louise took up her place at sixth form college. Her mind was awash with so many things she had a hard time focusing. She was working at a cafe too, and her life felt so fragmented. Other students and friends seemed to be happily living in the same bubble she used to inhabit. She didn't blame them, because how could they know? She would have been exactly the same. Nights out drinking, parties, and experimenting with alcohol and boys, was all a part of college. It was preparation for university. The thing Louise hadn't known then was that she wasn't going to go. She couldn't. She needed more time. She somehow got through her A Levels and got fairly decent grades, considering. A natural intelligence and a good memory more than made up for the circumstances of her life. She did well, but she was exhausted. It was as if she had spent the last two years existing on adrenalin alone. But then she crashed. Her body was so tired, and she couldn't think. She couldn't go off to university in that state. She took a year off, which stretched into two and then three. She met Jim and fell pregnant with Ella, and somehow the years had gone by, and she was twenty-six. Twenty-six and the urgency to correct herself, turn herself around, had come back stronger than ever. She wanted to survive and the only way she knew how was to study.

It was almost midnight when she finally closed the book. The curtains were drawn, and she had the light on in their tiny living room. Some of Ella's toys were stacked in the corner because there wasn't space for them anywhere else. Louise loved Ella so much, and she wanted to do this for her as much as herself. Ella deserved more than this. She wanted Ella to have all the opportunities she'd had in life. Louise's dream of going to Oxford was over. She had done well at sixth form, but not well enough to get into Oxford. Louise hadn't told Jim, but she had been looking at university courses. Ella was starting school in September, and then Louise would have the time to study again. There was a law degree at Kingston university, and Louise wanted to apply for it. She was too late to start that autumn, and she wanted to give herself the best shot at success, and so she was going to apply next year.

Louise wanted to become a barrister. That meant three years doing her bachelor's degree, and then postgraduate study, vocational courses, the Bar course, pupillage, and then finally she would qualify. It would take roughly five years. She would be thirty-two by the time she became a barrister. Ella would be almost ten years old. But it would be worth it. Then she could give them the life she wanted. They could afford a house, and to move somewhere nice where Ella could go to school without the fear of being attacked or knifed to death.

As Louise sat in her lounge that night, she thought about her past and her future. She wasn't going to let one destroy the other. She knew her life wasn't living in that house with Jim and popping out another couple of kids. She knew she could become so much more than she was. She felt like her life, and the life of her daughter depended on it. Once upon a time, chance, fate, a moment, had taken the life she had away. Louise thought about the tree again. She thought about how her childhood and adolescence were the trunk. How stable it was. Then she thought about all the branches that had led off that trunk, and where they had gone. She hadn't had the time then to choose the right branch. She wasn't thinking clearly enough to look up and see a clear route to the top. It had seemed too difficult. There were too many branches, and it was all too much. But when she looked up now, she had the time and the clarity of thought to see a route. She could see the stronger branches that would support them. She saw it all like a map in her head.

Louise closed her book, turned off the light, and went upstairs to bed. She checked in on Ella and she was sound asleep. She watched her little body for a moment. So small, and in a tiny ball, wrapped around her duvet, teddy still held loosely in her hand. Louise leaned down and gave her a kiss on the forehead. She left her room and tiptoed back across the landing to her bedroom. Jim was sound asleep, snoring loudly on his back. Louise got into bed and listened to all the sounds of life around her. Outside, she heard sirens, and someone shouted. Jim snored, and Louise thought momentarily of her father. She did still think about him. She wondered how he was and what he was doing. Occasionally, she thought of seeing him again, mainly out of curiosity, but the thoughts always subsided. Louise closed her eyes and slowly fell asleep, dreams about her future, and thoughts of the past slowly fading to darkness, and then she was asleep.

Part Two

11.

The past

Belinda's mum was in the bathroom, and she had locked the door behind her. Belinda could hear her crying from her bedroom. It wasn't the first time she'd heard her crying. It wasn't the first time that month. Things had definitely got worse. Belinda's brother, Jason, was in Dublin now. He was three years older than her and spent most of his time in town these days. He hadn't been home in at least four months, and even then it was brief and tumultuous. He had friends in Dublin and worked in a bar. He wasn't at university, but he liked the university girls. It was the main reason he worked where he worked, he had once told Belinda. Easy money, easy girls, he had said while taking a drag on his cigarette in their back garden. He was handsome, Belinda had always thought, and had the gift of the gab. 'He'll break hearts, that one, that's for sure,' more than one of their aunts had said about him. He was breaking away from their family. He had been stretching the cord between himself and them since he was sixteen, and old enough to make his own way in the world. He had little interest in staying around, which made Belinda sad because he was the one person in her family she truly loved. The only one who would stand up to their da'. Without him, Belinda stayed in her bedroom, waiting for the day when she could leave too.

The sound of her mum crying sounded like a wounded animal. A high-pitched wail and then a guttural grunt, followed by moments of quiet when Belinda hoped it was over before she started again. Belinda hugged her knees. She had been trying to read a book when she heard the shouting. Belinda hoped he didn't come into her bedroom. Even if it meant her mum would take the brunt of his drunken rage. It was her choice, Belinda told herself. She could always leave him, but she never did. Too weak. Too afraid.

Their house was on an estate on the edge of Dublin. A white and brown box surrounded by miles and miles of drab grey concrete. Even on the warmest days, it wasn't the sort of place that could look nice. A lack of trees and colour made the awful greyness of it seem worse. It was a desolate place. A war-torn town without the war. Every house was basically the same, every road and pavement like a depressing version of the future, where everything natural and beautiful was gone, and all that was left were rows of houses like small prisons. The only colour she saw on her street was the graffiti on the walls that were blank canvases for the bored and angry. It was ironic, thought Belinda, because they lived in Ireland, named the Emerald Isle because of its lush green rolling hills and valleys. It was so depressing that she was so close to such beauty, and instead she was trapped in the worst place she could imagine. She loved the days when they got out and into the country. Not that it happened often. She loved the greenness of it in the same way she hated the concrete greyness of where she lived. Their cramped three-bedroom terraced house. The grass that had once been in the garden was dead and covered in rubbish and cigarette butts tossed on the ground. A few broken beer bottles were against the fence, smashed in moments of anger, and left. A white plastic chair that had been stolen from a pub garden had been in the back garden for a year. It sat like a depressing art installation. Belinda hated everything about her house. It was devoid of everything, including love.

She winced as she heard his feet on the landing. He had been downstairs taking a break. Probably smoking a cigarette and getting some more energy for round two. He had returned home from the pub where he'd been all afternoon and evening, blind drunk, as usual. Belinda never understood how he could afford to drink so much when they barely had enough money to pay the rent. The electricity had been cut off more times than she could remember growing up.

Belinda sat on her bed, her knees hugged tight against her chest, hoping her door wouldn't open. The same feeling she had felt throughout her childhood. At least when Jason was home, and things got bad, she could run into his bedroom and hide. Her da' wouldn't usually bother her if she was with him. Two against one weren't good odds, and if her father was one thing, it was a classic bully. He only picked on her mother because she never fought back. The landing creaked, and then her door opened slightly. Her heart sank.

'Go away, Da',' said Belinda firmly.

She was sixteen now, and although her da' was a big man, he was drunk. If he came at her, she could defend herself. At least that's what she thought. The truth was, she couldn't. He was violent, and the alcohol just made him care less what he hit and how hard. He was a better fighter when he was sober, but he could do more damage drunk. He had been a boxer in his youth, and a life of fixing roads and digging holes had given him a hard body and a tough, cold mind.

'Who the feck do yer think ya talking to?' he slurred.

He entered her room, his big frame filling the doorway. He was a religious man. He went to church every Sunday before he went to the pub afterwards. A Catholic man who forced his children to go to church too. It was important. Where else could you have all of your sins forgiven?

'Just go to bed and sleep it off,' said Belinda.

'I'll do what I like. I'll not be talked to by the likes of you.'

He stepped into her room. Belinda's mother had stopped crying now. He had only hit her twice before she had escaped and locked herself in the bathroom. Her nose was smeared with blood, and she would have a black eye in the morning. Her body hurt from being pushed against the wall, but she was used to it after so many years. The years of being told it was the last time. He was sorry. He didn't mean it. It was the alcohol. A body continually bruised and broken. One day, he would do some real damage. But he loved her so much and she had got used to lying and covering it up to friends and neighbours.

Belinda sat up, preparing herself.

'You're drunk. Just leave me alone, Da'.'

He looked at her. Just like her mother. They had no idea how hard he worked for them. All the sacrifices he had made. They were never happy. None of them were happy. Well, he would make them happy.

'Why can't you just be happy, Linda, eh?' He always called her Linda, and she hated it. 'You've always been the same. Fecking miserable you are.'

'Da', just go. Please.'

He walked nearer. Her room wasn't big, and he was soon only a few feet away from her. She sat back against the wall, pushing herself away from him. He stank of cigarettes and alcohol. A horrible smell. She had promised herself so many times growing up that she would never smoke or drink. She would never be like him. She would never be like her mother either. Such a coward. Belinda shrank against the wall as her father approached her. He was almost forty, and the years of drinking and smoking had changed his face. When he was younger, he was like Jason. A handsome man, full of life and laughter. He loved a good craic and was known for being the life and the soul of the party. He sang and played guitar, but somehow over the years the drinking had turned him sour. Life hadn't gone the way he had planned. His dreams had faded into long, hard days of working, and months of unemployment and no money. He blamed everyone but himself, and inevitably, like his own father before him, he turned to violence. It had started with a few pushes, and then one day he had hit Belinda's mum. He had said sorry, and that it wouldn't happen again. It did, of course. Barely a month later. Fights with Jason followed, and then slowly over time, Belinda had felt his fury too. Just pushes and a few times he'd grabbed her and threatened to do more. But there was a carelessness in his eyes that night. It was as if he had stopped caring about the consequences because to him there were none. How much worse could it get?

'Yer think yer so fecking smart, don't ya?' He got onto the bed. Belinda pushed herself away from him and against the wall. She wanted to cry but didn't want to give him the satisfaction. She felt her entire body tighten up. 'With yer fecking books. Jesus, Linda, why don't yer get a fecking job to help yer family out, eh?'

'Because I can't wait to get away from you!' shouted Belinda. The rage at her father and at her life came out of her. She couldn't help it. 'As far away as possible. Just like Jason—'

Before she could finish, her dad had reached across the bed and grabbed her. She tried her best to resist him, but he was too strong. He pulled her body away from the wall.

'Don't mention that fecking boy's name! A waste of fecking space. No, yer going nowhere girl, yer staying here with me and yer ma, yer hear me?'

'No!' shouted Belinda.

He pulled her onto the floor. She hit with a loud thud and felt a dull pain in her back. He looked down at his daughter, the alcohol and anger like a fire inside of him. She was crying now, and he wanted to punch the tears out of her. She had never felt his rage. He grabbed her by the hair and pulled her up.

'Da', please,' said Belinda between the tears.

'Don't fecking cry.'

He pulled a hand back. He was going to punch those stupid tears out of her face. He pulled his hand back, ready to let her know who the boss of the house was. They had no respect for him, and how dare she talk about Jason in front of him. Well, he would show her. He would knock her into next week. She was crying even harder, and her body shook, and then she screamed out.

'I'm pregnant, Da'. I'm pregnant!'

He looked at her. His brain couldn't quite understand what she had said. Pregnant? How could she be pregnant? It didn't make sense. She was lying. A lying little bitch, just like her fecking mother. She thought he was stupid. Well, he wasn't. He wasn't stupid at all.

'Yer lying bitch,' said her dad, and then he landed the first blow.

Belinda had never felt the force of a punch before. It knocked her back onto the bed. She felt blood in her mouth. He came at her again. He called her a lying fecking bitch, and then he hit her. This time on the side of the head, and then he landed on a blow on her belly. She felt the pain shoot through her body. He hit her stomach again, trying to knock the lies out of her. She grabbed her pillow and was in a ball crying, her arms over her head trying to protect herself. One more punch landed on her leg before the noise from the landing as her mother screamed at her father to stop. Realising it was his chance to beat his wife again, Martin O'Leary left his daughter on her bed, crying, bleeding, and went after his wife instead.

Belinda was on her bed. She heard her mother's cries and felt the blood that was trickling down from her mouth. She felt a pain in her stomach. She grabbed her coat that was on the chair, stumbled, and then ran out of the house. She couldn't take it anymore. She was pregnant. It was her first-time having sex with Brian. She hadn't wanted to do it, but he had convinced her, and they hadn't used a condom because he said it would be all right. That nothing would happen. She didn't know where to go, but she felt the pain inside of her, and she was sure she was losing the baby.

She walked as far as she could until she came to her friend Becca's house. A slightly larger white and grey box. Becca's house was nicer than hers, and she had a decent family. They would take her in. They would help her. She had nowhere else to go. It was dark out. She felt the metallic taste of blood in her mouth. She cried as she rang their doorbell, hoping they would answer. The pain in her stomach got worse, and she fell to the ground as the door opened and Becca's mum stood there.

'Jesus, Belinda, what's happened to you?' she said.

Belinda remembered nothing much after that. She blacked out. The only thing she remembered when she woke up in the hospital was seeing her brother's face. He knew what had happened, he said, and he'd make him pay. Then they told her she'd had a miscarriage. The baby was gone.

12.

The present

When Alexander awoke the morning after Belinda's first night with him, she was still asleep. It was just past eight o'clock on a Saturday morning. It was cloudy but dry, and the merest hint of sunshine was just beginning to peek through the clouds. He went downstairs, made himself a cup of tea and looked out towards the garden. After her shower the night before, Alexander had made Belinda some food, and then she had gone to bed. He had checked on her twice during the night and she was sound asleep. Alexander couldn't sleep himself because he couldn't stop thinking about Belinda and what he was going to do with her. How long could she stay with him, and how could he get her the help she so obviously needed?

Alexander drank his tea and looked out at the garden. His mind wandered, as it often did. The guilt at what he had done still sat inside of him, slowly chipping away. It had never gone away. The pain had changed. The way he felt about himself, though, and what he had done was as strong as ever. The nightmares still visited him. If it wasn't for Laura, he might have tried to kill himself. But then again, he didn't think he had the courage to do that either. Instead, he just carried on living. It was all he could do. He lived but was numb to everything. At least he was until yesterday when he stopped Belinda from jumping in front of that train. When he woke up that morning, he felt for the first time in years that he had some sort of purpose. Someone needed him.

It was just past nine o'clock when Belinda came downstairs. She was in the pyjamas he had found for her. They used to belong to Olivia. A Christmas present. She had hardly worn them, but it was strange seeing Belinda in them.

She looked so different after her shower, a cup of tea, and some food. She looked younger, and she reminded Alexander even more of his own daughter.

'Can I get you some breakfast? Tea? Coffee?' said Alexander, nervously.

Belinda looked at him, and then she sat down.

'Why are you doing this?' she said.

'What do you mean?'

'Taking me in. Offering to help me. I'm no-one to you. Why are you helping me?'

Alexander didn't have a suitable answer to this that didn't involve a long explanation of his past. He couldn't tell her everything that had happened. It was impossible.

'I couldn't just let you kill yourself, could I?' said Alexander.

'But you didn't need to do this.'

'No, but I did. I just want to help, that's all.'

'And you want nothing in return?' she said, and gave him a look, which made him realise for the first time what she was hinting at.

'No, no, of course not,' said Alexander uncomfortably. He hadn't even thought about that, although now he did, he could see why she had to ask.

Belinda looked at him. She had little experience with men who didn't want something from her. Whether it was sex or someone to hit, men mostly wanted to take something away from her. Alexander just wanted to help, and that was hard for her to believe. He was a single, middle-aged man. He must want something.

'So, breakfast. I have cereal, toast, crumpets. Orange juice, tea, coffee?'

Belinda said she'd have a cup of tea and some toast. She just wanted to sit in front of the television and watch something normal. Something boring, actually. She wanted to drink a cup of tea and watch a television show that took her away from herself. Something that made her feel like a part of the world. It was one of the hardest parts about living rough. People didn't see her as part of society. She was an outcast. Less than. She hated the way people looked at her as they walked past on their way to work. She hated the feeling of it. She had promised herself so many nights as she lay trying to sleep that if she ever turned her life around, if she ever got a job and lived in a house again, that she wouldn't take any of it for granted. She would appreciate everything.

She went into Alexander's living room and turned the television on. She flicked between a few channels before she settled on a cooking show. A chef she didn't know was making hamburgers and she couldn't get her head around how quickly her life had changed. Yesterday morning she had woken up in the doorway of a shop, cold, wet, and depressed, committed to ending her life, and now she was in a lovely house, drinking tea, and watching a cooking show. It felt surreal.

'How's everything?' said Alexander.

He had walked into the room and sat down on the armchair opposite her. He still had so many questions, but he didn't want to push it. She would tell him everything in her own time.

'Good, yeah,' she said, taking a sip of her tea. 'I'm just watching this man cook some burgers. I don't think life gets any better than this.'

Alexander laughed. He didn't laugh often anymore, but he couldn't help himself.

'I have to go out this morning. Will you be okay?'

'I'll be grand.'

'I feel like I shouldn't leave you alone.'

'No, do what you have to do. I'll be fine. Promise.'

'There's food in the cupboards. Help yourself to tea and coffee,' said Alexander with a kind smile. 'I want you to think of this as your home.'

Belinda looked at the photos on the mantelpiece. The girl and the woman. She wanted to ask him, but she didn't feel ready yet. She was sure that when he was ready, he would tell her everything in the same way that she would too. When Belinda was growing up, she dreamed about living in a house like that. A nice house with good parents. A dad like Alexander who took care of her, who had a proper job and didn't drink. She didn't know how much his house was worth, but it must be a lot. She always thought she was quite intelligent and could have gone to university and got a proper career, but it hadn't happened for her. She hadn't had the opportunities like other kids. She had just been trying to survive.

Alexander smiled at her and then stood up. He told her he would only be gone for a few hours, and he would go shopping and come back for lunch. Maybe she might fancy a walk later. They could go to Richmond Park. This made Belinda smile. The thought of walking, smelling fresh air, feeling mud and grass beneath her feet. Birds swooping, blue sky and trees. It was so much of what she had always wanted. She told Alexander she'd love to and then he left her. She carried on watching television, made herself another cup of tea, found an apple and ate that while she watched another show.

Alexander got in his car. It was Saturday morning, and he would do the same thing he had been doing for the past few months since he'd found her. He felt awful for leaving Belinda alone, and he thought for a moment about not going, but if he didn't, he might not see her again for another week. He looked forward to it so much. It had taken him a while to track her down, but he finally had, and he wasn't going to lose that. Every moment felt precious.

The first time he'd gone to her house and then followed her to a park. It had been a Saturday morning, and he soon found out that she went to the same park every Saturday morning at about the same time. After a while he stopped going to her house and went straight to the park instead. It was a lovely little park with a football pitch at one end and a playground at the other. There was a cafe that served coffee and it was surrounded by lovely houses that were worth much more than his. He couldn't risk her seeing him, and so he stayed as far away as possible.

He parked his car across from the park under a tree. Before he got out, he had a look along the pavement in case she was still on her way to the park. Once it was clear, he got out and walked across the road to the edge of the park. He started as usual on the football pitch side. There was a game going on, which was good as it gave him more cover. A mass of young boys running around in too big shorts, chasing the ball in packs, while parents shouted from the side-lines, and an out of breath referee tried to keep up. He could easily walk amongst the parents watching their children without being spotted. He was wearing a baseball cap and sunglasses too, which added to his anonymity. He was just another face in the crowd. Another parent watching their child.

He looked across at the playground, and then he spotted her. As soon as he saw her, his skin prickled with excitement and a desire to see his daughter and his granddaughter. He wished more than anything that he could really see her again. Talk to her and meet his only grandchild. God, she was beautiful. Just like Laura when she was that age. There was a hole inside his heart that only they could fill. But he had to keep his distance. He had to respect her decision because if he ever wanted a relationship with her again, then he had no choice. No matter how much it hurt, and it hurt so much that just seeing them playing together brought tears to his eyes. The little girl must be about four. She ran around the playground, up a rope swing, and then down a slide. She laughed and started playing with a little boy of about the same age. Alexander looked towards his daughter. She was twenty-six and looked more and more like her mother with every year that passed. Sometimes when Alexander looked at her, he thought he was looking at Olivia at about the same age and it broke his heart. Seeing she was all right, and a mother made him so happy, and yet knowing it and not being a part of her life, tore him to pieces.

Laura was sitting on a bench reading a big, heavy hardback book. He wondered what she did for a living now. She was obviously still reading and learning, and yet the house she lived in was rundown and in a poor area of Croydon. He wanted to know so he could help her. Alexander had plenty of money and nothing to spend it on. He had thought about posting some money through their letter box, but if she knew it had come from him, he knew she wouldn't accept it. She had always been stubborn. Another trait she had got from her mother.

After about an hour, she got up and told her daughter it was time to go. She gave her a bag of crisps and a juice to drink before they left. Alexander watched them closely until they were out of sight. They left at the playground end of the park, and Alexander walked back around the football pitch to his car. He needed to go to the shop to get some food to bring home to Belinda. He didn't know what she liked, but decided to get some ham and cheese, and some good bread. They could make some sandwiches, and if it was still dry, he would take her to Richmond Park later. As he started his car and pulled away, he hoped Belinda was okay. He hoped she was still there and hadn't run away. The thought had crossed his mind, but he had done his bit. He wanted to help her, but she also had to want to be helped. He could make her food, give her a bed, and as much support as he could offer, but she was a grown woman and if she decided to go back to the streets, he couldn't stop her whether he wanted to or not.

13.

The past

It was all Olivia could think about while she made herself breakfast. While Laura pottered about in the kitchen, and while Alexander drank his tea and ate his toast. Olivia tipped a small amount of muesli into a bowl. She sliced a banana and put it on top and then poured some milk over. The message on Alexander's phone. *FYI No knickers tomorrow.* It had kept her awake for most of the night, while Alexander snored, the deep sonorous noise reverberating around the room. She lay there looking up at the ceiling, trying to make some sense of it. Today was the day of the no knickers, and everything inside of Olivia was telling her to confront him, ask him about the message, but her brain was telling her to wait. If he was guilty and she confronted him after breakfast, he would surely just make up an excuse. If it was a genuine mistake and there was a perfectly reasonable explanation, it would probably sound like an excuse, and she would spend the day mulling it over. It was taking every ounce of self-control she had not to say something. But she had to wait. She had to do this properly if she wanted to know the truth. She thought momentarily of her client, Susan Farringdon. She was torn between wanting to know the truth about her husband and being terrified of what it might mean if she was right. Olivia had felt pity for her. She had felt so sure that if she was in the same situation that she would handle it differently. So much better. But when it came down to it, was she any different?

'Do you have your lunch?' Olivia said to Laura.

'Yes,' said Laura, who was eating a bowl of sugary cereal. 'Don't forget we get out early today for revision. I'll probably go to Charlotte's house after school. I might even eat there tonight.'

'Just make sure you text me,' said Olivia, and Laura smiled at her as if to confirm.

Olivia looked at her daughter. She hadn't spoken to her last night after everything that had happened. She desperately wanted Laura to know that she knew, and it was okay. She wanted to make sure she was all right, and if they were thinking about sex, to be safe. She wanted Laura to know she was there for her. The truth was that Laura was going to Charlotte's house after school for revision. Despite everything with Tom, Laura was committed to getting the best GCSE results she could. She knew if she wanted to go to Oxford, then she would need to do really well, and she wanted to go to Oxford more than anything. Even more than she wanted to be with Tom. She hadn't completely lost her mind. The good thing was that Tom felt the same, and so despite their runaway hormones, they were both still thinking about the long-term plan.

'I'd better get a move on,' said Alexander, slipping the last piece of toast into his mouth. 'Or I'm going to be late.'

Alexander smiled at his wife, and she forced a smile back. She felt a sickness inside of her. Alexander couldn't be cheating on her. He couldn't. There must be some sort of explanation. There just had to be, and when she found out what it was, she would laugh to herself that she ever thought Alexander capable. But then she thought of the first couple she was seeing that morning. Greg and Julie. He had cheated on her multiple times, and yet he said he loved her and wanted to work on their marriage. Julie had left him countless times, but for one reason or another, kept coming back for more. It was a tale as old as time, but one that Olivia had no interest in being involved in herself.

Alexander and Laura said goodbye to Olivia. Alexander gave her a kiss, and she wanted to hold him, hug him, and tell him to stay at home for the day. They could stop life for a moment and spend the day together. When was the last time they had done that? They could call in sick and take the train to London. They could stroll around the National

Gallery, walk the Southbank with coffees, and get lunch somewhere fabulous and far too expensive. They could see the changing of the guard like tourists or sit in Covent Garden and watch the street performers. They could find a decent pub with a garden and just have a drink. When she looked into his eyes, she thought about saying it. *Let's just stop everything now and be us again.*

'What?' said Alexander.

'Nothing,' she said with a thin, uncertain smile, holding back the deluge of tears that sat inside her, threatening to explode at any moment.

'Right, better get off. Are you ready, Laura?'

'Coming,' said Laura, grabbing her school bag. 'Bye, Mum.'

'Love you,' said Olivia.

She gave her daughter a kiss on the head as she walked by, and then they were gone. Olivia just wanted to fall onto the sofa and cry. She wanted to succumb to the pain that was sitting in her heart. But she couldn't. She wouldn't let herself. She thought about tomorrow. Friday. The day that Alexander was going for drinks after work. She would find out either way tomorrow. If it really was just a few drinks with work and nothing untoward was going on, then she would confront him about the message. Either way, after tomorrow she would know whether she still had a marriage. It was only one day.

Olivia got herself ready and made the short walk to the end of the garden. She had a good forty-five minutes before her first clients of the day, but she liked to get down there early. She would make herself a cup of coffee, go through her notes from the previous sessions, and if she had time, she might pick up her book and have a quick read. It was all about getting in the right headspace. Calm. Relaxed. Clear.

Alexander was in his classroom. He couldn't help but sense that something was amiss. He had sensed it with Olivia all morning, and even last night before bed. Something in their little universe was off. But then again, it was probably just the guilt. The guilt of what he had done, and what he had yet to do. Surely Olivia didn't know anything. He had been so careful. She was good at detecting when something was wrong, and reading people, but she couldn't know any details. She couldn't suspect him of something, and anyway, what had he really done wrong so far? They had kissed, which was awful, and he felt terrible, but you didn't end a marriage over a kiss. You said sorry, you talked, and you moved on. Maybe you took a short break together. Perhaps it was all they needed. A long weekend in Paris to remind them how perfect they were for each other. The more he thought about it, the more he thought that's exactly what he should do. He shouldn't meet Sara tomorrow and instead surprise Olivia with a last-minute weekend away.

Alexander had a few minutes before class, and he looked up some last-minute deals online. They could go to Paris on the Eurostar and stay at a nice hotel near to the Eiffel Tower for a reasonable price. Alexander thought for a moment about a trip they had taken during the infancy of their relationship. It was during the summer after university ended and before they both started their careers. They set off for Paris together, so excited and full of love. Olivia had been before, but it was Alexander's first time in France. They had wandered the streets together, and it felt like a dream. How could life have ever felt that good? Perhaps they could reclaim that feeling again. The prospect excited Alexander. A weekend in Paris, eating croissants and sipping espresso. Sightseeing and strolling through Montmartre together before dinner at one of the old restaurants. A boat ride on the river Seine, and an afternoon strolling around the Louvre Museum. Something so very French. Just the thought of it made his heart swell with emotion and a nostalgia for the past. They could have that again. He hadn't gone too far with Sara. He could stop it now and go away with Olivia, and everything would be okay.

Alexander felt a presence at the door, and when he looked up, Sara had walked into his room. She closed the door behind her.

'Morning, Mr Burke.'

Alexander felt himself change the moment she was in the room. A heat rose inside him. There was just something about her that made him lose control of himself. He hated it but could do little to stop it. He closed his computer and Paris with it. Sara walked towards him. She checked that no-one was outside. The kids were still on the playground, and most teachers were in their rooms getting ready or in the staff room. The hallway outside his classroom was empty and quiet. In five minutes, it would be full of pupils loudly going to class. At that moment, they were alone. She walked up to him.

Today she was wearing a cream blouse that was buttoned almost to the top, and a cream-coloured bra underneath. She had a grey cardigan to go over the top for class. She was also wearing a knee-length grey skirt and a pair of black high-heeled shoes. Her hair was tied back in a tight ponytail, and she was wearing a pair of black-framed glasses. Her lips were red with lipstick, and Alexander could barely contain himself. All thoughts of Paris were immediately lost from his mind. She was only a few feet away from him. He could smell her perfume.

'I'm not wearing any knickers,' she said in a low, soft voice.

Alexander gulped. Why did she torture him so?

'Okay,' said Alexander, not knowing what else to say.

Sara looked around and listened for any noise in the hallway. It was quiet. She slowly reached down and pulled up the front of her skirt. Very slowly she edged it higher and higher. Alexander saw her legs and then her thighs. His penis strained at his trousers. His mind couldn't think clearly. His breathing got deeper. He knew at any moment that someone could walk into his class. They were playing with fire, but he didn't care. He couldn't stop watching her.

Her soft white thighs. Then she reached across and took his hand. He didn't know what to do. He wasn't expecting it. She took his hand and put it on her thigh. He felt something powerful shoot through his body. A sexual excitement. Her skin was so soft. His hand was about half the way up her thigh. Her hand was still over his. She moved it slowly higher.

'Keep your eyes on me,' she demanded.

He looked into her eyes. His hand was on her leg and getting higher. Surely, she wouldn't go all the way. Not in class. Not there. She moved his hand higher still. It was at the very top of her thigh now. Another inch, and if she really wasn't wearing any knickers, his hand would be there. He felt his knees tremble in anticipation. The thought of it shot fireworks through his brain, cracking and exploding, and sending shock waves of ideas flooding through his mind and down his body. She smiled, and then she took his hand and quickly put it against her vagina. Alexander was shocked. It was as smooth as her legs, completely waxed, and for a split second he felt it. He felt all of her, and then she took his hand away as quickly as she had put it there. She flattened her skirt down and then looked into his eyes.

'Friday,' she said with a delicious grin.

And then she turned around and walked out. He watched her go. Her bottom wiggled in her tight skirt, and he had to sit down at his desk. He was overawed with sexual feelings that he felt deep within himself. Feelings he thought were long gone from his life. He heard the bell go, and within a minute the school would be flooded with the noise of children. Alexander didn't know what to think anymore. He needed time and space to get his head together, but he had neither. His pupils would arrive any moment, and then before he knew it, the day would be over, and he would go home. A night with Olivia where he'd feel awful and he would definitely want to plan that weekend away, but the thought of Sara and her thighs would keep him from doing anything. Why couldn't he resist her? Was it just her age or her complete lack of fear of being caught? He didn't care. She excited him in a way he hadn't been excited in so long, and it wasn't Olivia's fault or anything to do with their relationship. It was Sara. He had never met a woman like her before. So beautiful, sexual, and unafraid. The things she had said she would let him do in bed. Alexander took a deep breath as his first class poured into his room. They were studying Henry VIII, which was one of Alexander's favourite historical periods, and one of his favourite figures. Such an interesting, complex character, and like him, one that had his problems with women.

14.

The present

Belinda walked through the garden. It was beautiful, exactly the sort of garden she wished she had growing up in Ireland. It was long and wide but got slightly narrower at the bottom by the large building that was so much more than a shed. It was so lush. Longish grass that probably needed a cut and lots of plants and flowers everywhere. It was a bit unkempt, wild almost, but she liked that. She felt the plants and flowers between her fingers and the grass on her bare feet. Nature. The garden she had as a child was a small, rectangular box with dead grass and broken furniture. It wasn't somewhere to dream. It wasn't a garden you could love or play in. Alexander's garden was perfect. She imagined herself as a young girl running through the grass, playing on the tree and exploring. Picking flowers and digging holes in the dirt in search of lost treasures. Making daisy chains. This was a garden for the mind and the soul. It was exactly what she needed to get better.

She wandered towards the bottom of the garden and the building. It was obviously not just a shed because it was so big and had two large windows at the front and a nice door. Like the rest of the garden though, it had become overgrown, and the windows needed a clean. Belinda put her hands against the glass and looked inside. She was surprised to see a beautiful living room. Belinda couldn't imagine why Alexander would have such a gorgeous room at the bottom of his garden. It had a grey sofa and opposite that was a large armchair, and in between them a small coffee table. In the corner of the room was a kitchen, and expensive looking rugs adorned the wooden floor. Belinda could imagine herself living in that little room at the bottom of the garden. She would be happy there amongst the foliage and vegetation. Reading books and dreaming. It was a million miles away from the shop doorway she had been sleeping in that was hard and cold, and where one night a group of drunken lads had pissed on her, laughing and calling her a piece of shit.

She looked around the back of the building, but there wasn't much except a fence and a gate. Beyond the gate was a lane with a few parked cars and beyond that more houses. She walked back up the garden path towards the swing. She ran her hand over the wooden seat. She felt the coarseness of it and imagined the fun it had experienced. The laughs of the children who had swung on it in years gone by. She sat on the swing, tested the strength, and it took her weight easily. She swung backwards and forward, and it felt wonderful. The green grass beneath her feet, and the blue sky above, she felt like a child again. She felt a pang of happiness. A nostalgia not for her own childhood, but for the one she dreamed about. She leaned back and looked up. Fluffy clouds and a plane that was coming into land at Heathrow Airport. It looked like it was going so slowly, as if it was going to fall out of the sky at any moment. She remembered swinging on swings when she was a child, but it was always on horrible concrete playgrounds covered in graffiti. Urban, cold, and hard. This was soft and beautiful, like a fairy-tale.

Belinda felt the swing beneath her and the sunshine on her face. She felt alive. She imagined herself growing up in that garden. Her name wasn't Belinda because she'd always hated that name. It sounded so old and unfashionable. It wasn't the name of a pretty girl. Instead, she was called something like Lottie or Kate. She swung and felt the wind on her face. She gripped the rope handles. She liked the feeling of them. Rough on her skin. She looked towards the fence and at the houses that seemed to stretch on forever. Each full of trees, life, and people like Alexander. Belinda felt a longing in her heart to belong to something like that. To have an identity. To be a part of something bigger than herself. She had felt such loneliness for most of her life.

It was a warm day, and Alexander walked out into the garden with two cups of tea. He saw Belinda on the swing, and his heart for a moment ached because it reminded him of moments from the past when he'd walk outside and see Laura there. He sat down at the small table he had on a wooden patio.

'There's tea and biscuits,' said Alexander.

She looked at him, and then after a moment she stopped herself, got off the swing and walked up towards the house. She wasn't wearing any shoes. Belinda would need some new clothes soon, as she had worn all the clothes that Alexander had found for her. He had washed them all already, and she was back to the original outfit he'd found on day one. It felt like a lifetime ago since she had arrived at his house, and yet it had only been four days. Four strange days since she could have died. She walked over and sat next to Alexander. She took a sip of her tea. There was something slightly old-fashioned about Alexander. Something stuck or perhaps lost in time.

They sat and drank their tea, enjoying the bright warm day, and they looked out to the garden, and watched birds swoop down and land in the tree and then take off again. It was so peaceful in the garden. You could barely hear anything but the sounds of nature. A distant rumbling of traffic and faraway life reminded them they were in London, but in that spot in the garden it was as peaceful as if they lived faraway in the countryside.

'I'm okay, you know,' said Belinda when they had almost finished their tea. 'You don't have to worry about me.'

Alexander looked at Belinda. She half-smiled at him, and he smiled back.

'Why did you do it?'

He finally felt like he could ask. Maybe she wouldn't answer or wasn't ready, but he felt like he could at least try to get something out of her. Perhaps he could help.

'Why did I want to kill myself?' she said, and Alexander

nodded. 'I'd just had enough, and I couldn't see a way out. I couldn't see this.'

'How long were you living rough for?'

'Five or six months, I think. It was the only thing left to do, but it ground me down being homeless. It took whatever hope I had left and destroyed it day by day until one day I woke up and realised I had nothing left. That was Friday morning.'

'God, that's awful. I'm so sorry.'

'It's all right, it's not your fault,' she said with a sad smile. 'It's just how life went for me.'

They sat in silence for a moment. Alexander looked at Belinda. Still so young. He couldn't imagine what had happened for her to feel so lost and broken that the only way out for her was suicide. He thought of Laura. He hoped she was happy.

'Do you think you might want to talk to someone?' said Alexander after a moment.

Belinda picked up a biscuit. Alexander had a good selection of biscuits. Chocolate ones, too. It had been so long since she'd enjoyed a chocolate covered biscuit and a cup of tea.

'Like who?'

'I don't know, exactly, a therapist or a counsellor, perhaps?'

'I don't think so. They can't explain to me what I already know. I didn't try to kill myself because of what was happening inside my head, so much as what was happening in my life. To my body. They can't help with that, can they?'

'No, I suppose not,' said Alexander tentatively, although he couldn't help but think that she should talk to someone who wasn't him. Someone who could actually help.

They finished their tea. It was still early in the afternoon, and Alexander had no plans for the rest of the day. He was going to make them dinner later. He had bought some sausages, and he was going to make some mashed potatoes. It was nice to have someone else to cook for. Seeing Laura every Saturday for the last few months had given Alexander a different perspective on loneliness. Now he had Belinda in his life, he had forgotten what it felt like to have another human so close to him. Perhaps it was something biological, something intrinsic to our survival. But once he had seen Laura and now he had Belinda, he longed not to be alone again. He wanted more human contact, not less. There was school, but that wasn't the same. Colleagues and students, but none of them filled the emotional hole that existed within him. The need to be needed, to feel some sort of love. Yes, it was that. It was love. For so much of his life, he had felt love, and then it was gone, and he longed for it again. He yearned for contact with Laura and to pick up his granddaughter. To feel their love.

'Can I ask you something?' said Belinda.

She looked at Alexander. At his face and into his dark, chocolatey eyes. His dark hair was slightly thinning, and at fifty-three, she could see the lines etched into his face. Life and experience. The bags under his eyes because he didn't sleep. The terrible sadness that lay within him.

'Of course.'

'Why do you have such a lovely shed at the bottom of your garden?'

The words in her wonderfully lyrical Irish accent drifted across to Alexander, and he heard them, and he thought about her question for a moment. Why was there such a lovely shed at the bottom of his garden? They had built Olivia's office when she had first started working from home. It was the perfect solution. She didn't want to rent a space for her practice, and so Alexander suggested building one in their garden. It had started off smaller, but over time, and with Olivia's imagination and interior design sensibilities running away with her, the entire project skyrocketed. The result had been a large office space with a kitchen, plumbing, electrics, and a comfortable, beautiful place where Olivia could do her work. She loved it down there. It was her space, and clients could easily access it from the lane behind their house. Alexander rarely went down there anymore. He hadn't opened it up in a long time. It was too painful. He remembered they'd had sex there once. Just after it was finished, Olivia was showing him around, and Laura was inside, and they had sex on the rug. It was spontaneous and amazing. Just the thought of it brought tears to his eyes.

'Because a long time ago we needed it,' said Alexander with an uncomfortable smile. He looked at her for a moment, as if he might say something else, but instead he got up and tidied away the tea and biscuits.

Belinda noticed that his entire face had changed. Her question had affected him so much that it lay across his face like a mask. An expression of anguish and pain. The look of a man who had experienced something truly awful. She felt it like an invisible force field that pushed her away. It was strong and it wouldn't be easy to break down. She let him get up and walk away. She wouldn't push it. But whatever had happened, it had been bad. It had destroyed him.

The moment Belinda had walked back into her house after losing her baby. The moment she had seen her da' again, and how he had blamed her and told her how awful she was for getting pregnant at her age and that losing the baby had been a penance from God. A punishment for her sins. How her mother had gone along with him and taken his side against her despite the pain that was still on her face, and the bruised body she let him still touch. Belinda had known pain. She understood it. We, he had said. A long time ago *we* had needed it. Belinda wondered who they were then, and perhaps more importantly, where they were now.

Alexander went inside. He put the teacups down on the side, and then he just stood there for a moment. He took a deep breath and tried to stop himself from crying. He stood over the sink and looked out of the window. Belinda was still outside at the table. If she stayed with him for a while, he would have to tell her. She would have questions. It had been such a long time since he'd had to talk about it. Ten years. It had been in the newspapers then. It was hard to believe. He pulled himself together and put the teacups in the dishwasher with the things from breakfast. He ran the dishwasher, and then he decided to see if Belinda was up to going shopping. Apart from their walk in Richmond Park, which she had enjoyed, she hadn't left the house. Maybe it was time she did. He needed the escape. He needed to get out and away from the confines of the house because sometimes the weight of it felt like it was crushing him.

15.

The past

The thought had been niggling Alexander all day. It had clouded his mind, coating him in a layer of uncertainty and worry. So, after school, he decided to do something. It was a matter of urgency. Especially after that morning when Sara had come into his room and done what she had done. He needed to define things with her. Nothing could be left to chance. He wasn't the sort of man to have an affair. He hadn't thought about it at all until Sara had come along. It was an opportunity. That was all. But now he couldn't stop himself, he had to make sure everything was clear.

He knocked on Sara's classroom door, nervously shuffling backwards and forwards on his feet, hoping none of the other teachers saw him. The last thing he wanted at school was gossip.

'Do you have a moment?' he said, popping his head around the door.

'Of course, Mr Burke.'

She was cleaning up her room. She had thirty essays to mark before the next day. She wasn't going anywhere soon. Alexander closed the door behind him and walked across to her desk.

'What do I owe the pleasure? I thought you'd be out of here like a shot today?' said Sara.

She looked at him with one of her smiles. Alexander thought she had one of the most beguiling smiles he had ever seen. There was just something about it that rendered him completely helpless. He hated himself for becoming the sort of weak willed 'typical man' he despised. Perhaps all men were intrinsically the same and couldn't stop themselves when it came to women who were far more attractive than they thought they deserved. Maybe it wasn't weakness, but just biology. He wouldn't be the last man in history to risk everything for a beautiful woman.

'I just wanted to clarify a few things,' said Alexander stiffly. He perched himself on the corner of her desk.

'It sounds very formal,' said Sara, looking up at him with her big blue eyes.

Alexander didn't quite know how to say what he wanted to say. He knew what he wanted to convey to her, but he wasn't sure what choice of words to use. He wanted to be completely clear, so they both knew exactly where they stood.

'The thing is,' said Alexander nervously.

'You're even more handsome when you're nervous.'

'The thing is, Sara. I want you, us, to be completely clear what this all means.'

'Riiiight,' said Sara, slightly confused where he was leading her.

She hoped he wasn't going to say something annoying and ruin everything. Alexander took a breath. He had to just say it.

'I'm never going to leave Olivia. I love her, and I love our life, and as much as I find you attractive, and I can't wait for tomorrow, that's it. I can't have an affair. I won't leave Olivia, and if you want more from me, then maybe we should just stop this now.'

He had said it. The thing that had been on his mind all day. They had never clarified what this was, and he didn't want Sara to get the impression that something more was going to happen because it wasn't. He didn't want it to get messy. It was a one-time deal, and that was it. Then he would go home and live out the rest of his days with Olivia because that's all he wanted. He didn't want to lose Olivia. He loved her. He loved the life they had built together. He just wanted one time with Sara, just to know, to feel what it was like, and then he would go back to Olivia. He didn't want to hurt Sara or for her to have expectations of something that wasn't going to happen. It wasn't fair, and so he wanted to tell her now before things went any further. Clarity.

Alexander didn't know how she would react, but he didn't expect her to laugh.

'I'm sorry, I shouldn't laugh because you were so serious about it.'

Alexander was confused.

'I don't understand.'

'I laughed because of course I know all of that, and I don't want a relationship with you either. I don't want to break you and your wife up and get caught up in a messy affair. This is just about sex. It's the thrill of the chase and the kill, and then everyone goes home, has a cup of tea, and moves on. Don't you see, Alexander, it's hunting. That's all. It's a hunt.'

He noticed she had a rather unsettling expression on her face. A smile that made him feel uneasy. The look of a big game hunter standing over a dead animal, a rifle in their hands.

'Right,' said Alexander. 'Good.'

He was caught off-guard by her complete lack of sentiment and emotion when it came to them. Sara wasn't like other women. All she wanted was sex. Hunting was the word she used to describe it. Was that all he was to her? Prey?

'Don't worry, Mr Burke,' she said, reaching a hand across and stroking the top of his leg. 'On Monday morning, it will be like it never happened, and it will never happen again. After tomorrow, life will get back to normal, and I'll be just a lovely little memory.'

Sara thought this conversation was so sweet, naïve, and somewhat quaint. Why did married men always get so caught up in it and have to have these conversations? The last one had told her he wanted to leave his wife, and that he hadn't been happy in years, and they could run away together, and she had to tell him it was off. She couldn't have men like that running around after her. She loved the thrill of the chase. It was a game. She was the hunter, and the men were the hunted. Some were easier than others. Some were quite a disappointment when it came to it, while others rose to the challenge. She had high hopes for Alexander, and maybe after tomorrow she would be rewarded. When she had arrived at the school, she thought he might be quite a challenge, but as it turned out, he was just like most men and quite easy to lure into bed. At least he wasn't like the last one. Alexander wanted once and then out. He couldn't stand the guilt. He was happily married. It was perfect for her. It was all she ever wanted. A fellow teacher. A lawyer, a banker, a footballer, or even a politician. It was all just a game to her. Power and the powerless.

Alexander smiled at her, and then he got up and walked out. He had nothing to worry about. Yes, things with Olivia were a little awkward, but after tomorrow, he would make everything right. He would book them that weekend in Paris. Maybe next weekend. It was perfect. A weekend to fall back in love again and put all of this behind them. It was clear, concise, and nothing would go wrong. After feeling nervous and worried all day, Alexander left school knowing that everything was going to be just fine. It was all down to planning, and he was sure he had crossed all the t's and dotted all the i's. Nothing was being left to chance.

Olivia chopped up the mushrooms and then put them in the frying pan with the onions and the peppers. She had a glass of wine, and she was listening to the first Coldplay album, Parachutes. She loved that album. She didn't much care for their later work, but that first album was so good and took her back to an exact moment in time. It was tender, sweet, and raw. It was youth. She felt like their mature albums were over-thought and tried to do too much. She loved how it made her think about those times. The start of a new millennium. Gosh, how different life had been then. How young she and Alexander were, how different life felt, and how quickly the time had gone.

The front door opened and then closed. The familiar sound of a bag being dropped, keys falling into the little ceramic bowl, and then Laura's voice.

'Mum, I'm home.'

'In the kitchen,' said Olivia.

She so desperately wanted to speak to Laura about her secret boyfriend. Alexander wouldn't be back for at least thirty minutes, and so this was the time. Olivia wasn't feeling so crushed emotionally as she did yesterday. With a whole day to think about the text on his phone, she had concluded that there must be a reasonable explanation for it. The more she thought about it, the more she came to realise that it was probably just her imagination running away with her. She knew Alexander. She knew every inch of his soul and every thought in his head. The drinks after work on Friday were also probably just that. It happened. Every few months, he would go out with a few of his colleagues for a drink. Her mind had just got a bit excited and now she was calm. It would be fine. She was still going to follow him after school tomorrow. Make sure he was definitely going to the pub and then that would be it. She would realise that he wasn't having an affair, and life would continue as before.

It would be like her cancer scare. Two years before, she had found a lump on her breast. A casual reminder in a magazine to check herself, and she hadn't thought for a moment that she would actually find something. The terror was swift and all-encompassing. Within moments she was convinced she had cancer and would be dead within months. A few visits to the doctor and it turned out it was just a benign cyst. But in those hours and days before she knew, it felt like her entire world was caving in around her. Her mind had gone straight to the darkest place imaginable without stopping for a moment to consider the alternatives.

'What's for dinner?' said Laura, walking into the kitchen. She went straight for the fridge and got out the orange juice and poured herself a glass.

'Something with mushrooms, onions, and peppers. I'm not entirely sure what yet.'

'Living on the edge, Mum.'

Olivia turned the heat down and then turned to face her daughter.

'Can we have a little chat?'

'Okaay,' said Laura, sitting down at the table.

Olivia walked across and sat opposite her daughter. Her beautiful daughter in her crumpled white school shirt, her tie loosely tied around her neck, and her hair that had been in a tight ponytail that morning, was loose and dishevelled. My god, she was so beautiful, thought Olivia. So much potential. When Olivia looked at her daughter, she saw so much of herself in there, and so much of Alexander too. Alexander hadn't quite reached the levels he wanted for himself. Olivia knew that. He hadn't gone to Oxford or Cambridge, and despite loving history, she didn't think he was completely happy at work. He had always wanted to teach at a higher level and maybe write a history book. When they were younger, he had so much ambition, and he hadn't quite fulfilled it. Olivia was more than happy with where she was. Her own practice, helping people fulfil their emotional and sexual needs. She wasn't a doctor on the frontline saving lives, but she was helping people. She made a difference. She couldn't ask for more. She wondered how far Laura would go. How much further could she reach?

'I know,' said Olivia resolutely.

'Know what?'

'About your boyfriend,' said Olivia, and she watched her daughter's face as it changed and fell flat in front of her. Laura had no idea that she knew. She was completely and utterly stunned. 'It's okay, Laura. It's fine.'

'I … umm … don't know what to say.'

Laura felt her skin prickle uncomfortably. God, she was so embarrassed.

'What's his name?'

'Tom. Tom Chance. He's in the same year as me, and he

wants to go to Oxford too.'

'Well, that's good,' said Olivia, smiling at her daughter.

A pause. A moment to gather their thoughts and questions.

'Does Dad know?'

'God no, and I'm not going to tell him if you don't want me to.'

Laura took a moment, looked down at her lap, and then back up at her mum.

'Thanks,' said Laura with a thin smile.

'Do you really like him?'

'I do,' said Laura, bursting into life. 'I really like him, Mum. He's so smart, and

funny and just … perfect.'

There was a pause. Olivia wanted to broach the topic of sex, but also knew how horribly

uncomfortable it could be. No teenager ever wanted to discuss sex with their parents, no matter how cool or 'right on' they thought they might be. Olivia was enjoying the closeness she felt to Laura at that moment. Sometimes, with Laura being so much like Alexander, so driven and emotionally closed off, she didn't feel like the mother she wished she was. She dreamed of one day being good friends with Laura. She thought about them meeting up for lunch in London when Laura was a barrister. She imagined the day when Laura might have a baby, and only her husband and Olivia were allowed into the delivery room. She wanted that connection with her. She needed that closeness. She didn't always feel it, and so she felt a warmth throughout her body when she did. A biological pull towards her only child.

'Are you having sex?' said Olivia.

'Mum!' said Laura, blushing suddenly.

'I have to ask.'

'No, we're not having sex,' said Laura, which was technically true. They hadn't had sex yet. A part of Laura wanted to ask her mum for advice. She wanted to talk to her about it openly and maturely because she had only spoken with Charlotte. It might be helpful to get her perspective too, but she was too shy. Too embarrassed to talk about sex with her mother, which Laura hated because she always thought of herself as strong and mature. She was intelligent and emotionally grown up. Yet when it came to it, she couldn't do it. So childish, she thought.

'Just promise me one thing.'

'Okay,' said Laura, still bright red and glowing inside.

'If you do have sex, you'll be careful. No matter what he says, use a condom, and if you need to go on the pill, tell me, and we can go to the doctor together. Promise me.'

'I promise.'

'Thank you,' said Olivia with a smile. 'Right, I'd better get back to dinner.'

Olivia stood up, relieved and happy that they had finally had the chat. She could relax. His name was Tom Chance, and he wanted to go to Oxford too. She wouldn't tell Alexander. It would be their little secret, and she rather liked that. Laura stood up and walked over to her mum.

'Thank you,' she said.

Laura gave her a hug, and Olivia inhaled all of her in. They were about the same height now, and when she hugged her, she felt the body of a woman. Olivia smelled the familiar smell of school on her. She loved that smell. She would miss it when it was gone.

'You're welcome, baby girl.'

Laura went upstairs to get changed before dinner, while Olivia went across to the fridge and found some sausages she'd bought earlier in the week from Waitrose. British pork, leek and chive. They sounded divine. There were some long rolls in the cupboard and some frozen chips in the freezer. They could have sausages in the rolls with the mushrooms, peppers, and onions over the top, and some chips. Alexander would be home soon.

Olivia got back to cooking and listening to Coldplay, and in that moment, in her world, she felt a calmness. She felt a stability, and a yearning for more of life. She had dreams of one day driving along the Italian coast with Alexander. Just the two of them in a little open top Fiat. Positano, Sorrento, and eating at little cafes in sleepy fishing villages. She wanted to go to Thailand and snorkel in crystal clear waters, and trek through steamy jungles. She had dreams of Australia, Fiji, and road tripping across America. She had dreams of things she wanted to do, a bucket list, although she hated that term, and one day she would do them all with Alexander. The love of her life. She couldn't help but dance around the kitchen as she cooked and listened to the music. She felt her hips move, and her feet tapped against the wooden floors. She felt alive and happy at the endless possibilities of her life.

16.

The present

'Ready, baby girl?' Louise said to Ella.

'Ready!' said Ella excitedly.

It was a warm Tuesday morning, and they were off to the park. Ella had Floyd the teddy in her hand, and Louise was making sure they had everything they needed. She was taking the buggy because it was too far for Ella to walk. She had tried it once, and Louise had carried Ella most of the way home. Louise made sure she had her book and a muesli bar for herself. She packed light coats just in case it rained. It was England, you never knew. Best to be prepared. A hangover from her own childhood.

On the walk to the park, Ella talked to her mum the whole time. She talked and talked, mainly about nothing, while Louise just listened. She loved her little voice. She knew it wouldn't be long before their almost daily walks to the park would be over and Ella would be off to full-time education. Louise wanted to relish them while she could because she knew that once they were over, she would miss them terribly.

Louise wasn't in the best of moods because she'd had an argument with Jim that morning. He had never taken her studies seriously. He joked she was always looking up at the sky while he was looking down at the ground. That Sunday, the plan was for Jim to take Ella to his parents for the day. They wanted to take her to a new indoor play park that had just opened up near them. They were going to have a Sunday roast, and it was going to be a lovely day for Ella. It was also going to be a rare day at home by herself for Louise. A day she could use to catch up on some reading. Her plans to apply for university next year were gathering pace inside her mind, and she wanted to be ready. She rarely had entire days alone, and she was really looking forward to it. But then, out of the blue, Jim said that maybe he'd drop Ella off, and they could spend the day together and do something fun. Louise immediately said no. Jim took umbrage with her, and the argument ensued. The result was that Jim would go to his parents, and Louise would get her day alone. She couldn't wait. Jim had gone off to work in a sulk.

'Here we are, baby girl,' said Louise, walking into the park.

The park was busier than usual because it was such a lovely day. Kids ran around laughing and screaming, and parents stood around feeding them and wiping their mucky faces. A few mums stood in groups chatting away, and once Ella had run off, Louise made her way to her usual bench. She took out her book, checked on Ella, who had found a little girl she knew, and then she dived into her book, The Rule of Law. It was suggested reading for the course she wanted to apply for.

Louise loved their trips to the park. The long walk there and back was good exercise, and it took up a good part of the day. Louise enjoyed the route. The same route she always took. She admired the houses and dreamed that one day she might live in one of them. She loved the park itself. Despite not talking to anyone, it made her feel like a part of the world. Beyond Jim and his family, she didn't have any friends or people she could call her own. But being in the park made her feel like she belonged to something.

'Do you mind if I sit here?' said a voice suddenly.

Louise looked up and saw a man standing there. A handsome man. He was tall with brown, biscuit coloured hair. It was short and slightly curly at the ends. He had the most incredible eyes that twinkled in the morning sun. They were a sort of turquoise and were so bright and clear, like a painting. He was wearing a light blue gingham shirt, and a pair of tight-fitting navy chinos, with plain white trainers. He looked about early thirties, and Louise wondered who he was there with. She hadn't seen too many dads on their own at the park.

'Umm, yes, of course,' said Louise with a smile.

Louise shuffled over slightly, and the man sat down next to her. She only realised then that he had a child's scooter with him.

'The scooter isn't mine,' he said with a smile. Louise laughed. 'My son, Josh, is over there.'

He pointed to a boy with the same colour hair, who looked far trendier than Ella in a pair of Nike trainers, blue jeans, and a striped polo shirt. He was running around with another little boy. They were playing cops and robbers. Josh was the cop, and the other little boy was the robber.

'How old is Josh?'

She closed her book without even thinking.

'He's four at the moment, five in September. He's about to start school, and I'm half dreading it, and half excited to have more time to work.'

'Snap. I have Ella, she's ...' she looked around quickly but couldn't see her. 'She's around somewhere. She starts school in the autumn. It's sad and scary, but I'll be excited to finally have time to study.'

She looked at him and smiled, and he smiled back. He really was very handsome. Strong, square, with a soft, almost boyish face. There was something kind about him, she thought. There was a moment of silence between them, and Louise looked out at the playground to find Ella. Sometimes she would vanish for what felt like an hour, and just as Louise panicked, her heart fluttering, her mind awash with terrible thoughts, Ella would appear again. It happened every time they went to the park. Today, though, she saw her right away. She was sitting talking with another little girl. She looked so happy and content. Louise hoped the rest of her life would be like that. Free from the torture and pain that she had endured.

'I'm Sam,' he said.

His voice was slightly posher than hers, but not overly posh. He may have gone to a public school, but probably not one of the more expensive ones. Definitely educated and nothing like Jim with his strong London accent, dropping h's all over the place, and glottal stops galore. For a moment, Louise wanted to say her name was Laura. Her actual name, but she couldn't.

'Louise,' she said instead.

'It's nice to meet you, Louise. You know it's awfully tricky this dad at the playground business. I see all the mums talking, and I can't just walk over and introduce myself without feeling like I'm on the outside.'

Louise laughed.

'Sorry, it's just ... I feel the same. I've been coming to this park for the last year, and I still don't know anyone.'

'I can't believe I haven't seen you here before,' he said, looking at her, a certain something in his eyes. Louise saw it but chose to ignore it. It was probably nothing.

'Well, now you have.'

'Finally a friend,' he said with a sweet, comforting smile.

They both looked off towards their children for a moment before they had the inevitable conversation about their life circumstances. Sam Gould was thirty-one, a single dad after a difficult divorce. He shared custody of their son Josh with his ex-wife, Vanessa, as he tried to navigate life post-marriage. He lived nearby in a two-bedroom flat, and he was a television scriptwriter. He'd written sketches and a few fairly successful radio sitcoms, and he was in the middle of writing a new sitcom for the BBC. He was, thought Louise, incredible. He was an actual comedy writer for television and radio. She knew those people existed, otherwise there wouldn't be anything on television, but she had never actually met one of them. He spoke with such passion about his work, and how he hoped his new sitcom would be his big break. He had had a few near misses with shows almost commissioned, but for one reason or another, they never quite made it. He was determined to make his way in the world of television.

'And what about you?' he said.

'What about me?'

'What are you studying?'

Her life was a patchwork of truth and lies. Telling him the whole truth wasn't an option, and there was the fact she was slightly embarrassed by her current situation. She knew she shouldn't be, and if Jim knew how she felt, he'd tell her to grow up and stop acting like a spoiled child. She had everything she needed. They had a roof over their head and food on the table. But he didn't know what she really needed. He didn't know the truth about Laura Burke and Louise Bailey, and maybe he never would.

'I'm going to study law next year, and then I'm going to become a barrister,' said Louise confidently. She loved how it sounded. The shape of the words, and how it changed his face.

'Wow, a barrister, impressive.'

'I have a long road ahead of me,' she said with a slightly self-conscious smile.

'It's better to have a long road ahead than behind.'

She looked at him as the sun caught the edge of his face, and she felt something inside of her she hadn't felt for a very long time. Perhaps not since before when she was with Tom Chance. The life that seemed so far away from her current one. And yet, sitting on that bench with Sam, something changed inside of her. She suddenly saw a clear path ahead. She saw all the possibilities that were open to her. With Jim, she felt trapped, as if life was already set in stone and it wouldn't ever be what she wanted. But with Sam, she felt it again. The same feeling she used to have when she was younger. The feeling that anything was possible. He gave her that, and the thought of returning home to Jim made her heart sink. She knew in that moment that despite trying for so many months and years, that one day she and Jim wouldn't be together. They couldn't. They wanted different things. The only thing they had in common was Ella, and that wasn't enough. It made her heart heavy because Ella loved her father, and Louise had always promised herself that no matter what happened, she would never get in the way of their relationship.

Ella and Josh both had a snack, and then they ran off together to play. Louise and Sam talked almost non-stop about so many things. They discussed favourite television shows for a long time, and she had asked him about his writing and what it was really like. He asked more about her interest in law, and it felt wonderful to talk about it openly with someone who actually cared. Someone who was interested and impressed. Someone encouraging.

'This has been really nice,' said Sam when they finally stood up to leave.

'It has.'

'Hopefully I'll see you again.'

'I'd like that.'

'Me too.'

They smiled at each other, their eyes for a split-second holding contact, and something passed between them. Something unspoken, but it said if there was ever hope of them being more than just two people who met in the park one day then they would like that very much. Louise hadn't mentioned Jim, and she wasn't wearing a wedding or an engagement ring. As far as Sam knew, she was single, and he had told her everything. There was something there. Something solid and tangible. But in that moment, a flash of a memory went through Louise's mind. A feeling that hadn't gone away. The moment when she knew her life wouldn't ever be the same again, and she looked at Sam and thought there was no way she could be with someone like him if he knew the truth. Lie after lie and she had forgotten the truth because the truth was too hard to comprehend. Instead, she took shelter with Jim, unhappily hiding in plain sight. She hoped to one day step out of the shadows and become someone that Sam might think about like that. She dreamed.

'Come on, baby girl, time to go,' said Louise.

Ella, tired after all the running around, jumped into the

buggy, and Louise made sure they had all of their stuff. She looked at Sam and he looked back at her. They both smiled, and then she turned around and walked away. Back towards home that was so far from the park. So far from the life she wanted. Ella was quiet all the way home. Louise walked and looked at the houses, and thought about Sam, and she couldn't help a few tears that leaked out and down her face. She wiped them away as soon as they came but found that more came soon after.

One Lie

17.

The past

Belinda arrived in London full of hope. After the miscarriage, Belinda realised she couldn't stay living at home and so she started working on a plan to escape. After her father had hit her once, it was as if he'd broken down a barrier and he had a clear run at doing it again. At first her plan had been to move to Dublin with her brother, Jason, but the plan quickly evolved to moving to London instead. She had an aunt there who she contacted via her brother. She had a spare room that was available to rent and could take her in for a few months until she got herself sorted. Belinda jumped at the chance. The multi-coloured dream of London felt like something incredible compared to the drab greyness of home.

It was a chilly morning when she finally packed up a bag of things and left the house. Her father was at work, and her mother was out shopping. She left a note that just said 'goodbye' and that was it. She was going to spend the night in Dublin with Jason, and the next day she was going to get on a plane for London. Jason had helped with some money and paid for the flight. She felt like a refugee escaping a war-torn country, slipping out quietly in the dead of night.

It was her first time flying. It was only a short flight, but Belinda couldn't believe it. She spent the entire flight staring out of the window at the ground below and at the sky in complete awe. As they got nearer to London, she saw the green fields of England for the first time, and the houses that seemed to stretch on forever. She saw the snake-like river Thames and then finally the Houses of Parliament, Big Ben, The London Eye, and Belinda felt overawed with a sense that her life was only just beginning. The small, grey box she had grown up in, and her terrifying father, felt a million miles away. That dull, depressing life full of hate and nothing but bleakness was gone, and it had been replaced by London and everything it had to offer.

Her aunt's house was near Upton tube station in East London. It was a nondescript house on one of those streets full of terraced houses. Stacked together like Lego. A small brick wall enclosed a tiny front garden that had been concreted over years ago with weeds that had grown through the cracks. It had uPVC windows that were installed in the 1980s when they were all the rage, and Artex ceilings and wallpaper in every room. Despite its less than aesthetically pleasing interior, Belinda was happy to be somewhere she felt safe. Her aunt, her mother's sister, who hated Belinda's father almost as much as Belinda, was widowed, and so filled her house with tenants. It was an unofficial bed and breakfast, and so all types of people were coming and going, and Belinda was just another face. She had agreed to take Belinda in because she knew how awful her father was and agreed to keep her existence there a secret. She only wished that Belinda's mother, her sister, would leave him and join them too. Belinda was happy for the first time in as long as she could remember. It was a feeling she had forgotten existed.

The house was loud and chaotic, and Belinda loved it. She had the smallest room at the top of the house, with just a single bed, a wardrobe, and a simple desk. It was more than she needed because she didn't have much stuff. Only the bag of things she had brought over from Ireland. A few clothes, a copy of The Bible, and a framed photo of her and Jason when they were kids. She had stolen it from the lounge in her old house.

She was only seventeen when she arrived in London. She had some money from Jason, but not much. It wouldn't last long, and she needed a job quickly. She was in London though, and surely anything was possible. She lacked education and work experience, but she had a drive to succeed born from the years she had spent in Ireland. The first day in London, she had spent wandering around like a tourist. She saw Buckingham Palace, walked through Green Park and Hyde Park, and the streets of Soho and Covent Garden. She strolled by the Thames and thought about the sort of life she wanted in London. She was going to work every hour possible to make sure she had everything she wanted. The miscarriage had left a scar on her, and the only way she could think about healing it was to keep busy.

It didn't take Belinda long to find a job. It was nothing much, just answering phones in an office. The man who had interviewed her loved her accent and said she'd do great on the phones, but if she worked hard and showed initiative, then she could work her way up. The job was in Farringdon, and so every morning Belinda would get the bus from her aunt's house in Upton to work. After growing up on the edge of Dublin, London felt like a tremendous release for Belinda. Just the sheer size of it baffled her, and the number of people, noise, and the energy of it. She felt like she had been locked away in some far-flung part of the world, cut off from everything, and suddenly she was in the centre of it all.

Her days started early, and ended late, but gradually over time, she worked her way up from receptionist and learned other positions within the office. It turned out she had a real aptitude for computers. At twenty-two years old, Belinda had grown into herself. The life she had in Blanchardstown felt like it had almost never happened. She occasionally thought about her parents, and she hoped her mum had the courage to one day leave her father. She thought about Jason in Dublin and wondered what he was doing, and she hoped he was happy. She had spoken to him a few times on the phone, but he was terrible at keeping in touch. Every time she rang him, he was busy or drunk. Belinda sank herself into London. By twenty-three, Belinda was living in a flat share in south London, she had a job working in the IT department of a financial analyst company in the City, and life for Belinda was full. It wasn't everything she ever hoped for, because she had never really had hopes, her father had seen to that, but she had a life. A proper life. She had a few friends and a job that paid well enough. The only thing she didn't have was love.

It was a Friday night, and Belinda was on the train heading out of London Bridge station and towards home. She had gone out for a few drinks after work. Not that she drank much. Belinda still didn't like to drink. She had two glasses of wine in three hours, while her office colleagues drank three times as much. Some of them had talked about going on somewhere else, and that's when Belinda had decided to go home. It had been a long week, and she was tired. She wanted an early night and a relaxing weekend. Her flatmate was away all weekend visiting her family in Yorkshire. Belinda thought of walks in the park and watching television in her pyjamas.

The train was fairly quiet, and it wasn't long before she noticed the man opposite her. He kept looking across at her. He was interested in her. Belinda wasn't an expert with men by any stretch of the imagination, but he didn't hide it well.

'Sorry, do you mind if I join you?' he said after a few furtive glances.

'And why would you want to do that?' said Belinda.

He laughed. He was dressed in a suit, no tie (that had been taken off a few hours earlier) and he smelled of cigarettes, but he was handsome, and he had one of those smiles. Deep dimples in his cheeks, and dark eyes like night-time pools that swallowed her up. Belinda felt there was something there, even if she didn't know quite what it was.

'I'm Liam,' he said in an English accent. She wasn't sure where he was from exactly. She had heard so many accents in London and couldn't quite place them all yet. She knew it was definitely northern. Manchester? Leeds?

'Belinda.'

'Irish?'

'You're a smart one,' she said, and they shook hands and smiled at each other.

He sat across from her with his smile and dimples.

'So, Belinda, what do you do?'

'IT. You?'

'Sales.'

'Makes sense.'

'What's that supposed to mean?'

'Well, you have to be quite confident to talk to a complete stranger on the train. That and the cheeky smile equals sales.'

Liam laughed, and Belinda liked how confident she felt talking to a stranger on the train. She hadn't had much experience with men, but she had grown in confidence the longer she had lived in London. They sat on the train and talked. Belinda's journey was only twenty minutes. She enjoyed talking to Liam. He was twenty-five, and originally from Sheffield, but had moved to London after university for a graduate job in sales. He lived in East Croydon in a shared house with three other men, and he wanted to take Belinda out. She looked at him, unsure whether meeting up with a complete stranger was a good idea, but he seemed nice and funny, and he gave her his number if she wanted to call him tomorrow. No pressure. She didn't know if it was a sales trick, but if it was, it had worked. The train slowed down as Belinda's stop approached. She stood up, ready to get off, and Liam looked at her.

'Call me,' he said.

'Maybe I will,' she said, attempting a coquettish smile.

'I really hope so, Belinda from Ireland.'

She smiled at him and then walked towards the train door. The train slowed to a stop, and Belinda stood by the door. She waited for the door open button to light up. She had a quick look back towards Liam, and he was looking at her, and she felt it. The thing. The excitement of attraction. She would call him in the morning. She was sure of it. She smiled as she got off the train and walked the short walk back to her flat. Life had taken her by surprise yet again.

She got back to her flat, walked into the lounge, kicked

her shoes off, and then sat down on the sofa. She would get up, make a cup of tea, and watch some television soon. She just needed a moment. As she sat down, her phone buzzed with a call. She didn't know who it was. The number wasn't one she recognised. She answered anyway.

'Hello?' she said.

'Is this Belinda O'Leary?' a woman's voice said. She was Irish.

'It is.'

'I'm Roisin. You don't know me, I'm a friend of your brother.' Her voice was cold and sad. 'I'm sorry to have to tell you this, but it's about Jason.' Another pause, and then, 'he died tonight.'

It took a moment for Belinda's brain to catch up with what she had said. Jason had died. Her brother was gone. The beautiful boy with the brilliant smile who had always saved her.

'Hello?' Roisin said. 'Are you still there?'

A moment passed.

'How?' said Belinda. Her voice sounded like it was so far away.

'We're not sure yet. He'd been drinking, and there was some sort of accident.'

All the information washed over Belinda. All she knew was that the one person in her family she truly loved and was desperate to see again was dead. Roisin said she'd call back in the morning with more details, and Belinda said goodbye. She sat there for a moment, and then she burst into tears, her heart breaking for the second time in her life.

18.

The present

Alexander was awoken by a piercing scream that broke through the silence of the night. He groggily opened his eyes and looked across at his alarm clock. 3.22 am. Perhaps it was just a dream. Surely no-one would scream at such an hour. Then he heard another scream. This one really woke him up. A fear ripped through his body. All the worst-case scenarios were already flooding his mind. It was pitch black. There was hardly any light from the moon. It was one of those nights. He quickly got out of bed. Should he grab something? What if there was an intruder? Another blood-curdling scream tore through the house again. Alexander looked around for a weapon. There was nothing. He would have to go in alone. He was terrified of what he might find when he walked into her room. He had a flashback to a night ten years before. Before she left. Before she knew. Laura waking up in floods of tears, crying her heart out. Alexander had gone to help her, to soothe her tears, but he couldn't, and he had just held her as she wept. His baby girl.

Alexander opened his door and turned on the light. The door to Belinda's room was directly opposite his. He walked across the landing until he was in front of it. He took a deep breath. His heart was pounding in his chest. He opened the door, not sure what he might find. It was dark and warm in the room, and he looked towards the bed where Belinda was sitting up.

'Are you all right?' he said when he realised there was no-one else there.

Belinda started crying. Big tears that cascaded down her face. Her entire body shook. For a moment, Alexander wasn't sure what to do. He stood watching her, and then he walked over to the bed, sat down, and he reached out both arms, and she fell into him. He hugged her, and she wept into his shoulder. It was the first time they had had any real physical contact since the day on the railway bridge.

'It's all right,' said Alexander. 'It's okay. I'm here. You're safe.'

The same words he had said to Laura so many years before.

He felt her body shudder against his, and it took quite a while for the tears to subside. She must have had one hell of a nightmare. They sat together in that dark room for a few moments. She was against his body, and he had his arms around her. She was in the pyjamas he had given her. The pyjamas that belonged to Olivia. He felt the fabric of them and Belinda's body beneath, and for a moment he imagined it was Olivia instead. What he wouldn't give to feel her body again. To hug her. He wished more than anything that it was Olivia inside those pyjamas and not Belinda. He closed his eyes as he hugged her and imagined. He thought of Olivia. His mind drifted.

After a minute, she pulled away and wiped her face with the sleeve of her pyjamas. He looked at her through the soft darkness.

'I'm sorry,' she said.

'It's okay. What happened?'

'I had a dream my da' was back. He came here to bring me back to Ireland. To our old house. I didn't want to go, but he was going to make me. He hit me again and again.'

'You're okay. You're safe here. I promise.'

They sat quietly for a moment. It was almost three thirty in the morning. Alexander knew he wouldn't be able to sleep again. He had a hard enough time sleeping as it was. He never used to have insomnia, but since everything happened, sleep was the one thing that eluded him. He was better these days, but he still had some nights when he could barely sleep for twenty minutes before he was awake again. When he would just lie there in silence staring up at the ceiling before he would inevitably get up and walk around the house in the hope it might make him tired again. It never did. The thoughts and memories were too strong and kept his head full. They kept him awake. Instead, he'd read or watch television. In summer, if it was warm enough, he'd sit in the garden and wait for the sun to come up. He loved the birdsong and the feeling of a new day when anything was possible before the reality of it would hit him again.

'Do you want a cup of tea or something? Some warm milk?' said Alexander.

'Warm milk?'

'It's something my mother used to give me when I couldn't sleep.'

'Tea will be fine, thank you.'

Alexander saw her smiling through the darkness. He stood up. He looked down at her for a moment. She suddenly looked so small. So fragile. She had lost a lot of weight living on the streets. She had never been a big person, but she had lost whatever fat she had, and now had a slight frame, and her face had changed shape altogether. When Belinda had first looked at herself naked in Alexander's bathroom mirror, she hardly recognised herself.

'Did he hit you?' Alexander said.

'My da'?'

'Yes.'

'Just the once. It was enough.'

Alexander couldn't fathom why any parent would hit their child. You brought them into the world, and your only job was to love them, and give them everything you could of yourself. To protect them. Alexander had tried to be the best dad possible. He had failed, but he had tried and would never have hit Laura. With all of his heart, he couldn't imagine it. To strike something you loved so much seemed impossible to him.

Alexander walked downstairs to make them both a cup of tea. There was something he liked about the house in the middle of the night. It was strange how the same house in the day could feel so different at night. Even London itself felt different to him. The noises weren't the same. There were nights after it happened when he couldn't sleep, and he'd get in his car and just drive. Sometimes he'd drive through the very heart of London. Across the Thames and into the city, past Buckingham Palace, through Westminster and into Chelsea. He preferred London at night when it was almost empty. A few people left over from clubs, drunk and staggering home, and the homeless. Street sweepers and the night people, as he called them. But on the whole London was dead, and it was nice to drive the streets that by day would be packed with cars, buses, and people that were suddenly empty.

He turned the kettle on, got two mugs from the cupboard, and put tea bags in both. He looked out at the darkness of the garden and saw his reflection in the glass of the doors. Then, after a few moments, he saw Belinda's reflection behind him like a ghost. He turned around.

'You all right?' asked Alexander.

'Yeah, just a bit shaken up, you know.'

'I know,' said Alexander because he did.

He had had so many nightmares about that night. Ones that had woken him up in terror, and others where he'd woken up crying without even realising why. Certain dreams he'd had again and again, like films he had watched over and over, while others were gone before he'd even had the chance to remember them. Night was always the worse part of the day. The quietness and stillness of it made the thoughts seem so much louder. By day it was easier to lose yourself in life, but at night, alone with his thoughts, sometimes they drowned him.

He made them tea, and they sat down at the table.

'He used to hit my ma all the time,' said Belinda. She looked across at Alexander. 'Sometimes so badly she couldn't leave the house for a week or more because of the bruises.'

'That's awful,' said Alexander. He felt sick just thinking about it.

'She would never leave him, though. I'd be in my bedroom, and I'd hear them arguing, and I'd be waiting to hear the first punch. Ma would scream at him, and he'd be shouting at her. I didn't mind the shouting. It was the good bit, really. It was when the shouting stopped.'

Alexander looked across at Belinda. She took a sip of her tea. He thought she might be crying, remembering such an awful part of her childhood, but her face was still and cold.

'When my brother Jason was at home, I'd sneak into his room. He'd tell me to be quiet, and he'd hide me behind him on his bed. If Da' ever tried to lay a finger on me, he'd have to go through him first. That's what Jason was like.' She smiled. 'I loved him so much.'

'Where's he now?'

'He died. A few years ago. He'd gone out for the night in Dublin. He'd got drunk, and then he'd gone missing. They found his body in the river. They don't know what happened.'

'I'm sorry.'

He could see the pain stamped on her face. She smiled. A sad, forlorn smile.

'He used to call me his little darlin'. Come here, little darlin', he'd say. He was a brilliant brother. He was the only good thing about my childhood.'

Alexander left a pause. He watched her face for a moment. He took a sip of his tea.

'And what happened the one time your dad hit you?' he said finally.

He couldn't look at her, and instead sipped his tea and watched their reflections in the glass.

'Jason was gone at that point, and I think he finally got bored of only hitting Ma. I was the next thing. He was drunk, as usual. He only hit Ma when he'd been drinking. I think he liked to use it as an excuse. He wouldn't do it if he was sober. It was the demon drink that made him do it. The truth was that he was just a violent man who'd made nothing of his life.'

She stopped talking for a moment. Alexander looked across at her. He wanted to help her. To comfort her. He felt so awful. No-one should have to go through something like that. It was no wonder she had ended up where she did.

'I was only sixteen,' said Belinda, and suddenly her face changed, and a tear slipped out down her cheek. She quickly wiped it away, but it was followed by another and then another. 'I lost my first baby that night. He punched me so hard in the stomach I had a miscarriage.'

In all the words she said, and that broke his heart, Alexander heard her say she had lost her first baby that night. That meant she had lost another. He wondered more about her story, and how she had come to be on the bridge that morning. It was clear to Alexander that she had lost a lot and perhaps as humans we could only lose so much before we lost all hope of ever getting enough back to make up for it. Alexander got up and walked around the table and gave her another hug.

'I'm sorry for everything you've lost,' he said. 'I promise I'll do everything I can to help you get something back worth living for.' He found himself struggling to hold back the tears because he realised he wasn't just talking to Belinda, but to his daughter too.

After another cup of tea, Alexander told her to come outside with him. It was chilly, and so he grabbed a couple of blankets from the cupboard. They went outside into the garden. It was still dark, but the first hints of sunshine were beginning to crack through the clouds. He told Belinda to sit down, and he put one of the blankets across her legs. He sat next to her, and they listened to the birds singing, and eventually the sun came up. Alexander loved that time of day so much and experiencing it with someone else made it even better. They sat together in their chairs with their blankets over their laps and looked up at the sky as it ever so gradually changed from darkness to light. Birds flew past, and chirped, and they sat in silence and just watched it all unfold before them. A new day. A fresh chance to do something meaningful. To release some of the demons that haunted them. Alexander thought about sixteen-year-old Belinda back in Ireland, losing a baby, and the pain she must have felt. He thought about the second baby she had lost and wondered when it was and with whom. He felt her next to him, and then he looked up at the sky and thought about Laura and his granddaughter. He needed to see her again. He had to make up for everything he had done. For every moment that she had felt pain, he wanted to give her ten more when she didn't. They sat in the garden and watched the day begin together. The sky slowly changed colours, the clouds drifted from grey to white, and the gun-metal sky to blue.

19.

The past

Everything felt wrong. Belinda woke up that morning with a pain in her stomach, and she knew that something wasn't right. She was alone in bed. Liam had slept there, but his side was just a messy sheet and a pillow with an indentation of where his head had been. Gone again. It seemed he spent more time away from her these days than with. It worried her so much that when she had the baby, she would have to do it alone. A single mother in London. No support. No help. Liam was more interested in going out and getting drunk and probably sleeping with other women. She didn't have any proof, but he was gone so often it was the only logical conclusion.

The pain came again. A sharp pain in her stomach. She was almost twenty weeks pregnant. It wasn't a planned pregnancy. Belinda wasn't on the pill because her body didn't like it. It made her feel awful. It gave her migraines, and it changed her body. Stupid hormones. And so they used condoms. They were always careful until one night when they weren't. It was Liam's fault. He insisted they do it without a condom, and he'd be careful. He wasn't. She had thought about the morning-after pill but had reasoned the chances of being pregnant were slim. It was the wrong time of the month and he had mostly pulled out on time. Belinda was shocked when she was pregnant, but not unhappy. After her first miscarriage, she had long harboured wishes to be a mother. It felt like she was righting a wrong. Liam, who had been one hundred per cent into her and them, suddenly pulled away. He didn't want children. He didn't want to be tied down. They weren't even married. He had even claimed she had trapped him, despite it being his choice to have sex.

The pain came again, and Belinda knew she needed help. She had to go to the hospital. For a moment, she thought about calling for an ambulance, but she felt silly. What if it was nothing? She didn't want to waste their time. Another silly mum, panicking because of a bit of pain that was perfectly normal. It was probably just cramps. She would get dressed and go to her GP. She had her twenty-week scan coming up, and at the last one everything was fine. She got herself dressed, got her stuff, and walked down the stairs, out of their flat and onto the street. She took a deep lungful of air. It was going to be all right. The sun was shining. Nothing bad happened on days like that. The surgery was only a ten-minute walk away. She could do it. She took a few steps, and then the pain came again, but this time it was much stronger. She fell to her knees on the street. Her hands instinctively going to her stomach, trying to protect her baby.

'You all right, love?' said a passing woman. She was in her sixties with grey hair.

'I don't know. I don't think so. I'm pregnant.'

'I'll call you an ambulance. Just stay there and relax, love.'

She put her shopping down, took out her phone and rang for an ambulance. A few

other people came over to enquire if she was all right. Take a few deep breaths, someone said. The pain shot through her stomach, and she screamed out in pain. Something was wrong. Where was Liam? She needed him. She needed someone.

'Call Liam,' Belinda whimpered to the woman, who took her hand and held it tightly. Belinda passed the woman her phone. 'He's the father.'

'All right, love. They'll be here soon,' she said, taking the phone from Belinda.

She had a kind face. The face of a woman who had lived a tough life. A face of someone who had seen things, raised four kids of her own, and had ten grandchildren. Kind and strong. She held Belinda's hand and looked into her eyes.

Belinda wished she was her mother, and then another pain like a flash of lightning shot through Belinda's body. Belinda felt herself losing consciousness. The pain was too much. A feeling in her body that her baby was gone. Her body ached, as if it was already in mourning. Belinda began to cry. She wasn't fully lucid, and yet she knew deep within her mind that her baby was dead. She felt dizzy. She felt outside of herself.

'Just hold on,' said the woman, who held her hand.

But it was too late. She felt the blood on her leg. The blood of her dying baby in her underwear. Belinda cried. It couldn't be happening again. Then she lost consciousness.

Belinda awoke in the hospital. She was in a bed in a room by herself. Liam wasn't there. A nurse came in and then left. Belinda tried to sit up, but she couldn't. Everything hurt. She had some wires attached to her and a machine. A drip was in her arm. Finally, a doctor came. Dr Richardson. Belinda would never forget his face. Older, narrow, grey hair, and a pair of glasses on a thin nose. An expression on his face she never wanted to see again.

'I'm afraid baby wasn't alive by the time we got to you,' he said in a calm, clear voice. 'They died before we could do anything. I'm so sorry.'

The doctor explained she would need to have a C-section to remove the baby, and that they should do it soon. Lots of words. Meaningless to Belinda, because all she heard was that her baby had died. She was only twenty-five, and she'd already lost two babies. It was all too much. Liam eventually came, but he offered very little. He couldn't deal with it. He couldn't help. He left before she was wheeled away for surgery. He came back the following day to take her home, and that was it. He carried on as if nothing had happened. He kept working late and drinking and staying away, and Belinda mourned the loss of her baby. She wasn't coping. She felt the depression linger longer than usual in her mind. Terrifying thoughts and ideas kept her awake and unable to function. She couldn't go back to work or leave the flat without having a panic attack.

Time slipped by until one day Liam came home from work. He had been drinking. He smelled like her father.

'Look at the state of you,' he said. 'You need to get up and take a shower, get dressed, and get back to work.'

'I can't,' she mumbled, wrapped in bedding that needed a wash.

The depression was like a physical thing that affected every part of her body. It was like a flu that kept her in bed, tired, and trying to unsuccessfully fight it. She was sick and knew there was nothing she could do about it. Lost in a maze, unable to find a pathway out. The dazzling lights of London had all gone out. It was just black.

'You have to, Belinda, because I can't do this anymore.'

'Do what?'

'This! Us! I'm tired of it, and I'm done,' he said. His words were like cold, sharp knives that cut through her. 'I'm done with you. We lost a baby, I get it, but it's been months and you're still just lying there. You don't have a job. You haven't washed in I don't know how long. I can't deal with you. The rent on the flat is up in two weeks, and I'm moving out.'

She looked at him. He seemed so far away from the man she had met on the train. When her life finally seemed to be going well. Before it all fell apart.

'I can't do it,' she whimpered.

'Neither can I. Two weeks and then you'll be evicted. You need to get yourself together. Go home. Do something.'

And then he packed up his things and left. She would never see him again. Belinda was alone in the flat. She had two weeks to do something. To get a plan together. She had no-one. She had a little bit of money, but not much. She could go home to Ireland, but she couldn't. It wasn't her home anymore. She could return to her aunt's house in East London, but she couldn't do that either. She couldn't face her. She didn't want her to see her in the state she was in.

And so she slept, and did nothing, and the two weeks came and went, and finally she had to leave. She packed up as much of her stuff as she could and walked out. She had nowhere to go. With the last of her money, she found a cheap hostel for a week, and then she was homeless and penniless. If she had a clear mind, she would have been able to do something. She might have been able to get a job, go to her aunt's house, or stay with a friend for a few weeks. With a healthy body and mind, she wouldn't have done what she did. Belinda started sleeping rough. Every day was like a fog. She woke up, cold and shivering in doorways, and she told herself that she would get out of it soon. She would turn it around. She would get her life back. She just needed a bit more time. Tomorrow.

Months went by and Belinda's situation got worse. Her mental health declined, and she stopped telling herself that it would get better. All she thought about was her baby. After the C-section, they had given her the option to hold her. It was a little girl. As difficult as it was, Belinda knew she had to hold her baby. She wouldn't be able to forgive herself if she didn't. They handed her to Belinda, wrapped in a blanket, and she was so small. She weighed almost nothing. All the potential. All the life she would have given Belinda. She cried and cried. Her little girl. She kissed her head. In the weeks after, Belinda did nothing, but on one of those days she went out and got a tattoo. She had to find a way to remember her, and so she got the tattoo on her ankle. *Rachel.*

The day that Belinda woke up and decided to end her life, she had been living rough for six months. She had stopped caring about herself. She just wanted to be with her daughter again, and the only way was to die. She wondered if she thought about it, whether she would be scared. She thought that perhaps the idea of it would shake her up and make her do something, but it didn't. The idea was nice. A long sleep. She had had a terrible life, broken up by moments of happiness, but ultimately if she died no-one would care and she could finally be at peace. She could stop fighting the demons that wouldn't leave her alone.

She left her small jumble of things in the doorway where she had woken up that morning. She knew how she was going to do it because she had planned it the day before. She knew trains went under that bridge every fifteen to twenty minutes. It wouldn't be a long wait. The walk there was surreal, as if she floated. She was quite happy it was all going to be over. She wasn't sad for her life. She was only sad for the life of her daughter. She thought briefly of her brother, Jason. She remembered his face. Such a handsome boy. She remembered his voice and how he used to hold her hand when they went shopping. What had his last moments been like? Had he died painfully? She hoped not. God, she missed him. If he hadn't died, she could have gone to him for help. He would have saved her again like he did once before. She thought of her parents getting the news that she was dead. Her father wouldn't care. Her mother would be broken. Two dead children and an abusive husband. If only she had left him when she had the chance. Perhaps both of her children would still be alive.

Belinda reached the bridge. It was only then she realised she wasn't wearing any shoes. She felt relieved. The pain inside of her was just too much. She cried for her daughter. For the loss of her life. She got up onto the bridge. The train would be coming soon. The train that would end her life. Twenty-six years old. It wasn't long, but longer than so many children that never even got the chance. She heard the train in the distance. She wasn't afraid. She was prepared to die. And that's when Alexander came and saved her. He took her hand and held it and gave her a second chance. If it wasn't for him, she would be dead. That much she knew. Alexander Burke rescued her when all seemed lost. He was a good man. Perhaps the only good man she had ever met.

20.

The present

Louise stood in front of the cafe and looked at the menu.

'What do you fancy?' said Sam with an eager smile.

'I want a hot chocolate,' said Ella.

'Is that okay?' Sam said to Louise.

She looked down at her daughter and smiled.

'Just this once,' she said.

'Yes!' said Ella.

'Me too!' said Sam's son, Josh, quickly.

'Fine,' said Sam, smiling at his son. 'And what about you?'

'Just a latte please,' said Louise.

'And cake? You must want a piece of cake. They all look delicious,' said Sam.

Louise looked at the cakes. He was right. They did all look absolutely wonderful. They were at the cafe in the park, and Sam said he'd buy them all coffee and cake. Ella was thrilled because she never got anything from the cafe because it was too expensive. Louise didn't often get a coffee because she didn't have the money. It was the third time she had met Sam at the park, and he had offered, and despite turning him down once, he insisted. Ella and Josh had quickly become good friends, and Ella spoke about him all the time. For the first time in a long time, Louise felt that pull of attraction towards someone. She looked across at the cakes.

'How about that one?' she said, pointing at an indulgent looking chocolate cake with fresh cream on top.

'That one it is,' said Sam with a smile.

'I like cake,' said Ella with a cheeky smile.

Josh and Ella burst out laughing like it was the funniest joke ever. Louise looked down at the kids and smiled, and then she looked at Sam, who was already looking at her. His eyes met hers, and they both held the look for a few seconds before they fell into coy smiles. Louise had started putting on a bit of makeup for the park and dressing in slightly smarter clothes than usual. She noticed Sam looked handsome that day too. Freshly washed jeans, an ironed shirt, and his hair had definitely been done. Whatever it was between them, it was mutual. The only problem was that she hadn't mentioned Jim yet, and she knew at some point she would have to. He had to know about Jim, but she also wanted him to know that she was going to leave him. It was complicated. That's the expression she thought she might use. It was mainly complicated because he was Ella's dad, and she loved him to bits. He loved Ella too, and she would never want to get in the way of their relationship. Louise wanted an amicable separation. It was hard imagining how it would all work without anyone getting hurt, but she knew it was impossible, and the person getting hurt would be Jim.

They got their drinks and cake and sat down. The cafe had a few wooden benches that looked out towards the park. Ella and Josh immediately started drinking their hot chocolates. The girl at the cafe had made them not so hot, especially for the kids. She had also added whipped cream on top, which Ella scooped up with her finger and ate with a huge smile on her face. Louise loved this. She loved having coffee out and seeing the kids happy and getting along. She wanted holidays like this. A week or two away somewhere fun where the kids could just be kids. She didn't have that with Jim, but she could see it with Sam. She looked across at him, and she could see it all. Him writing his sitcoms, and her a barrister. They could live somewhere nice, like the houses around the park, take holidays abroad, and give their children the best life. In time, Sam would become like a dad to Ella, and she would become a mum to Josh. A blended family. A modern family. It was possible.

The kids quickly finished their hot chocolates and wanted to play, but Louise and Sam were still working on their coffee and cake. They all got up and walked over to the park so the kids could get their energy out. They found a bench and sat down. Ella and Josh immediately started playing hide and seek while Louise tucked into her cake.

'They get on so well,' said Sam wistfully, looking towards the kids.

'They do.'

There was a pause as they both had sips of their coffees.

'Just like us,' said Sam after a moment.

He looked at her with a smile. But it was different. It was serious. A smile that meant more than just a smile. Louise wondered if that's how her father's affair had started. A smile across the playground. A kind word. A smile that lingered a little bit too long. Louise had never asked him the questions because she had never wanted to know. But now she was thinking about another man the way she should have been thinking about Jim. She had become just like her father. The one thing he had done that had altered the entire trajectory of her life. The thing she had hated him for, and now she was doing the same. She felt awful. Awful for how she felt about Sam and the thoughts she had about Jim. For not telling Sam the truth. His smile changed everything in her head because she knew what it meant. It was that sort of smile.

'Look, Sam, there's something I need to tell you,' she said after a moment.

The casual, flirty tone of her voice changed, and her expression hardened.

'Oh,' said Sam. His voice was flat. 'This is where you tell me you're married, right?'

'Not quite,' she said with a thin smile. 'I am with someone, but it's complicated. It's Ella's father, but we're not married.'

'Right.'

His face changed too. The realisation that all the thoughts and daydreams he had about the girl from the park perhaps weren't going to be fulfilled. He had already thought about how he was going to ask her out. How he was going to broach the topic of them without coming across as creepy. Despite his age, and being married, the thought of dating again terrified him. He hadn't dated since his ex-wife, but here was this woman suddenly. This beautiful, funny, intelligent woman who had dreams of being a barrister, and he could imagine a life with her. Her and Ella and him and Josh. A family. The thing he had wanted with his wife, but it hadn't worked out. The wholesome, middle-class dream that had disintegrated into arguments and shouting matches and sleeping with their backs turned away from each other in cold silence.

'I'm sorry. I should have told you sooner, it's just ...' she stopped for a moment. She felt like she might cry, but she couldn't. Not in front of Sam.

'Complicated?' said Sam, finishing her thought for her.

'I don't love him,' she said quickly. 'We only stayed together because I had Ella, and now we're sort of trapped in this relationship, but it's not what I want.'

'And what do you want?'

Louise wanted the life she had dreamed about as a teenager. She wanted a career she loved and one that afforded her the life she had always dreamed about. She wanted a husband she loved and who loved her, children, and a house. She knew from her own experiences that all of that wasn't always enough to make people happy, but it was a start. She thought the most important thing is that she made her own money, so that whatever happened, she didn't have to rely on other people because no matter how much you thought you could, you couldn't rely on people. People always let you down. Maybe if she knew Sam long enough, he'd let her down too. She felt like it was inevitable, but also that she had no choice but to give him the chance to prove her wrong.

Before Louise had the chance to respond, she heard a child crying and knew immediately it was Ella. She knew her cry and before she had had time to think, she was running across the playground. There was no other sound in the world that hit her heart like the sound of her daughter's tears. She found her on the other side of the playground. She had fallen down, and blood ran from a cut on her knee and down her leg. Tears pooled in her eyes and then slid down her face. Josh looked on and Ella tried to tell her mum what had happened between heavy sobs.

'I… was, trying to climb … and I fell and …'

'It's okay, baby girl, let's get you all cleaned up, shall we?' said Louise calmly.

Sam was next to her, and he and Josh walked with Louise, who was carrying Ella in her arms, back to their bench. Louise carried a small medical kit in the buggy, just in case. Ella was still crying and holding her leg, although from previous history, Louise knew that as soon as she had a plaster on her knee, she would be running around again within moments. She wiped the cut with a wipe and then put a plaster over the top. It was one of Ella's favourite plasters. Peppa Pig. As soon as Louise put on the plaster, Ella smiled.

'There you go, baby girl, all better,' said Louise.

She gave her a magic kiss on top of her head too.

'Thanks, Mummy.'

Ella wiped the tears from her face, had a sip of water, and then she and Josh ran off again. Within seconds they were laughing and screaming, and it was as if Ella had never fallen over. Louise loved how a simple plaster could make Ella feel so much better. If only her life were that simple. Perhaps Sam could be the plaster she needed to make her feel better. To heal the wounds that had been open and hurting for so long. They sat down on the bench again. Louise took the last sip of her coffee. Sam did the same. They sat in silence for a few minutes and watched their children playing. Eventually Louise spoke.

'I just want to be happy,' she said. She didn't look at Sam because she couldn't. 'I just want to wake up one day and feel really happy.'

Sam looked at her. He could see the pain wrapped around her eyes, and he could sense it in her voice. He didn't know her whole story. He barely knew her at all, really. But he knew that given the chance, he wanted to make her happy. She had a vulnerability about her. She had obviously spent time building a wall around herself for protection, but he could see that behind it, she was just scared and unhappy. Like so many people, they appeared one way and when you got to know them you realised they were something else entirely. He knew there were layers to Louise. She had stories and things had happened to her he didn't know about. He had only just found out about her boyfriend and the father of Ella, but they had something. He could feel it, and he wanted to know what it was. He knew it was going to be messy and difficult, but sometimes they were the things in life worth fighting for. Sam wanted to fight for her. He wanted to be the person who woke up next to her the day when she felt really happy.

They eventually packed up their stuff and said goodbye. It had been another day together, and Louise was feeling things for Sam. She hadn't intended to feel the things she did, and she had no intention of cheating on Jim, but she also knew the feelings were strong.

As she walked home, she thought a lot about her father. Had she been unfair to him? At the time, she couldn't understand why he had done what he did. She couldn't look at him. She hated him with a raw anger she had never felt towards anyone or anything else in her life. She hadn't seen him in years, and maybe, she thought, it was time to see him again. To talk. He had never even met Ella. He had made a mistake that Louise had never fully understood, but now she had met Sam, she was beginning to understand how it was possible. People made mistakes. They were human. Just because her father's mistake had had such far-reaching consequences, it was still just a mistake. A mistake she might make herself given half the chance.

She circled the questions and the answers through her

mind, again and again on the walk home. She didn't come to a successful conclusion, but she knew one thing for sure. She was tired of being Louise Bailey and wanted to be Laura Burke again. If she was ever going to be truly happy, she needed to be herself. It was the only way.

Part Three

21.

The past

It was Friday morning, and Alexander was awake early. It was still dark outside as he lay in bed and watched his wife sleep next to him. Today was the day he was going to cheat on her. The thought kept running through his mind. It was the thought that had woken him up. Could he do it? Alexander wasn't the sort of man to sleep with other women, and he loved Olivia. He didn't understand the motive behind sleeping with Sara. What was the point? Surely what he had to lose was exponentially greater than what he had to gain. It made no sense. If he had to explain himself to someone, perhaps a marriage counsellor, if it all went wrong, he didn't think he could. It was just pure physical want versus everything else in his life. As he lay there watching Olivia sleep, a part of him still didn't believe he would do it. It still didn't seem real.

To Alexander, Olivia was just as beautiful as ever. She had aged, as had he, but with the lines and wrinkles, and her body changing, she had become even sexier to him. He should tell her more, appreciate her more, he thought. He was turned on his side, his head on his pillow, watching her. She was on her side too, turned towards him. Alexander heard birds singing outside and the gentle hum of early morning traffic. The early commuters heading off to work. Alexander had always loved the morning. The pre-dawn light and the quietness of life before the world awoke. There was something refreshing about a new day, and the hope it brought with it. Olivia's eyes opened, and she looked at Alexander.

'Morning, beautiful.'

'Were you watching me sleep?' she said, slightly groggily.

'Maybe.'

He reached across and ran a hand through her hair. It was so soft, and it reminded him of all the times they had been in bed together from when they were young until now. It made him think about all the years they had been together. He could stop everything with Sara now. He could make the right decision. Be a good husband. Be a good man because that's all Alexander had ever wanted to be. He wanted to be successful, happy, and all the rest of it, but most importantly, he wanted to be a good person. At that moment, he was all of those things. Despite the kiss with Sara, he had never so much as thought about anyone else. He was happy with Olivia, and they would grow old together. That had always been the plan. It was true that recently things between them had been a bit mundane, but marriages fluctuated, didn't they? There were highs and lows, and flat passages of time, but ultimately, you stayed with it because the highs outweighed the lows. The peaks were high enough to compensate for the lows of the troughs.

'I'm so happy it's Friday,' said Olivia.

She rolled on her back. She was wearing a thin cream coloured t-shirt and no bra underneath. Alexander let a hand slip underneath her t-shirt and onto her stomach. He felt her smooth skin and then his hand wandered up towards her breasts. He felt the soft sponginess of one of them and then let a finger slowly glide across her nipple that instantly became hard at his touch. She didn't move and kept looking up at the ceiling of their bedroom. He took one milky white breast in his hand and gently massaged it, letting the whole thing fill his hand. Olivia had always had incredible breasts. Alexander had loved them from the very beginning of their relationship. They were perfect. Smaller and perkier then, but fuller now with small pink nipples.

'Our dates tomorrow night,' she said.

'Let's head into London. Really make a night of it,' said Alexander.

Olivia smiled to herself. If only he knew what she had

planned.

He reached his hand across and felt the other breast. The nipple. She moved slightly. She twisted her back, and her breathing changed. Were they going to have sex? Alexander hadn't thought about it until that moment. They hadn't had sex in the morning for a long time. Years perhaps. He felt himself get erect just thinking about it. He kept massaging her breasts. If he had sex with Olivia, he definitely couldn't meet Sara later. He wouldn't need to. He let his hand move down towards her knickers. Alexander suddenly felt an overwhelming desire to have sex with his wife. He needed it. He needed her. She turned her head slowly and looked at him. Her eyes met his, and all the years between them seemed to be in that gaze. He wanted her more in that moment than he had wanted her in years. Maybe it was because of Sara and what they had planned, but he thought it might somehow save them. His hand went down towards her knickers, and he felt the top of them. He played with the lace in his fingers. Alexander felt a rush of relief wash over him. He didn't have to go through with it. He could tell Sara it wasn't going to happen, and he thought she would be fine with it. It was about the chase. She had said it herself. The hunt. She would move on to someone else. Alexander had got close to the edge, but he hadn't fallen off. He ran one finger along the top of her underwear. He felt young again.

'Alexander,' said Olivia, slightly breathless.

She put a hand over his. She stopped him from going any further.

'What?'

He felt the relief wash away.

'Not now. Tomorrow,' she said with a smile.

'Oh.'

'Sorry.'

'It's fine.'

He took his hand back, and Olivia had to get up and use the toilet, and Alexander lay in bed and looked out towards the window. If only she had had sex with him. If only they had done it, then maybe he could have said no to Sara. He could have turned her down. He still could. He wanted to be a good man, but the longer he lay there and stared towards the window, the more he thought about Sara, and the more he realised how difficult it would be to say no. He also realised that perhaps he just wasn't a good man after all.

His phone was on the side, and it buzzed with a message. He quickly grabbed it. Olivia was still in the bathroom. Despite telling her not to message him, it might be Sara. She seemed to enjoy the thrill of almost getting caught. He opened his messages quickly, and it was from Sara. But it wasn't a written message. It was a photo. He opened it, the excitement building inside of him. It was the first time she had sent him a picture. The photo took a second, and then it was in front of him. Sara had obviously just taken it. She was in bed, and it was of herself naked under the sheets. Alexander could see the bottom of her breasts, the merest hint of a nipple, her smooth, lean stomach, and then down towards the darkness of her vagina. She wasn't wearing any knickers, but she was under the sheets, her legs apart. Alexander felt himself get aroused again. She had an incredible body. It mesmerised him. He imagined running his hands down that body. He thought of his head between those legs. He heard the toilet flush. Olivia would be back any moment. He quickly deleted the photo, and then he put his phone back on the side just as Olivia walked back into the room to get ready for work.

Olivia put two slices of bread in the toaster and flipped the switch on the kettle. She had a long day ahead of her. She had five clients, each lasting an hour. Fridays were usually her busiest day. People needed time off work to come and see her, and so Friday was normally the day they chose. Five clients meant at least six hours in her office. Then she needed to get to Alexander's school to follow him to the pub. She couldn't stop thinking about it. Perhaps she shouldn't do it. It was ridiculous. If one of her clients confessed they were going to follow their husband, she would tell them not to do it. Nothing good would come of it. She momentarily thought of Susan Farringdon. She had wanted to follow her husband on a night out, and Olivia had talked her out of it. Mistrust was never a healthy emotion. Talk to them. Listen. Communicate. All the things she knew and preached were firmly against following Alexander. Maybe she wouldn't. They had a date tomorrow. Perhaps she would talk to him then. Tell him she'd had some silly thoughts, and that she was sorry, and knew that he would never do something like that. They would talk about it and move on. Just like her cancer scare. This was just another one of those life moments.

Olivia was in a daze when her toast popped up. She was staring out of the window at the garden. It was a bright, cloudless day. Two birds were in the tree, squawking away.

'Mum, your toast,' said Laura, who had walked into the kitchen.

'I was miles away,' Olivia replied.

'Looked that way.'

Laura made herself a bowl of cereal and sat at the table eating while listening to the radio. The kitchen radio was always tuned to Radio 2 in the morning. Olivia buttered her toast and then put on a thick layer of marmalade. She finished making her tea and sat at the table with Laura. Alexander was still getting ready for work. On the radio they were reporting the latest weather and travel. There were long lines on the north and south circular. A crash on the A40 had led to increased traffic queues going in and out of Oxford. There was going to be a high of nineteen and a low of ten degrees with a chance of rain in the south later. Then a song by a band that Olivia had never heard of. She ate her toast and looked across at her daughter. Olivia knew her daughter was growing up fast, and in two years she would be off to university, and she might never live at home again. She was gradually losing her. It was like a grief that was slowly gripping Olivia.

'I think we should go away somewhere nice this summer,' said Olivia.

'Oh yeah, what do you have in mind?' said Laura.

'I don't know. Spain? Portugal? Italy, maybe. Where do you fancy?'

'Charlotte's family went to Mallorca last year. She said it was so nice.'

'Then Mallorca it is.'

'Mallorca is what?' said Alexander, walking into the room, adjusting his tie.

He was in his favourite navy-blue suit with a striped, red tie.

'We're going to Mallorca for a holiday this summer,' said Laura.

'I just thought with Laura going to sixth-form that it might be our last chance to have a proper family holiday together,' said Olivia.

'I think it's a great idea,' said Alexander.

Olivia looked at him and smiled. She loved him in that suit. So bloody handsome.

'Sweet,' said Laura, finishing up her bowl of cereal. 'I'll start looking at new bikinis.'

Olivia laughed, and Alexander put some bread into the toaster.

'Leaving in fifteen minutes,' Alexander said to Laura as she made her way upstairs.

'I know, Dad,' said Laura, who was desperate to get upstairs and get everything ready.

Alexander walked across and sat opposite his wife.

'Mallorca, eh?' he said.

'I just thought it would be nice. One last family holiday together before she gets too big.'

She looked at her husband, and the thought of going to Mallorca together made her feel warm and dizzy with excitement. She had really wanted to have sex with him earlier. She almost gave into it, but she wanted to wait until tomorrow night. She wanted it to be special. She had arranged for Laura to spend the night at Charlotte's house, and Olivia had booked a hotel in London. She had really splashed out and booked a room at the Langham hotel. It was very expensive and luxurious, but they needed it. She had even bought some racy new underwear. She wanted to reclaim the magic and put a spark back in their love life. As hard as it was say no that morning because God she had wanted to, it would be better if they waited for their dirty night away in a five-star hotel in central London.

Upstairs in her bedroom, Laura was packing her bag. A change of clothes, lipstick, perfume, hairbrush, toothbrush and toothpaste. Everything had to be perfect. She had butterflies in her stomach already. She couldn't believe she was going to have sex with Tom later. It was finally going to happen. She had spent so long thinking about it and dreaming about what it would be like. She made sure she packed everything at the bottom of her bag, and then her folders and books on top. She looked at herself in the mirror. She had washed her hair last night, shaved everything that needed to be shaved, and straightened her hair that morning. It was currently down, but she would put it up in a ponytail for school. She took a deep breath as her dad shouted up the stairs that it was time to go. Time to head off to school. She couldn't wait for it to be done so she could head off to Tom's house. She would be so nervous, but he was kind, gentle, and he wouldn't rush her. He'd probably get roses and put the petals on his bed or something.

'Come on, Laura!' Alexander shouted up the stairs again.

'Coming,' she shouted back.

She was ready, or at least as ready as she would ever be to lose her virginity. To change her life forever.

22.

The present

Louise looked at her face in the small mirror in their bedroom as she applied her makeup. It wasn't often she got dressed up for a night out on the town. Jim's parents were babysitting, and Jim said he had something special planned. When he had told her they were going out, she wasn't overly excited. Since she'd met Sam, he was all she could think about. That and the inevitable end of her relationship with Jim. She just had to work out how and when to tell him. She had things to get in place first. If she left Jim, she had to have somewhere to go with Ella. The problem is that she had no money of her own. Everything they had was with Jim. She hated that she relied on him for everything, and if she wanted to go back to university, she couldn't work full time. Louise felt trapped, and she needed a fool-proof exit strategy.

Louise looked at herself. Despite everything, she still thought she looked quite pretty when she made the effort. She hadn't gone overboard on the makeup but the small amount she had on, plus straightening her hair, and the little black dress, and she felt vaguely human again. Sometimes, when it was just her and Ella all day, she barely got out of her pyjamas. Her hair was perpetually in a ponytail, and she never felt glamorous or sexy. Tonight, she felt a little of both.

'Blimey, you look nice,' said Jim, walking into the room behind her.

'Thanks,' said Louise, turning around to face him.

Jim didn't scrub up too bad either. He was wearing his one suit and his nice aftershave. The one she had bought for him last Christmas. He walked over and gave her a kiss.

'Are you going to tell me where we're going yet?' said

Louise.

'Not yet, babe. Mum and Dad just arrived. They're downstairs with Ella. You ready?'

'I just need to grab my coat and put on my shoes.'

'I'll be downstairs,' said Jim, before he added on his way out. 'You look blindin'.'

As he left the room, she felt a pang of guilt. He was a good man and didn't deserve what was going to happen to him. But then she thought of the other life. The one she was supposed to have. At twenty-six, she would have been at the height of going out in London. A trainee barrister, a group of professional friends, expensive restaurants, and trendy clubs. That should have been her life instead of the one she had, trapped in that tiny house with Jim. It was hard for her not to think about it. Not to think about him too. She had been thinking more and more about seeing her father recently. It had been almost ten years since the last time. She had hated him so much for what happened. For what he did. But you can't feel the same for so long. Her hatred had dissipated and now she didn't know what she felt for him. He was her father, and in a world where she didn't have that many people, surely she should cling onto him.

'Ready, babe?' Jim shouted up the stairs.

Louise took one last look in the mirror, and then she walked downstairs. The narrow stairs that led to the hallway and then the front room. The tiny box that had far too much stuff in it. Packed with Ella's toys, a second-hand sofa they had got from one of Jim's cousins, a coffee table they had got on sale from Argos, a television that was far too big for the room but was given to them by Jim's brother, and the large recliner chair that Jim's parents had given them just so Jim's dad had somewhere to sit whenever they came over.

'There she is, and doesn't she look pretty?' said Jim's mum, Sally.

'Thanks,' said Louise, feeling a little self-conscious.

'A real picture,' said Phil, Jim's dad.

Louise smiled, and then Ella came running over and gave

her an enormous hug.

'Nanny says we're going to watch Frozen,' said Ella excitedly.

'Lucky you,' said Louise.

'Right, we'd better get off,' said Jim.

Everyone said goodbye, and Ella gave her parents' huge kisses before Louise and Jim stepped outside. It was a clear, bright evening, and they were going to get the train into London. Louise loved going into London. She dreamed about the day when she would work in central London. A barrister. Coffee out and lunches with colleagues. The hustle and bustle of professional life. She yearned for it. Even the long hours. They held hands and walked towards the train station, the early evening sunshine clinging on, and it gave both of them a bit of a glow.

Jim had something to tell Louise. He was excited. He knew she had been a bit off recently, but he hoped that after tonight she'd get back on track again. She just needed something to be excited about. He had big plans for the night ahead. They were going to get the train into London Bridge and then walk down to the Thames. They were going to have a couple of drinks at a pub by the water, and then they were going to get dinner at a steak restaurant nearby. Jim loved a good steak, and it was a properly posh place that Louise was going to love. Cocktails, steak, and then he was going to share his news. As they got onto the train at Croydon, Jim couldn't help but smile. It was going to be a good night. One they had needed for a long time. Yeah, things were definitely looking up, thought Jim as they stepped onto the train.

The Southbank was busy, as usual. Lots of after work suits were drinking in the pubs, and the restaurants were full. Smartly dressed women sipping on wine, while loud city boys brayed and laughed loudly, smugly confident in themselves and everything around them. Tourists from all over the world stood next to them, speaking in five different languages, working out what to order and how to say it. Jim stood at the bar, an imposing figure, Louise thought as she sat at a small table and watched him. Big, broad shoulders, and a shaved head in the suit that made him look a bit like Jason Statham. He was a handsome man. That had never been the problem for her. Jim was good looking and tall, and he had so much going for him. For the right woman, thought Louise, he would be a real catch. It was why she felt so guilty because every day they were together, he could be off finding someone else. Every day that she kept silent, kept telling him she was fine when she wasn't, was another day that he could move on. She wanted him to be happy. A part of her loved him, but he wasn't the man she wanted to spend her life with. Jim would never make her completely happy, in the same way that she would never love him the way he deserved to be loved. In a way they were both trapped. Her in a relationship she didn't want to be in, and him in a relationship he wanted to work, but that never would.

'Here you go, babe,' said Jim, putting her glass of white wine and his beer down on the table. 'They really take the piss with the prices. You won't believe how much these cost.'

Jim took a long sip of his beer, while Louise looked around the pub at the suits and the women talking about work. People with careers and hopes. She knew Jim hated these people, but they were her people. One day she would be one of them. She loved the bright lights of the city. The money and power and everything that came with it. She longed for intellectual conversation and dinners in expensive restaurants, and it might be slightly superficial, but she wanted nice things. She wanted a house with space and pretty decor. She thought about sitting in the pub with Sam and how different it would be. How different life might be with someone like that. The things they would talk about, the dreams they might have, and the places they'd go.

'I can't wait for dinner. I'm starvin' Marvin,' said Jim. 'Where are we going?'

'Just a place,' said Jim with a sly wink.

Louise smiled at him and took a sip of her wine. She enjoyed the noisiness of the pub. Most of her life was so quiet, and the only noise she heard was children's television and the neighbours arguing. She loved how loud the pub was and the voices she heard.

'So, what's tonight all about?' said Louise.

'You'll have to wait for later.'

'You can't just tell me now so I can stop thinking about it and enjoy myself?'

Jim looked at her. He had always been terrible at keeping secrets. It only took him a moment to crumble.

'Fine. The reason we're out tonight.' He couldn't stop himself from smiling. 'I've managed to book a week's holiday for us. You, me, and Ella, we're going down to Devon in June for a week. We've got a lovely little caravan right near the beach. It's going to be amazing, babe. There's a playground for Ella, and loads of kids' activities, and the beach for us, and there's a pub on-site.'

Louise looked at Jim, and she could see how happy he was. He had obviously been planning it for a while, and he genuinely thought it would make her happy. It was all she needed. A good holiday, a few days away, a bit of sunshine, and everything would be as right as rain. If only he knew what was going on inside her head. She looked at him, and how happy he was, and it made her even sadder. She couldn't help it, but a few tears leaked out.

'What's up, babe?' said Jim.

'I'm sorry.'

Jim was so confused. He'd just told her they were going on holiday for the first time as a family. She should have been over the bloody moon. He didn't understand Louise sometimes. Louise excused herself and went to the ladies' toilets. She needed a moment to gather her thoughts. She had so much she needed to say to Jim. She needed to tell him about going to university, about the dreams she had for her future, and how he wasn't a part of them. She hated that a week's holiday in a caravan was the thing he was so excited about. She longed for holidays abroad, and something so very different from Jim. She hated herself for feeling so much annoyance towards him when all he was trying to do was make her happy. But she couldn't tell him any of it yet. She needed more time to get things in place. She needed time to prepare herself. She washed her hands and looked at herself in the mirror. Next to her was a woman of about the same age as her. Long, blonde hair, dressed for work, and out having fun. Louise wondered what her situation was. Was she single? Did she have children? What sort of work did she do? Where did she live? She looked across at Louise and smiled. Louise smiled back.

'Love your dress,' said the woman in a home counties voice.

'Oh, thanks,' said Louise. It was the only nice dress she had.

The woman was pretty, and Louise imagined in another world, another time, that they might be friends. Flatmates that brunched together on Sunday mornings in Clapham.

'Off out somewhere fun?' said the woman.

'Just with my boyfriend.'

'Oh, right, well, have a good night.'

'You too.'

The woman took a small bottle of perfume from her handbag, sprayed it on her wrists, and then spread it across her neck.

'You never know,' said the woman on her way out. 'I might get lucky.'

Louise smiled at her. How different their lives were. How different Louise wished her life was. But she needed to control herself. She needed to go out there and tell Jim she was fine. Just shocked and overawed. She couldn't leave him yet. It wasn't possible. Choices. Moments. She had made so many mistakes over the past ten years, she didn't feel like she had the room to make anymore. She hated keeping so much of herself from Jim, but it was the only way to protect herself and Ella. She wiped her face, reapplied some makeup, and stood up tall. You didn't get to be successful by wallowing in pity. You didn't get what you wanted in life by saying everything that was on your mind. She had to be strategic. She had to think of the long-term plan. In the long run, it would be better for all of them. That much she knew was true. She would be herself one day, but at that moment, she still needed to be Louise Bailey, the woman who didn't really exist.

23.

The past

Olivia settled into her chair and waited for her first client of the day. She had just finished her coffee and was trying to clear her mind in preparation. Gordon was forty-seven, originally from Leeds, he had moved to London twenty years ago. He ran a cafe in Dulwich, was married to Clare, and they had three children. Gordon's problem was that his wife didn't fulfil his sexual needs, and so he regularly cheated. His cheating had started once the internet had caught up with his needs. Before that it was just porn and fantasy, but online meetups and sexual partner apps had given him the opportunity to fulfil everything he had dreamed about. On one hand, he was a cafe owner, devoted husband and father, and on the other, he met women for casual sex who liked a bit of bondage. He was an interesting case.

Gordon sat on the sofa opposite Olivia. He was average height with short dark hair, blue eyes, and he was in good shape. He ran marathons and was quite slim. He was dressed in a pair of black jeans, brown shoes, and a blue shirt. He was a good-looking man; Olivia had thought the first time she met him. Looking at him, you wouldn't think for a moment he was a sexual voyeur. That he spent nights away from his family tying up strangers and wearing latex face masks with things shoved up his anus.

'How are you today, Gordon?' said Olivia.

She had her notepad on her lap to write her observations, comments, and remind herself of important information. She did the same with every client. She would often write single words. Under Gordon's page, she had written the following words: Strength. Obsessive. Mother's death. Strangulation. Power. Family. Young women. Dual personality. Truth.

'Okay,' said Gordon. His voice always surprised Olivia. It was deeper than you'd imagine. 'I, umm, had a date a few nights ago.'

'And how was it?'

'It was,' he stopped, searching for the right word. 'Ground-breaking.'

'In what way?'

'She got me. She understood me. We did things I hadn't done before. She took things to another level for me.'

'And how did it make you feel?'

'Good, yeah,' he said, and then he left a pause before he continued. 'I'm seeing her again tomorrow night.'

'Oh, right.'

She was surprised because Gordon's golden rule had always been the same. He never had sex with the same person twice. It wasn't about an emotional connection. It was always about the sex. This one was clearly different.

'You know that breaks your rule.'

Gordon shifted uncomfortably in his seat. He looked at Olivia. He wasn't sure what he should say next. He liked Olivia. She understood him. He didn't want to let her down. He realised that seeing the same person again might lead to something more than just sex, but it had been mind-blowing. It had changed his perspective, and he had to have it again.

'I know, but like I said, it was special.'

Olivia wrote a word down in her notepad. Changing. He was changing. Breaking his own rule. Once he had done that, he would find an excuse to keep breaking it until all the rules he had made were null and void. It was a slippery slope. Olivia knew it was a big moment for them.

'Have you thought anymore about what we discussed last time?' said Olivia.

She had brought up the idea of Gordon confessing everything to his wife. His guilt had taken a strain on his life, and as a result his sexual fantasies had become more extreme. Olivia feared that something bad might happen to Gordon if he didn't face up to what he had been doing. He needed to confess what he had done to release him from his own self-imposed prison.

'No, not really. I just can't. Not at the moment.'

'I really think you should give it some more thought. What you're doing isn't sustainable. You can't keep living two separate lives. You can't keep lying to your wife and meeting up with women in secret. It's taking an emotional toll on you whether you realise it or not.'

Gordon told Olivia all about the woman from the other night. Like him, she was also living a lie. A married woman who didn't get what she needed at home. She wasn't fulfilled and just needed that release. She had a high-pressure job, and it was the only thing that helped her cope. Olivia tried her best to focus but drifted off and started thinking about Alexander, and about whether he could be having an affair, or was it like Gordon, just sex? Was this other woman fulfilling the sexual needs that she couldn't? Did she even know what his sexual needs were? Here was a man in Gordon, who had a wife and three kids, and ran a cafe, and no-one in his life knew anything about his sexual fantasies. No-one in his world knew that when he was going out to the gym or wherever else he said he was going for those two or three hours, he was meeting strangers in rooms and performing acts of bondage with them. It was a secret that had led Gordon to Olivia. So many of her clients raised the same question again and again in Olivia's mind. The question that terrified her. Do we ever really know anyone properly?

Alexander was in his room getting ready for his first class of the day when Sara Coupland walked in. She closed the door and walked up to Alexander's desk. He was sitting down, going through a pile of essays that had been handed in the day before. He needed to get them marked before Monday.

It was a hefty pile, and it would take him most of the weekend. He was trying to get a head start.

'Good morning, Mr Burke,' said Sara with a smile.

'Miss Coupland.'

Just her presence in the room raised his heartbeat and stiffened up his body. He could almost feel the chemicals in his body changing. She did things to him he couldn't explain or control. He wished he could. Yes, she was beautiful, but it was more than that. She had something that connected with him on levels he didn't understand. It was something physical. Something biological. It was as if she reached inside of him and altered his DNA. It was far too simple to just say that she was sexy, and he was weak. Both of these things were true, but it was more than that. She rendered him helpless, and she knew it. It was a game to her and one she knew how to win.

'Are we still on for tonight?' she said.

Alexander took a moment to answer, and then he did. His voice was croaky and unsure.

'Yes, of course.'

'At any point you can say no. I'd hate for you to feel like you're trapped.'

'Then why did you send me that photo this morning?'

She smiled.

'I just wanted to give you a glimpse of what you had to look forward to.'

Alexander noticed as she said this that she moved her lips in the most seductive way. She spoke with a softness, so she sounded younger and more alluring. She was wearing a blouse and a grey skirt, and it seemed impossible that despite what she said that Alexander could say no to her. He was trapped in every definition of the word, and that's exactly how she intended him to feel.

'I don't feel trapped.'

'Good,' she replied, and then she smiled, blew him a kiss, turned around and walked out. He watched her walk away. The way she moved her bottom. She knew he was watching her, and she liked it. It was as if every movement, every word and expression had been designed to convey one simple feeling. Sex. She was pure sex. She loved it and Alexander knew he would too. He thought about the soft curves of her breasts, her body on top of his, her nipples in his mouth, and her legs wrapped around the sides of his head. He tried not to think about it, but he couldn't help himself. It was just one night, and then he would get back to normal again. He craved normality. The days when he could focus on school and work, and then go home and not feel gut-wrenching guilt because Alexander knew that after it had happened, he could put it away. He would compartmentalise it. Sara would just be something that had happened. A memory. A moment. And then he would get back to being himself again, and perhaps an even better version of it. He would be more attentive to Olivia. He would spend more time making her happy in the bedroom and out. After today, Alexander thought, life would be a lot better for everyone.

Laura sat in class and stared out of the window. It was maths, her least favourite subject. Luckily, she had a natural aptitude for numbers, and so even though she didn't enjoy it, she found it easy enough. From her seat she could see a tree gently swaying in the breeze. Tom Chance was in another class at that moment. Laura had to stay away from him at school. She didn't want her father getting in the way of her and Tom. Why did he have to be so bloody strict? Why couldn't she have a boyfriend like all of her friends? Laura was daydreaming about next year and sixth form. It would still be school, but it would be so different. She and Tom could actually be girlfriend and boyfriend. They could hang out, go on dates, and sleep together like proper grown-ups. Life was going to be so good; she could barely contain her excitement.

Laura looked out of the window, and she couldn't help

but smile as she thought about Tom. God, he was gorgeous. Laura had known for a while that when she lost her virginity, she wanted it to be with someone special. She didn't want it to be with some random person she didn't even care about. Charlotte had lost her virginity to Simon Harris after they had been barely going out for a month. Two days after they had sex, he dumped her for Rebecca Thompson. Despite her bravado, Laura knew that Charlotte deeply regretted it. It was her first time, and it hadn't been special or memorable at all. Laura knew it would be special with Tom. It would be something she would look back on in years to come, and she would never regret it. Perhaps she and Tom would still be together in ten years. Could you imagine? She would be a barrister and him, whatever he wanted to be. They would have the most amazing life. She looked at the clock on the classroom wall. It was eleven o'clock. School was over at three-thirty, and then she was going back to his house. She watched the clock ticking down until the end of the day when she would become a woman. The feelings inside of her were so strong that she could barely sit down, and she couldn't concentrate on anything. Her mind was a whirlpool of emotions and feelings, and she couldn't stop them getting away from her. Tom Chance was everything at that moment. He was her life and nothing else mattered.

24.

The present

Belinda walked up the stairs and looked at the framed photos on the wall. Someone had obviously spent a great deal of time and effort choosing the photos, framing them, and hanging them in the right places. There were photos of a much younger looking Alexander, smiling and looking happy with a woman who must have been his wife. There were numerous photos of a young girl who looked so much like Alexander she had to have been his daughter. Belinda slowly walked up the stairs, running her fingers along some of the photographs, until she stopped at the last one. It was a photo of Alexander with his wife and daughter outside a cottage, and in the distance you could see white cliffs, and a wide, flat beach. It was a bright day, and it looked as though they were the happiest little family in the whole world. It made Belinda wonder even more about what had happened to Alexander and his family. Why was the house empty? What had happened to his wife and daughter? Why was Alexander so sad?

It was Saturday morning and Alexander had left Belinda home alone again to go wherever it was he went every Saturday morning. Belinda had been feeling marginally better the last few days. More at ease with herself. She had started thinking about the next part of her time with Alexander. The first week had been about trying to calm the voices in her mind and relax. Alexander had left her alone when she needed some space, and he had been there when she needed someone to talk to. She had started cleaning the house. She felt like she should do something to repay him, and the house needed a decent clean. She had started on the dusting, and she was going to go through the entire house before she started on the garden. She liked to be useful, and the work helped relax her mind.

Belinda looked at the photo. She didn't recognise the place, but it looked beautiful. She thought to herself that she'd like to go there one day. She wanted to stand by that cottage and look out towards the white cliffs. She wanted to feel the sunshine on her face, and the salty sea wind in her hair. It occurred to Belinda as she continued walking up the stairs to her room that she had had a thought about the future. She had plans and things she wanted to do. She knew at that moment that she didn't want to die anymore, and she had Alexander to thank for that. He had not only saved her life, but he had given her one.

Belinda looked out of her bedroom window at the world. She couldn't see much but an ordinary suburban street; trees, cars, people, and in the far distance, the very tops of buildings that reminded her she was in London. She used to get the train into London every day when she worked there. She sat for a moment and thought about those days. The days when she was happy. Before Liam and before Rachel. Before she ended up on the streets. It reminded her that she was a fighter. She had got away from her dad and made her way to London, and she had made a life for herself. Just because it had fallen apart, it didn't mean she still wasn't a fighter.

Alexander was back at school, and so Belinda had time and she had been thinking about getting a job. She needed to move on with her life. She couldn't stay with Alexander indefinitely. Eventually, she would have to move out, and she would need money to do that. She had no idea what she would do. Could she return to her old life working in the city, or would that be too much of a reminder of what had happened before? Perhaps she could do something else? She was still only twenty-six. She had so many years ahead of her. She didn't have much of an education, but she had experience. She must be able to do something with herself. She wanted to be useful. She wanted to work hard again because she knew how much enjoyment and fulfilment she got from it. She also needed to be busy, so she didn't have time to think. Belinda needed something to keep her mind moving forwards instead of constantly looking back.

Alexander had been gone for a few hours already, and she wasn't sure when he would be back. It was grey and drizzly outside, the sort of day to stay in and watch television, drink tea, or read a book. While she was alone in the house, she wandered into Alexander's bedroom. She didn't know what she was looking for or what she thought she might learn about him, but she felt a curiosity about his life and what had happened to his family.

She opened the wooden door and walked in. It had the same light brown carpet that the entire upstairs of the house had. Downstairs it was all wooden floors. It was quite a large master bedroom, and in the centre of the room was a King-sized bed with a blue duvet that had been made and tucked in tightly. On either side of the bed were white bedside tables, each with their own small reading lamp. There was a large window that looked out over the garden. Belinda had a quick look out of the window, and the views across the other gardens and houses were very suburban. Unlike her window, where you could at least see the merest hints that you were in London, this view could be of anywhere in England. Against the wall were two wardrobes. Belinda opened one, and it was almost empty. A couple of dresses, a coat, and a few pairs of women's trousers lay on a shelf. It had a musty smell, as though it hadn't been opened in a long time. She opened the other wardrobe, and it was full of Alexander's clothes. Suits, shirts, ties, trousers, and a few pairs of jeans and jumpers folded up. She ran her hand along the clothes and felt the different fabrics on her skin, before she closed it, and sat on the bed for a moment.

The house was so quiet she could hear the clock ticking in the hallway downstairs. She got up and looked quickly through the drawers next to the bed. They were mostly empty. A watch, some batteries, and a couple of books. There wasn't much. She was about to leave his room and head downstairs when she decided to have a quick look under his bed. It's where, she thought, people might keep their secrets hidden away. She remembered once when she was little going under her parents' bed with Jason. They were looking for their Christmas presents, and they found them all wrapped up in a little pile. They hadn't touched them, but they knew they were there. She kneeled down, and that's when she saw the stack of photo albums that were under the bed. She thought for a moment about whether she should look at them. They were obviously under the bed for a reason. But the more she looked at them, the more she realised she couldn't help herself. She wanted to know more about Alexander, and he hardly ever spoke about himself and any questions she had asked him were quickly batted away. She reached in and pulled the albums out.

There were eight albums in total. They were mostly the sort of albums she had seen at her own house growing up. Flowery covers full of family photos, most of which were badly taken of people half out of shot or not even looking at the camera. These were old photos before digital cameras and camera phones. Photos that were taken in hope and printed out, the best of the worst chosen and stuck in albums to reminisce about years later. It seemed in some ways so old-fashioned now. She flicked through some of the albums, and they were mostly of a baby and then a young toddler, and a very young Alexander and his wife. Typical family photos. Nothing out of the ordinary. Belinda flicked through a couple more, and they were much the same. There must have been a point when they stopped taking photos with a camera or printing them out because they stopped when the girl was about ten or eleven. Her last year at middle school, and then no more photos. Belinda came to the last album, and it was then that she realised it wasn't really an album at all. It was more of a scrapbook. The front cover was empty, just a brown cardboard colour with wire spiral binding. She supposed the idea was to design your own cover, but they hadn't done that. Belinda opened the first page and was shocked to see what was inside and staring back at her. She immediately felt a chill down her spine, and her hands froze. Inside was a newspaper clipping glued to the first page. She couldn't believe what it said, and the photos that were on it. She flicked quickly through the rest of the scrapbook, and it was filled with more newspaper clippings, and articles, and then finally some cards and letters that had been glued inside. Alexander's name was in some of the articles, and also his wife, Olivia Burke. Her photograph was next to the article. Belinda was stricken with horror. As she looked at the pages, with each one her heart sank more and ached with grief, she heard Alexander's car pull up in the driveway outside. The gravel underneath the wheels of his car crunching in the gentle rain.

Belinda didn't have long until he would be in the house. She wanted to check one thing before she put the albums back. She searched desperately through all the newspaper articles until she found what she was looking for. The date on the newspaper was almost ten years ago. Belinda couldn't believe it. The same year she had run away from Ireland and arrived in London. Ten years of pain and anguish. She quickly slid all the albums and the scrapbook back under the bed where she found them. Then she quickly walked out of the room and across the landing as the front door opened. Belinda couldn't see Alexander. She had to go into her room and wipe the tears from her face. She couldn't help but cry because she couldn't believe what she had seen, but it made sense why Alexander was the way he was. Why a heavy sadness sat inside of him like that. She wished she hadn't looked under his bed and seen what she had seen because it would be impossible to be around him knowing what she knew. She had seen the truth in black and white, and it had ripped a hole in her heart. She could only imagine the size of the hole in Alexander's heart, and how impossible it would be to fix. How something like that could destroy you forever with no chance of redemption.

25.

The past

David and Lydia were the last of Olivia's clients before lunch. They were the couple that had reminded her of her and Alexander. A professional couple in their forties, and out of the blue he had cheated, and now they were trying to put their marriage back together. Somehow reassemble the jigsaw pieces of their old life, but the problem now was that some of the old pieces were missing, and they had new ones in their place. That's the thing about marriage, when it's good and everything is how it should be, it's like the perfect jigsaw puzzle. But once you remove pieces and start exchanging them with new ones, it's never quite the same.

Lydia looked on edge. Her knee quickly bobbed up and down and she picked aggressively at her nails. When she walked in, it looked like she had been crying. Her pale face was flushed with red. She had lost weight because she couldn't eat. She didn't get any enjoyment from it. She also wasn't sleeping, and so had dark bags under her eyes. David looked lost too. This is what happened when you took away pieces of the jigsaw puzzle. None of it made sense anymore, and you were left scrambling, hoping that the edges at least stayed together.

'How are you today?' Olivia asked Lydia. She looked at her, but Lydia kept looking down at her hands. Picking away at her already broken nails.

'I just don't know if I can keep doing this,' she said, on the verge of tears. 'It's just—'

'Has something happened?' said Olivia calmly.

She sat with her notepad next to her. A tear leaked out of Lydia's eyes and stretched down her face before letting go and falling onto her lap. David looked away. He had seen enough tears already and couldn't face anymore. He was losing hope.

'The other day I was on Instagram,' said Lydia. 'And someone posted a quote. It said, what a wonderful thought it is that some of the best days of our lives haven't happened yet. Do you know what I thought? I thought to myself that it isn't true for me. I know the best days of my life have already happened. I know that I'll never be as happy as I was.'

'Oh, Lid,' said David, his head in his hands.

For once, and perhaps for the first time, Olivia saw him crumble. His face fell flat, and he looked like he might cry too. He had always maintained an air of stoicism at their sessions. David was from one of those great old English families. Educated at a boarding school in Kent, Oxford university, and then straight into the city. David had never had the time for emotions or flights of fancy. He had that gap year before university and that was it for frivolity. He was solid, like an old oak tree. He didn't melt. During World War One he would have been an officer, keeping his troops together and giving them confidence to give up their lives for Queen and country, and shooting the cowards who tried to run away. Perhaps it was the problem for men like David. Without a war or anything to give their lives meaning, they got bored and had affairs instead.

The rest of the session was mainly Lydia talking about her fears that no matter what David did or said, she would never be able to trust him again. The pain was too great. David, looking and sounding broken, did his best to convince her that there was hope. They had to keep trying. Keep believing. For their children, if not for him. Olivia did her best to sit in the middle of them and ask the right questions, but she couldn't help but drift off and think about her and Alexander. It was Friday. The day. She needed to decide what to do. Her brain kept telling her to forget all about it. It was nothing. Go about your day, Olivia, and tomorrow was their big date. A night at The Langham Hotel, dinner somewhere expensive, and sex to keep the fires burning. Stop thinking ridiculous thoughts about an affair. Keep the jigsaw puzzle together. Don't end up like Lydia and David.

But then her heart, and that voice in her head that had told her to be careful, don't let things fall apart, wouldn't let her stop thinking about it. He's just going to the pub. What was the big deal? All she had to do was drive to his school, park across the road, and when he left, just follow him to the pub. Once he was there, she could go home, make dinner, have a glass of wine, and relax. She was torn. Olivia decided to call Jenny and meet for a coffee. She needed to run her worries past someone. Someone she trusted. She needed a filter because she couldn't trust the voices in her head anymore.

David and Lydia left after their session, no closer to any sort of resolution or hope for their marriage. It had been a year since David's indiscretion, and they still couldn't find a way to make it work. Olivia wondered in cases like theirs whether it was time to give up, accept that they needed to end their relationship and move on, because maybe, despite what Lydia thought, better days could be ahead. Perhaps she could meet someone else and be even happier with them. The same for David. Perhaps it was time to put the puzzle pieces back in the box and start on a new one.

It was another grey, drizzly day outside, and Olivia sat inside the coffee shop. She was hungry and grabbed a sandwich and a coffee. She sat for a moment and watched people coming and going. Young people, older people, people alone and together. A man sat in the corner reading a newspaper and drinking a coffee. A young woman sat reading a book, nibbling on a cookie. Olivia glanced momentarily to see what she was reading. The cover looked interesting, and Olivia made a mental note to check it out later. She had just finished a book and needed a new one to read. Olivia liked to get out in the world like this. She needed to get away from her office sometimes and remind herself of the world. Of all the possibilities. She took a sip of her coffee, and the door opened, and with it a cold gust of wind and a splattering of rain, and then Jenny appeared. She was wearing a green Barbour raincoat that she took off and put over the chair opposite Olivia. She put her yellow umbrella down and smiled at Olivia.

'What a ghastly day,' said Jenny.

'Coffee? And it's definitely my turn,' said Olivia, standing up.

'Go on then. I'll have a latte, and perhaps a flapjack or something.'

Olivia got up and got her friend a coffee and a fruit and nut flapjack before she sat down again. Jenny took a sip of her coffee and had a bite of her flapjack.

'So,' said Jenny after a moment. 'What's going on? You sounded a bit off on the phone. Is this still about the Alexander thing?'

'Today's the day. He's going to the pub tonight, and I'm trying to decide whether to follow him or not. God, even hearing myself saying it out loud sounds ridiculous. Follow my husband like a crazy, insecure wife or a shit spy.'

'I think that's your answer right there. Just answer me one question.'

'Go on.'

'Do you trust him?'

Olivia didn't need a moment to think about it.

'Of course, I trust him. Completely.'

'Then you know what to do,' said Jenny with a comforting smile.

'Thank you,' said Olivia. She already felt so much more relaxed about it. She just needed to talk to someone. To hear the words out loud. 'I've booked us a room at The Langham Hotel in Fitzrovia tomorrow night, and I'm bringing some new underwear.'

'Oh, good for you,' said Jenny with a smile. 'The last time I tried some saucy underwear with Greg, it worked a treat. A weekend in Bath. Bath '09. Gosh, that was a fun weekend. It feels like a lifetime ago now though.'

'All the more reason to do it, don't you think?'

'Yes, it probably is time to slut it up a bit, and maybe take the old man away,' said Jenny, and the friends laughed. 'A naughty weekend in Bath sounds absolutely divine at the moment.'

After coffee, they spoke about their much-needed spa weekend and promised that they would definitely do it soon. Jenny had a busy few weeks ahead, a conference in Birmingham, and a birthday to plan for one of the boys, but after that they would definitely pencil something in. They hugged outside the coffee shop before saying goodbye. Jenny told her to be sensible and trust in Alexander. Olivia completely agreed and said she definitely wouldn't follow him. She was going to get a takeaway pizza and a bottle of wine and watch a bit of telly. Laura was going to Charlotte's house after school, and so Olivia had a bit of time for herself. She thought she should probably try on the new underwear again, just to make certain, and perhaps have a decent shave. She might even have a bath with candles, a book, a bath bomb, and a glass of wine.

She had needed coffee with Jenny. It was so easy to listen to David and Lydia and to let the paranoia get the better of her. Alexander and Olivia were not David and Lydia. They were nothing like them, and they wouldn't end up like them either. She was going to trust her husband and be happy. The Instagram post that Lydia had mentioned shot through her mind: *What a wonderful thought it is that some of the best days of our lives haven't happened yet.* Olivia knew that was definitely true for her and Alexander. They had so many great days ahead of them. She had so much she wanted to do, starting with Mallorca that summer. Her life was brilliant and thinking that Alexander was cheating on her had been a blip. A silly thought that had spiralled out of control.

Olivia drove back to her house in the drizzly rain with a renewed sense of hope. She had been a fool, but that happened in her line of work. If she wasn't surrounded by couples who needed her help, who had cheated or been cheated on, by people with strange sexual desires and appetites, and by the constant threat of divorce and unhappiness around every corner, then she wouldn't have thought twice about Alexander. She couldn't second guess herself. The universe, as if to prove a point, played their song on the radio as she drove home. Ever Fallen in Love (With Someone You Shouldn't've) by the Buzzcocks. It made her smile, and she put the windows down and let the wind and rain hit her face as she sang along with the song because she knew she had definitely fallen in love with the right man.

26.

The present

Louise had started meeting Sam at the park on a regular basis. They had swapped phone numbers and messaged each other often, although Louise was careful in case Jim saw them. Not that he was ever on her phone or even knew the passcode. She had recently changed it without telling him just to be on the safe side. Not that anything had happened with Sam physically, but in her mind it had, and that was why she had to be careful.

It was a gloriously sunny day as Louise and Sam sat in the park. Ella and Josh were scampering around playing a game that involved Ella shouting loudly, and Josh seemed to be a pirate. Louise and Sam watched them and laughed. It was nearing lunchtime, and Louise knew it was almost time for them to head home. They had been at the park for two hours already. Ella would be tired, and Louise had some housework to get done before the weekend. She looked across the bench at Sam. She hated saying goodbye to him.

'We should probably—' said Louise, but before she could finish, Sam interrupted her.

'Do you fancy coming back to my flat for a spot of lunch? I have far too much food in the fridge that needs to be eaten, and we can't do it on our own. Plus, I have a new espresso machine, I'm dying to test out on someone.'

He spoke quickly and slightly nervously. He knew it was a line they hadn't crossed before. It was dangerous. She was with someone, he was divorced, and kids were involved, but at that moment he didn't care. He just wanted to spend more time with her.

'Look, Sam—'

'Before you say no, I have four doughnuts from this incredible bakery just around the corner, and I swear to God that they're the best doughnuts I have ever had. Cross my heart,' said Sam, and Louise couldn't help but laugh.

'How good are they? Really?'

'I mean, on a scale of utter shit to just had a food orgasm they're definitely orgasmic.'

'Well, I can't turn down the chance of a food orgasm now, can I?' said Louise. The word orgasm danced suggestively between them.

She smiled, but inside her heart was beating faster than it had beaten since the last time she'd tried to go for a run, and her tummy was in knots. She desperately wanted to go back to Sam's flat and have a peek at his life, but she also knew she shouldn't. It was dangerous. It wasn't time yet. He didn't even know her real name or the truth about what had happened. She didn't want to keep lying to him. She didn't want to keep lying to Jim either. The truth was she was tired of living the life she had created for herself, and she needed to be free again. She looked at Sam in his black polo neck jumper, dark blue jeans, and brown leather brogues, and she wanted to be a part of his life. She wanted it so badly, but he had to know the truth first, and the truth wasn't easy.

When they told the kids they were going back to Sam's flat for lunch, they both whooped with joy, and then ran around in excitement. The chance of a playdate at his own flat was all too much for Josh, and the opportunity of a playdate at Josh's flat was far too heady an idea for Ella. Louise already knew that she would have to tell Ella not to tell Daddy about it. It would be their little secret. She hated having to tell Ella to lie to her father, but it was the only choice she had. Once they had all calmed down and were ready to go, they set off towards Sam's flat.

It was only a short walk from the park on a beautiful, tree-lined street full of expensive looking houses, all immaculate with Range Rovers and sports cars parked outside. It was the sort of road Louise had looked at online and dreamed about living. How often she had peeked on Rightmove and searched houses in that area. Sam's was a ground floor, two-bedroom flat, and so it came with a compact garden that had a lovely deck with a built-in barbecue. From the moment Louise walked in, she was captivated. It was just beautiful. Despite it not being any bigger than her house, and in fact it was probably smaller, it felt so light and airy. It felt spacious, and it had been decorated beautifully. The refinished wooden floors went throughout, and the kitchen had been completely re-modelled with gorgeous green cabinets, white tile backsplash, stainless steel appliances, and plants galore. The living area had a large, grey sofa, and a yellow armchair that looked very comfortable. The whole flat had a contemporary but vintage feel to it. The framed prints on the walls were very cool, and it felt to Louise like the exact opposite of her house with Jim. She loved it and wanted to move in immediately. It made her feel an embarrassment towards her own house, and a sadness that she knew she would never be able to live somewhere like that with Jim. They just didn't have the money, and Jim didn't have the taste.

'Oh my god, it's gorgeous,' Louise said as they walked through into the open-plan kitchen and living area. A few large, leafy plants stood in plant pots to add a splash of colour, and she immediately noticed the large American style Smeg fridge in pastel blue.

'It does the job,' said Sam modestly.

The truth was that he'd spent a great deal of time and money making the flat perfect. He had bought it six years earlier with his then wife, and it had been almost abandoned. It was a hovel, and so they'd bought it for next to nothing, and Sam's father was very handy, and together they did most of the work themselves. Now it was perfect, and he had bought his ex-wife out of her half of the flat and it belonged solely to Sam. The value had more than doubled since he'd bought it.

Louise sat down at the island in the kitchen. The kids had already run off to Josh's bedroom and were playing

Lego.

'There was definitely talk of coffee and doughnuts,' said Louise with a smile.

'Coming right up,' said Sam with a smile.

He went across to the counter and started fiddling with a very expensive looking espresso machine. A red stainless steel cruise liner of a machine. It was something that Louise could only dream about. One day she would have a place like that. A coffee machine like that. One day she would have everything she wanted. She just had to keep focused on the long game. The big plan. No more stupid mistakes. Louise excused herself so she could use the toilet, but she just wanted to see if it was as nice as the rest of the flat. She peeked in on the kids first, and they were happily playing in Josh's room. A large bedroom with a cool bunk bed with a play area on the bottom. He had artwork on the walls, and his bedroom window with white shutters looked out on the street. Unlike Ella's bedroom, everything was put away nicely, and he had a vintage wooden wardrobe in the corner. It was a gorgeous little room, and there was a large J for Josh on the door. She walked across and into the bathroom, which was just as lovely as the rest of the flat. It had symmetrical Victorian tiles on the floor, there was a rolled bathtub under the window, and there were more plants and cool artwork on the walls. One of the pieces of artwork was a framed poster, and it said in bold, black capitals: WORK HARD & BE NICE TO PEOPLE. Louise loved it. She loved everything about Sam's flat, and it only made her desire for change and to be herself again that much greater. It also made her desire for Sam stronger too.

They settled on the soft, grey sofa to drink their coffee and eat their doughnuts. The kids were happily playing, the occasional giggle or bout of laughter being heard in the living room, and Sam and Louise sat and talked. It was one of the things she loved most about him. They could just talk, and it was so easy and nice. The way it should be when you're with the right person.

'So ...' they both said at the same time, and then they laughed.

'After you,' said Sam.

'I was just going to say,' said Louise. Her skin flushed. They both put their coffees down on the coffee table at the same time. She felt it. The sexual attraction between them. 'That it's nice hanging out at your lovely flat.'

'Well, my lovely flat and I love having you here.'

They turned their bodies to face each other. Their legs were crossed towards each other, the smell of coffee hung in the air. They were silent for a moment. They were close to each other, and Louise felt the urge to lean in towards Sam. He felt the same, and so they both did. Their heads leaned in closer and closer. The air between them fizzed with sexual tension. Barely an inch away and she could smell his aftershave. Woody, masculine, with hints of citrus. She could feel his breath on her. Their lips came together. Soft, supple, and full of want and something so much deeper. They wanted each other. They kissed for a minute until the noise of their children woke them up and they pulled apart.

'I'm hungry!' said Ella, dashing into the room, her face flushed red.

'Me too!' said Josh loudly.

Louise and Sam looked at each other. They couldn't help but smile. It had been one of those kisses. As soon as their lips met, they both felt it. The longing to keep doing it. The need for each other. Sam got up and started making the children lunch, and Louise watched him. So easy and happy around the children. He was so relaxed as he made them both sandwiches. Ham, cheese, lettuce, tomato, cucumber, and butter. Ella hated lettuce, tomato, and any sort of salad, but at Sam's flat, she ate it without complaint. He cut up an apple for them, some carrots, and a handful of crisps. They sat down at the dining table and ate and talked, and Sam got them a glass of water each. Ella also refused plain water at home but drank it between talking quickly and incessantly with Josh. Louise watched them all, and a sadness took over her heart. A deep pain that made her want to cry. She felt a terrible agony because at that moment she had the exact life she wanted. That and her plans to study law and her life for the first time in over ten years could be perfect. But was it possible? What would happen when she told Sam the truth? Would Jim let her leave with Ella? She didn't want to break his heart but knew she would. The pain of seeing everything she wanted so clearly and being so close to it broke her heart. She had already lost so much in her life; she didn't feel like she could lose anything else.

Sam finished up with the kids and then walked over to the sofa. He picked up his coffee, sat down, and looked across at Louise. They both smiled at each other. They knew the kiss had changed things between them. It had changed both of their lives, and there was no going back.

27.

The past

Laura got up, grabbed her bag, and started walking out of class. It was the end of the day and it had finally arrived. Her body was too full of excitement, wonder, and nervousness that she could barely feel her feet as she walked out. It felt like she was floating. Other pupils followed her, and the school halls that moments ago were deserted were suddenly full of noise and chaos. It was the weekend, and everyone was jubilant, but none more so than Laura and Tom. Laura saw him in the corridor. They both looked at each other across the minefield of school children and smiled. Laura would leave school with Charlotte, but once outside, Laura would meet up with Tom and head off to his house. His parents wouldn't be home until nine o'clock.

'It's finally here,' said Charlotte, surprising Laura from behind.

Laura was lost in her own little world, dominated by thoughts of Tom Chance and of sex. What would it be like? How would it feel? What would they do afterwards? God, it was just too much. Laura spun around.

'I'm so nervous.'

'Don't worry, you'll love it,' said Charlotte, seemingly as excited as Laura.

The two friends walked out of school together, riding the wave of teenage bodies that took them out to the pavement. Charlotte lived further away from school than Tom or Laura, but she liked the walk. She liked to wander home slowly. She had her ear buds, and would listen to music, and let her mind drift off and dream. She had recently been thinking about a gap year after sixth form. An older sibling of a good friend had just left for a year around the world, and Charlotte loved the idea. She had mentioned it to her parents, and they had agreed that if she got good A Level results, and she still wanted to do it, they would help pay for it. She dreamed.

'Make sure you message me as soon as the deed is done.'

'Sure,' said Laura, who was feeling more and more nervous. 'What if I do it wrong?'

'Trust me, there isn't much you need to do, Law. All you need to do is get him ready, make sure you're ready, and then just lie there. It will be painful at first, tell him to go slow, but then you'll start to enjoy it.'

'But,' said Laura, her mind flooded with questions. Suddenly all of her confidence and bravery were drifting away. Was she doing the right thing? Was Tom really The One? Charlotte stopped walking and turned to her friend.

'Just stop thinking and enjoy it, yeah? It's Tom Chance. You're so lucky. Do you know how many girls at school wish they were you right now?' said Charlotte, not telling her friend that she was definitely one of those girls.

Laura took a deep breath and looked at Charlotte. She had been her best friend since primary school. They had been through so much together, and she loved her like a sister. She just needed to calm down. Everything was going to be fine. It was just last-minute nerves.

'You okay?' said Charlotte.

'Just a bit scared. But I'll be fine.'

'You'll be more than fine in a few hours,' said Charlotte, and then she laughed her big laugh, and the two girls walked arm in arm along the street to meet Tom, who was waiting on the corner, just as nervous, just as worried and excited as Laura. It was a big moment in both of their young lives. The moment. Tom's mates had been giving him a hard time for weeks about Laura. When were they going to do it? Was he gay? Was she gay? Was his penis just too small? Typical schoolboy banter. He had brushed it off. They were just jealous, he thought, because all of them would love to be with Laura. She was The Catch. The most beautiful girl at school, and not only that, but the smartest, funniest, and she was his girlfriend. He didn't want to mess it up. He wanted it to be perfect for her. He wanted it to be the best day of her life.

He took a few deep breaths and bounced up and down on his feet. He needed to calm down. He needed to relax. If his mates could do it, then so could he. He waited on the corner until he finally saw Laura coming. More deep breaths. He smiled at her as she got nearer and did an awkward little wave he hadn't planned on.

As soon as Laura saw Tom, her nerves dropped slightly. It was Tom. He was so lovely, and he looked more nervous than her. Poor thing. Laura reminded herself that this was her choice, and she wanted to do it. Just before they reached Tom, Charlotte stopped and turned to Laura.

'Okay, Laws, this is it. Good luck.'

'Thanks.'

'You'll love it and make sure you message me right after. Like as soon as you're done.'

'As soon as we're done. Promise,' said Laura with a smile.

Charlotte gave her a big hug before she walked off, and left Laura alone, standing on the pavement. Laura looked at Tom just ahead of her, smiled, and walked up to join him.

'All right?' said Tom.

'Yeah, you?'

'Yeah, good.'

They both smiled and then started walking off towards his house. Their hearts were full of passion and excitement, their stomachs knotted in nerves, because they both realised that what they were about to do was a big deal. You only got to lose your virginity once, and it had to be perfect. They were the same in that respect. Tom had to be the best at everything too. Head boy, captain of the cricket team, and the highest marks in every subject. Tom Chance was the best at everything he did, and he wanted to be the best at sex too. Whatever that meant.

In his classroom, Alexander sat at his desk, tidying up before the weekend as he always did. Only this wasn't an ordinary weekend. This wasn't an ordinary Friday. Sara had texted him her address earlier. He looked down at his phone and at her address. Could he do this? Could he cheat on Olivia? It wasn't like he'd had a few drinks and his moral compass was a bit tipsy. He was stone cold sober, and he had to drive to her house and have sex with her. It was a hard thing to comprehend. The more he thought about it, the more he had no idea what to do. One moment. One decision. As he sat there, his phone buzzed with a message. It was from Olivia.

Have fun at the pub tonight. Looking forward to our date tomorrow x

Every single word drove a dagger through his heart. How could he cheat on her? She was his wife, and he loved her so much. She had planned a date for tomorrow night. Only a truly terrible human being would go to Sara's flat. Only a monster could do something like that. But then he started thinking about Sara, and how he would never get that chance again. He was forty-three years old. If he was lucky, he'd live for another forty years, and in that time, he would only ever have sex with Olivia. Today was his last chance to sleep with a twenty-eight-year-old woman, who under any circumstances, he thought, would be out of his league. Those legs, those breasts, and the way she knew exactly how to turn him on. The photo she had sent him that morning. It was burned into his brain. They had only flirted at school, and there had been the kiss, but he could only imagine the things she would do to him once they were alone. How could he turn that down? And it was just once, and then that was it. If Olivia didn't find out, and she wouldn't, then what was the harm? She might even understand. His last chance to be with someone else for the rest of his life. Think of it as a gift. A once in a lifetime opportunity.

Alexander stood up and grabbed his satchel from the floor. He got his jacket from his chair and put that on, and then he walked out. He hadn't decided in his head because he couldn't. There were too many thoughts. Too many arguments on both sides. He could spend weeks going backwards and forwards without coming up with a clear decision. The truth was that Alexander couldn't decide, and so he decided to just leave school, get in his car, and let his heart decide for him. He couldn't rationalise it. He couldn't debate his way out of the situation he had got himself in. He would just get in his car, drive, and see where he ended up. As he walked out of school and towards his car, he imagined himself typing out the text to Sara. *Sorry, couldn't do it. Too much of a coward. It's just not for me. Best, A x.* Or something like that. That's what the good version of him would do. The version of himself he thought he was.

Alexander Burke opened his car door and got in. The sky was overcast with leaden clouds and spots of rain had begun to fall. He closed the door and then put his satchel on the seat next to him. He put the keys in the ignition, turned the car on, and sat there for a moment. A horrible sickness sat in his stomach. He felt the weight of history on his shoulders. He put his hands on the wheel and felt his grip tighten immediately. Nervousness. Tension. This was it. Home or Sara's flat? The decision. Perhaps the biggest decision of his life. He pulled the sun visor down and looked at himself in the little mirror. Could he really cheat on the woman he loved so much? It seemed impossible, but that was the plan. It's all he had thought about for the past few weeks. Every waking second and she had been on his mind. Sara Coupland. That body. The things she would do. Alexander wasn't the sort to cheat, but how could he turn her down?

He checked his mirrors, lifted the handbrake, and started to drive. He backed out of his parking spot, drove out of school, and onto the main road. There were still lots of pupils milling around, and cars parked on both sides of the street. He used the wipers to wipe away the rain that had covered his windscreen in a thin layer, and then he was off. In about half-a-mile was the turning. Left to home or right to Sara's flat. A literal fork in the road. Two pathways that might define the rest of his life, or perhaps not. It was only one night. Not even a night. Maybe an hour or two. And then he could move on. Get back to normal. Be his old self again. Olivia would never find out. He drove. The decision was getting closer and closer.

Olivia sat in her car and watched the droplets of rain fall down the windscreen. It wasn't raining heavily, but enough to have to use her wipers. What was she doing? She had told herself all day to let it go. She'd had such a lovely lunch with Jenny, and after that had felt calm about everything. She was fine. It was fine. Alexander wasn't the sort. She had the image of running herself a hot bath, filling up a glass of wine, maybe candles (why not?), and reading her book. How relaxing it was. That's what she should have been doing at that moment. That's exactly where she should be, and she wasn't really sure why she wasn't. It hadn't been a conscious decision to get in the car, and it definitely hadn't been her plan to drive to Alexander's school and park across the road. She was waiting for him to leave. She knew that. There was a part of her that just needed to know. Wait for him. Follow him to the pub. Watch him go in, feel a pang of relief, tell yourself that you knew all along, and then go home.

The end of day bell rang, and children quickly started pouring out of school like rats fleeing a sinking ship. Jumping overboard and doing their best to survive in the harsh, icy waters. Laughing, singing, running, walking slowly and talking to their friends. Olivia watched them like someone watching animals at the zoo. She hadn't been there at the end of school for a long time. When Laura was in middle school, Olivia would always pick her up at the end of the day. Gosh, that felt like a lifetime ago now. Laura was so small then. So innocent.

Olivia watched, and then she saw Laura. She was walking with Charlotte. The two of them caught up in their own conversation. Their own little world. Olivia watched her daughter for a moment. On the cusp of adulthood. On the brink of becoming a woman, and yet as she watched her walking along the pavement in her school uniform, the backpack they had bought together in Marks and Spencer last summer swinging backwards and forwards on her back, she also looked so young. Still her baby girl. Gosh, she loved her so much.

Laura walked off, and Olivia's eyes drifted back towards the school. She didn't know exactly how long he would be. She turned the radio on and listened to some music to help pass the time. A few newer songs came on that she sort of knew and then a couple of classics from the 80s and 90s followed. Her mind drifted backwards and forwards before she finally saw Alexander walk out and towards his car. It was a strange feeling watching him like that. Her natural instinct was to go to him, tell him exactly how she was feeling, and that she was sorry. It was all just a silly mix-up and some middle-aged worries. A blip. He would laugh and call her silly, and that would be it. But she didn't. She sat in her car and waited. After a minute his car appeared and then pulled out onto the road. She had a quick look in the mirror to check for cars, and then she started after him. She had never tailed anyone before, but she had watched enough television shows to know to stay back, not get too close. He drove, and she followed, telling herself that it would be all right. Everything would be fine. Just the pub and then home.

28.

The present

The house looked much the same as it did in Belinda's mind. A nondescript terraced house on a street of similar houses. The front garden with a small brick wall, and the same white, uPVC front door. Belinda hadn't been back to her aunt's house in years. She had visited once with Liam, but not since she'd got pregnant with Rachel and all the subsequent events that had followed. She was nervous. She had travelled from Alexander's house in Richmond, all the way to Upton on the train and underground. She felt like she had to get in touch. She wanted to feel the connection to her old life again. To Ireland. Despite all the pain and heartache it had caused her, she couldn't ignore it. It was a part of her, and if she was going to move on with her life, it was something she had to face.

Belinda had felt anxious about going on public transport again and being around so many people. It had been a while since she had felt like a proper part of society. Alexander had insisted on giving her some money. He gave her enough for her train and tube journey, and extra for coffee and lunch. She was wearing clean, smart clothes, her hair had been washed, and she looked and felt like a new person. The woman who had been sleeping rough in doorways and tried to jump in front of a train wasn't just gone, it was as if she had never existed. After the initial anxiety, and once she was sitting on the train watching houses, buildings, parks, and roads flash by, Belinda felt that rhythm of normality again. She remembered how many days she had sat on the train and gone to work in London. The feeling of holding a warm cup of coffee in her hand. It felt good. But mostly it was the feeling that no-one was looking at her with disgust or contempt. She was just another ordinary person in London, and she loved that feeling. It glowed inside of her.

Belinda walked up to the front door she had walked up to so many times before and rang the bell. The light in the hallway was on as it always was, despite it being early afternoon, and bright out. Eventually through the thin glass in the door, she saw the shape of her aunt appear. Belinda hadn't decided yet just how much she was going to tell her. Homelessness? Suicide attempt? Living with a stranger in south London with a dark secret? She didn't have to tell her anything. The door opened and her aunt was suddenly standing in front of her.

'Jesus, Belinda,' said her aunt as soon as she saw her.

Belinda smiled.

'Hello,' said Belinda cautiously.

Her aunt was a short woman, and just over fifty years old now. She looked a lot like Belinda's mum. The same hair and eyes. Even the way she stood in the doorway reminded Belinda of her mother.

'Where the hell have you been? I tried calling you and trying to find you, but nothing. It's like you just vanished.'

'Why don't you put the kettle on, and I'll tell you everything.'

Her aunt told her to come in, and Belinda followed her inside. It was nice hearing her aunt's strong Irish voice. She hadn't heard a voice like that for a long time. The house was exactly the same as it was when Belinda had stayed there. The same curtains, wallpaper, and Artex ceilings. The same smell. It was a house lost in time. Belinda's aunt still ran it as an unofficial bed and breakfast, but it was quiet at that moment. She only had two lodgers, and they were both at work. Two young men, both from Ireland. Belinda walked through the house, and memories of the first day she arrived from Ireland flooded back to her. It didn't feel that long ago.

Belinda followed her aunt through into her kitchen. Her aunt filled the kettle and flicked the switch to turn it on, and then she turned to face Belinda.

'I tried so hard to find you.'

'I know, I'm sorry.'

There was a brief pause, and Belinda felt something change between them. A heaviness sat in the room. A frisson of tension electrified the air around them.

'I have some news,' said her aunt. Her face stiffened up. An expression that Belinda had never seen before came over it. A dark, heavy cloud. Belinda felt an uneasiness. She leant back against the side. 'It happened six months ago now, and I tried to call you and let you know, but the number I had didn't work and anyway ...' She stopped for a moment, took a small breath, and then said very matter-of-factly. 'Your father died, Belinda. He had a heart attack, and he died.'

Belinda felt something slowly seep into every fibre of her body. It was like her veins were being filled with a drug and it gradually began to take effect. If she hadn't been leaning against the side, she might have fallen down, but as it was, she just leant further back and felt the side jut into her back. She went ever so pale as the blood drained from her face. Her father was dead. The man who had cast such a shadow over her life. The man who had made them all so miserable, who had effectively killed her first baby, driven Jason away, and forced Belinda to run away to London, was gone. It was such a relief, as if given the news that you were in remission from an incurable cancer. Belinda hadn't realised the weight she carried around with her. The weight of her da'. Even all of these years later, and after so much tragedy, he was still a constant source of pain in her life. But just like that, it was gone. She took in a deep breath and felt the tears rush down her face.

'Oh, Belinda, love,' said her aunt, and she walked over and put her arms around her, and Belinda fell into her. She squashed herself against the woollen fabric of her aunt's jumper. She felt the coarseness of it, and she wept and felt the wetness against her own skin. It wasn't grief, it was relief. The hold he had over her was gone. Her whole body felt weak, and her aunt walked them over to the table, and they sat down. Her aunt got Belinda a box of tissues, and she blew her nose and then wiped her face dry. Finally, she spoke.

'How's ma?' she said quietly.

'She's grand. Like I said, I tried to find you because she wanted you to go back to Ireland, for the funeral and that. No one came, you know. It was just your ma and me, a couple of cousins and that was it.'

'I'm sorry.'

'It's okay, love. I'm just glad you're all right. Truth be told, I was worried you were dead,' said her aunt, and Belinda smiled at her.

'I'm not dead. I just needed some time to figure things out.'

'And how's that going?'

'I'm getting there.'

'Well, maybe now you're back, we can call your ma because I know she's worried sick, she is. Do you want to call her with me?'

Belinda hadn't given any thought that morning when she had woken up to speaking with her mother. It had been ten years without a word between them. Their last conversation had been something of a non-event. Belinda knew she was leaving, and she wanted to tell her she loved her and hoped that one day she would leave her da' but she couldn't. She didn't want her to suspect anything. And so when her mother had asked Belinda if she needed anything from the shops, Belinda had said no. Her mother said she'd be back in a couple of hours, and that was it. Belinda watched her mother walk out of the house, her raincoat on, and with her shopping bags in hand. She watched her close the door, and she didn't say anything. She didn't know if she'd ever see or speak to her again. She felt sorry for her, and she hated her just as much. She hated that she let him win. That she wouldn't leave him or protect her children from him. But she also felt pity because it wasn't her fault she was weak. It wasn't her fault she was just so afraid.

'I don't know,' said Belinda. 'It's been such a long time.'

'Then at least let me call her and let her know you're okay. She's been worried sick, she has, especially after what happened with your brother. You're all she's got.'

Belinda nodded, and her aunt got up and finished making the tea. She gave Belinda her cup, and then she walked over and got her mobile phone that had been charging on the side. Belinda took a sip of the tea. Thick, dark brown Irish tea. Strong enough to stand a spoon in. It was the only way that Belinda could drink her tea. She felt the warmth of it hit the back of her throat and it helped. It seemed impossible that her father was dead, and that her mother was on the end of another mobile phone in Ireland. That life with those people felt like a different lifetime to Belinda. Despite only being twenty-six, her life had already been divided up into segments. There was her childhood in Ireland with Jason and her parents. A miserable, unhappy time for the most part. Then there had been her escape and London. For years, she was happy there. Working hard, creating a life, and falling in love. She thought at the time that she had finally found happiness, but then that all fell apart so dramatically, and she had ended up living rough and then trying to kill herself. Now she was just starting out on the next bit. Her recovery, as she called it. Perhaps before she could move on completely, she might have to go back and right the wrongs of the past.

Belinda's aunt held her phone out and told Belinda she would put it on speaker so she could hear her ma's voice. Belinda nodded in agreement. She couldn't imagine how her mother would sound now. She thought she knew in her head, but it was just memories. The gentle lilt of her voice that she hadn't heard in so long. The mobile phone rang, and then after a few rings, Belinda's mother answered.

'Hello, Therese, I was just thinking about you,' said Belinda's mother.

Hearing her voice sent chills and memories through

Belinda's body. Belinda didn't want to, but she couldn't help but cry. She silently wept, wiping each tear away as it fell down her face.

'Is that right, Mary? Listen, I have some news. You'd better sit down,' said her aunt.

'Oh, Christ, is it Belinda? Please tell me she's all right because I couldn't face it—'

'She's fine. She's here with me now, she is.'

There was silence on the other end of the line. A sudden quietness. Belinda looked towards her aunt, who was standing and holding her phone in the palm of her hand. The quietness lingered for a moment, and then they heard tears.

'Mary, she's fine. I told her about her father. She knows what happened.'

'I know, I just can't ... can she hear me?' said her mother, a deep anguish in her voice.

'She can.'

Another silence. Belinda's mother blew her nose. She composed herself. Belinda imagined her in their old lounge in Blanchardstown. The same red carpet. The same horrible curtains. The horrible dreariness of it.

'Belinda, love,' said her mother finally. 'I'm so sorry for everything that horrible man did to you. For all the years that you had to put up with him, and I don't blame you for running away. I was sort of glad, to be honest. You didn't deserve that. None of us did. Are you okay, love? Are you well? Please, just say something so I can hear your voice.'

Belinda wiped another tear from her face before she spoke.

'Hi, Ma.'

It's all she could say, but it was enough. Her mother broke down into floods of tears and Belinda did the same. Her aunt sat down and put the phone on the table between them, and then she placed a hand over Belinda's. Three women together across two countries, who had lost so much, but at that moment they had each other. A bond of a shared history and blood, and the man who had torn them all apart was finally gone, and they could be together once more. It did something to Belinda's heart that she hadn't experienced before. A feeling that only came from the love of family. From a feeling deep within her that she belonged to something. A bond that stretched from Dublin all the way to London and brought them together in a moment of pure love.

29.

The past

Everything would be all right. The same words Olivia had been telling herself all day. Keep calm and carry on. That most English of expressions that was never actually used during the war, as Alexander had delighted in telling her once. She was in her car following him. She was staying as far back as she could. It felt wrong to be spying on her husband, but at the end of the day, she was certain it was nothing. He was driving ahead of her and had stopped at the road that ran perpendicular to the road they were on. Left was home and right was towards the pub. He put his indicator on to turn right. He was about to pull away and so Olivia sped up a little bit. She didn't want to lose him in traffic. She had the radio on and the Eighties classic, Sweet Dreams (Are Made of This) by the Eurythmics came on. Olivia had always loved that song. She tapped her fingers on the steering wheel. It reminded her of good times. Of being young and carefree.

Olivia pulled out onto the road and found herself a car behind Alexander. The pub he was going to was about a mile away, but the turning for it was coming up soon. Olivia knew the pub well. It was a nice old pub, and they had gone there for dinner recently. It had been the day that on a whim they had decided to drive to the coast. Olivia had always wanted to go to Seven Sisters Country Park in Sussex and see the white cliffs and the quaint little cottages that sat by the beach. It was a gloriously warm day and so they set off early, and drove down from London, stopping off just once at a service station to get coffee and something to eat. Once there, they set off on foot until they reached the cottages. It was even more beautiful than she could have imagined. There was a slight breeze, but otherwise the sun shone on them as they stood together as a family and marvelled at the view in front of them. It was the very best of British. After a long walk they made their way back to London and had dinner at the pub Alexander was heading towards. It had been one of those days when life felt perfect. A day she would remember for a long time.

The turn to the pub was coming soon. The car in front of Olivia was driving slowly, and Olivia was trying to see in front of them. If Alexander turned there, then Olivia could relax. There wasn't much else down that road apart from the pub. If he turned, which he would, she would keep on driving and go home. The warm bath was waiting for her. She had a bath bomb from Lush she had been meaning to use for a while. Annie Lennox continued singing Sweet Dreams (Are Made of This), and Olivia was starting to relax. The car ahead of her slowed down, and Olivia assumed it was because Alexander was turning onto the road towards the pub. But then Olivia realised it was the car ahead of her that was turning. The car disappeared around the corner, and that's when Olivia saw Alexander's car ahead of her. Her heart sank in her chest. Where was he going? What was he playing at?

Olivia drove on, speeding up slightly. She didn't want to lose him. Olivia felt her hands tremble slightly. Her heart raced, and her mind was awash with confusion, and she quickly spiralled. She had spent the day convincing herself that she had nothing to worry about. She wished she had stayed at home and taken that bath. But now she couldn't stop. She had to keep going. She had to find out where he was going. She kept driving. Sweet Dreams (Are Made of This) ended and A Spice Girls song came on, but Olivia wasn't listening. Her mind was focused purely on Alexander. Why would he lie to her? Had he lied to her before? No, stop it, she told herself. They had been happily married for eighteen years and as far as she knew, he hadn't lied to her about anything important. Perhaps there had been a few white lies here and there, but nothing big. Gosh, she had lied to him before. Didn't everyone slip in a little white lie here and there? But this was different. He wasn't going to the pub. *No knickers tomorrow.* The smell of perfume. The blonde hair on his jacket. It couldn't be the worst, could it? It couldn't be the very thing that would destroy everything they had spent so many years building up.

A thought of that day at Seven Sisters Country Park came back to her. Alexander, Olivia, and Laura were standing in front of the cottages waiting to take a photo. She had asked a passing stranger to take their photo for them. She was a kindly looking older woman who was out walking with her husband and their little Jack Russell called Jackie. The woman took their photo, and when she gave Olivia her phone back, she looked at her and said, 'you have a beautiful family'. Olivia remembered looking at her and thinking that yes, she did. She was so lucky. She had a beautiful little family. A wonderful life. Sat in her car, following Alexander, she had the terrifying thought that what if her beautiful little family was nothing more than one big lie.

Alexander eventually stopped and parked his car. Olivia parked a little bit behind him and across the road. She slouched down slightly in her seat so he wouldn't be able to spot her. She watched him. He was stopped. He hadn't opened the car door. She could see his silhouette through the side window. She didn't know where they were. It was a fairly ordinary street of quaint Victorian terraced houses. Olivia turned her car off and watched him. He didn't move. A middle-aged man walked past with a dog. The dog tried to stop to wee, and the man dragged him on. Olivia could barely breathe. Her chest was so tight, and she felt a tension, almost a pain in her heart. Could he be cheating, and if so, with whom? He wasn't ever gone long enough to have a full-blown affair. It had to be someone at school. A teacher? Perhaps a parent.

Slouched down against her seat, Olivia sat and waited until finally someone appeared. She couldn't quite see who it was at first. Blonde hair. Younger. Her face for a moment was half hidden by a lamppost. Was it her? Alexander's car door opened, and he got out. He looked quickly along the road and then he was on the pavement next to her. Olivia sat up so she could see better, her heart thumping in her chest. Her hands shook with the realisation that her husband was meeting a woman. He had lied to her. Her whole life like a pack of cards began to fall, slowly one after the other. She looked at the woman closely. She recognised her. She had met her before, and then it came to her. Sara Coupland, the English teacher that had started that year. But she was so young. What would she see in Alexander? Surely someone like her could get her own boyfriend. She remembered meeting her and thinking how pretty she was. How young and beautiful, and it had made Olivia feel self-conscious of herself and the middle-age years she was hurtling towards.

Tears suddenly stung her eyes. Her whole body trembled in shock. Across the road, Sara had her arm around Alexander, and then she leant in and kissed him. There on the street in front of Olivia. It was like a punch to the stomach. Olivia felt winded. Sara took Alexander's hand and walked him towards a house. Alexander took one last look outside as if he was checking he wasn't being followed, and then he disappeared inside.

'No, no, no, no!' said Olivia to herself, tears streaming down her face. She hit the steering wheel with her hands in anger. A scenario she had listened to in her office before. Clients who had followed spouses and said how awful it was, how it had broken them, and she had listened and gave her advice. But now she was one of them. She had to do something. She was in the eye of the storm, and it was very different to listening to it calmly in her office. The advice she would have given herself would have been to go home. Think about it clearly. Don't react with passion because nothing good ever happens when you do that. You need to calm down. You need to think of the long-term plan. *What was the plan?* Olivia tried to clear her mind, to think, but she couldn't. *Think. Think. Think.* What was the plan? The anger was too much, and it rose up inside of her like a drug that overtook her mind and body and had her opening her car door without even thinking.

Olivia marched across the road, past her husband's car, and stood by the front door of the house. Such a handsome door with a brass knocker and letterbox, and a stained-glass window above the door. Olivia froze for a moment. The anger that had raced throughout her body for a split second stopped and melted away, and the rising reality of the situation hit her. The moment she knocked on the door. The second that Sara or Alexander opened that door; she couldn't take any of it back. Tears still leaked out slowly from her eyes. Her hands were shaking. Knock on the door and confront them or go home? She knew what she would tell herself. She knew the advice. What was the plan? She knocked loudly on the door. The heavy knocker felt cold and solid in her hand, and it had a gloriously satisfying feeling as it thudded against the wooden door.

There were two thin slits of glass in the doorway. They had the same stained glass as the window above the door. After a moment, the figure of Sara appeared. Olivia didn't know what she was going to do. She had lost all sense of self-control. The door opened, and Sara appeared, her face immediately changing when she realised who was at the door. God, she was young. Beautiful, yes, but so young. She was wearing a blouse, buttoned down a good two buttons less than was needed, exposing a bra beneath. She was about the same height as Olivia.

'You bitch!' shouted Olivia, her voice coming from deep inside of her.

Sara looked momentarily lost and shocked. She didn't know what to do. She had never been caught out before. Rule number one of sleeping with married men: never get caught. Alexander quickly appeared from behind Sara. His face dropped in shock.

'Shit, Olivia …' said Alexander. 'Jesus, love.'

Olivia cried harder than before. Her body shook. She wanted to punch him. To hurt him in some way. How could he do that to her? Had it happened before? Had it been happening since the start of the school year? All over Christmas when they had been so happy. When he was slicing the turkey, wearing his festive paper hat and crap Christmas jumper, and Olivia had laughed at a stupid cracker joke, and she had thought how happy they were. Was he shagging her then? When they went to Seven Sisters and that lovely old lady had said what a beautiful family they were, was he sleeping with her then?

'I hate you,' Olivia snapped at Alexander. 'I hate you!'

She couldn't stand there any longer. Her body wouldn't stop shaking and she couldn't stop the tears. She had the sudden urge to get as far away from Alexander as possible. She would kick him out, change the locks, and then divorce him. That would teach him for sleeping with that girl (because that's what she was, a girl!). Olivia ran back towards her car.

'Olivia, please, don't. Wait. Let's talk,' shouted Alexander, following her, but she didn't care. She didn't care what he thought. She got to her car, got in, and put the keys in the ignition. They were shaking so much it was hard to get them in, but she did. She locked the car as Alexander approached. 'Please don't leave. Olivia. Stop. Olivia. Let me explain. I love you.'

Alexander pleaded with her, but it was no use. Olivia took one last look at her husband, started the car, revved the engine as she struggled to get it into gear, and then she pulled out. Alexander backed out of the way, and then she drove off. She drove, floods of tears streaming down her face. She just had to get away. As far away as she could. Nothing else mattered.

30.

The past

One mistake in all of those years. That's all it was. One moment of absolute madness. One lie. Alexander watched Olivia drive away, her car speeding out of the street, and he couldn't move. He stood on the road and just watched. He had been caught out. Why hadn't he just gone home after work? Why had he even driven to Sara's house? Would he have gone through with it? He didn't have any answers, and especially not to the most important question of all: how did Olivia know? He had been so careful. He had deleted every message Sara had ever sent him. They had been discreet at school. He didn't understand. Sara walked over and stood next to him.

'You should go after her, Alexander. I'm sorry. I don't know what happened.'

'Me either. I don't know how she found out.'

'That doesn't matter now. You need to sort it out.'

'I just need a moment,' he said slowly, trying to clear his mind.

Alexander felt like someone had punched him in the face. He felt groggy. His vision was cloudy, and he felt a pain in his chest. The pain of knowing that his life, the life he loved so much, had changed forever. That it wouldn't ever be the same again, no matter what he did. For a moment, he felt like he couldn't hear properly. Every sense had been damaged by what had happened. He couldn't breathe, and he had to take a few deep breaths to compose himself.

'Are you okay?' said Sara.

'I should go.'

Sara didn't know what to say, and so she said the only thing she could think of.

'I'm sorry.'

Alexander looked at her as though she wasn't there, and then he walked towards his car. He just needed to talk to Olivia. He hadn't slept with Sara. He had just made a mistake. An error in judgement. He thought he wanted to have sex with her, but the truth was, as he walked into her flat, it had felt all wrong. He was going to leave. He wasn't going to go through with it. He couldn't. He needed to talk to Olivia. She would understand once she had calmed down and knew all the facts. He had just been a silly old man who had been momentarily attracted to something new and sparkly, but he wouldn't have slept with her. He realised as he stepped into Sara's flat just how much he loved what he had, and how he didn't want to lose it. Olivia would come around.

Alexander started his car as Sara walked back inside of her flat. The worst had happened, and now she just hoped it didn't affect her work life. She hoped his wife didn't cause a fuss, or that Alexander didn't somehow blame her for this. She enjoyed teaching at that school, and she didn't want to move yet. She had just got settled. She felt sick to her stomach. She needed a drink.

Alexander pulled away and started driving towards home. He went slowly because he wasn't thinking clearly, and his head still felt like he'd been punched. Just take it easy, he told himself. He assumed that Olivia would have gone straight home, and he needed time to think. He needed to know exactly what he was going to say, and how he was going to say it. His marriage was on the line and didn't have any margin for error. He needed to get his story straight.

Alexander slowed as traffic built up, and then he stopped as the cars did ahead of him. He was trying to focus his mind on what he was going to say when he realised that something must have happened. No-one was moving on either side of the road. After a few minutes, someone got out of the car ahead of him. Alexander turned his engine off and got out too.

'What's happened?' Alexander said to the person ahead of him.

'An accident, I think,' said the woman. Late fifties, wax jacket, and leather driving gloves.

He looked ahead of him, and a long line of cars had stopped, and no cars were coming in the opposite direction either. That's when he heard the voices of worry and concern. Alexander walked slightly faster towards the front of the cars to where most of the people were gathered. And that's when he first saw the car. The car that had veered off the road and ploughed headlong into a tree. The front of the car was smashed up, almost embedded into the tree. It was hard to see where the car ended, and the tree began. Then he saw the body on the road. A girl. A teenager in school uniform, and a man next to her shouting to keep away. He was a doctor. An ambulance had already been called. Another man was in front of the smashed-up car. He was an off-duty policeman. He told everyone to keep back. Keep away from the scene. His face looked strong and authoritative, but also hollow and white with shock. He had seen something awful. It was the scene of a disaster. It took Alexander a moment to realise, but slowly his mind clicked into gear. The car embedded in the tree with smoke coming from the bonnet was his wife's car. Alexander stopped thinking, and he began to run.

Olivia was fourteen when her father finally left the house for the last time. Her mother had found out he had cheated again. Olivia didn't know the details, but she knew he had had an affair before. He had begged and promised it would never happen again. Her mother, too afraid of a life without her husband, took him back. A last chance. He had promised. For a while they were happy, but a few years later he was at it again. He just couldn't help himself. Olivia's mother found out, and after a blazing row, had kicked him out. She couldn't live the rest of her life knowing that he would cheat again. Nothing was the same after that day. Olivia remembered saying goodbye to him at the door while her mother cried in the kitchen. He promised he'd still see her all the time. It wouldn't change things between them. He would always be her dad, no matter what. She barely saw him after that. The last she'd heard he was living in Bristol with a new woman. Her mother never got over it, and when she got cancer a few years later, it was like she was almost happy to give up. She died broken.

As Olivia drove towards home, she couldn't help the tears that ran down her face. As soon as she wiped them away, more came. They were unstoppable. They crashed down her face and all she could do was drive on. She just wanted to get home. Despite her thoughts that maybe Alexander was cheating on her, she didn't really believe it. He was the love of her life. What had happened to her mother wouldn't happen to her. She had watched as her mother fell apart, drifted into isolation, crumbled until she wasn't even a shell of her old self. Olivia was just a teenager and had her own life and couldn't wait to leave for university because she couldn't bear to be around her. The awful sadness of her. Was history going to repeat itself?

She drove on. She was halfway home before she realised she hadn't put her seatbelt on. She was so lost in her own world she hadn't thought about it. She didn't care. She would be home soon. She just needed to be home. As she drove, her phone rang. It was in her handbag on the seat next to her. It was probably Alexander. She wanted the ringing to stop. She wanted to scream into the phone and tell him to stop calling her. That she hated him. She fumbled her hand across to retrieve the phone from her handbag. She tried, but as she grabbed her phone and tried to pull it out, it fell down by her feet. It kept ringing. She could get it. She reached down, but her hand couldn't quite get it. It kept ringing. *Stop ringing!* She took her eyes off the road for a second and bent down to get her phone. She had it. She was about to answer it when she looked up, and that's when she saw the girl right in front of her. There was no time. No time at all. And she was going too fast. Before Olivia had even realised what was going on, the girl's body slammed against the front of her car, and Olivia panicked and tried to swerve out of the way at the last moment. It couldn't be happening. She felt the impact with the girl, and seconds later, Olivia's car ran off the road and straight into a nearby tree.

The impact was instant, and her car was travelling too fast, and it smashed into the old oak tree that had been standing in that same spot for over a hundred years. Olivia didn't have time to think. There were no last thoughts or worries. She didn't have time to worry about Laura's future or to think of Alexander. The car hit the tree and Olivia's body was thrown forward and through the windshield of the car and smacked against the tree with such force that she didn't feel a thing. She was dead before she'd even had time to comprehend that she was about to die. One moment she was alive and the next nothing. Not even a second to think or to feel anything. The car was embedded in the tree. The girl she had hit lay in the road, twenty feet away, her body battered and bruised, blood seeping from her head. She did have time for one last thought. One last breath. And then she was gone too.

Laura lay in Tom's bed in the dark and looked up at the ceiling. She couldn't believe that they had finally done it. Sex! She had lost her virginity. It was, actually, a little disappointing. It was supposed to be this huge deal, and it had been nice, but it wasn't like she felt that different afterwards. She wasn't suddenly hurtling towards adulthood in a new way that she hadn't even considered before. She felt the same, but with the knowledge that something small had changed in her life. More of a slight shift than a giant alteration.

Tom had been very nice about everything. He had taken

his time and asked her if she was sure more than once. It had all been over quickly once they started. Laura had heard from more than one person and read about it online, and most said it was a bit of a let-down the first time and then it got better. She supposed they would be doing it a lot more now they had done it. Tom was in the bathroom, and Laura picked up her mobile phone from the side. She had promised she would text Charlotte as soon as she had done it. The deed. She couldn't let her best friend down. Charlotte would be so excited. Laura tapped out a quick message to her friend.

We did it. Not life changing, but nice. I'll call you later. L x

She pressed send and then waited for Tom to return to bed. She would stay there for another hour before going home. She was hungry and her mum had mentioned something about getting a takeaway. She did feel a little different, she thought. She'd had sex, and it was with Tom. It had brought them closer together, and with summer approaching, they could finally be a proper couple. Maybe Tom could come over to her house for dinner. Meet the parents. Laura smiled to herself as Tom walked back into the room. Exciting times ahead.

A mile away, a phone buzzed with a new message, and it was picked up by a policewoman. It was amazing the phone had survived the impact. The screen was cracked, but it had survived, unlike the poor girl who owned the phone. It made the policewoman incredibly sad. The phone had a new pink and glittery case. It reminded her of her own daughter's phone. The policewoman had a quick look at the message.

We did it. Not life changing, but nice. I'll call you later. L x.

A poor friend, the policewoman thought. They had put a sheet over the girl's body, so no-one could see her. It was horrific. The policewoman kept the phone so they could return it to her parents. Such a tragic waste of a life. Two lives. Gone. Just like that. And then there was the man, who was the husband of the dead woman. He was still crying. She could hear his howls. It was so guttural. Like a wild animal. The policewoman didn't know what had happened, but she knew in that moment that many lives had been changed, altered, forever.

Part Four: After

31.

Laura came home to an empty house. She was confused because it was past seven o'clock, and someone should have been there. She knew her father was out, but where could her mother be? She checked her phone for any messages, and she had none. It was strange enough that Charlotte hadn't replied to her text, and now her parents were nowhere to be seen. She put her school bag down by the foot of the stairs and walked through into the kitchen.

After they'd had sex, Laura and Tom lay in bed for a while. They talked, kissed, and cuddled. It felt grown up. She still couldn't believe they had finally done it. Afterwards, Laura went into his bathroom and looked at her face in the mirror. She just had to look at herself and see if she looked any different. She knew it was silly, and she didn't look any different, but inside she was. Inside, it had made her fall more in love with Tom. Perhaps he really was The One. She hated it when other girls talked about their boyfriends as if they were on the verge of getting married. Laura realised they had to get through sixth form, and then university, and even if they survived that, which was already five or six years away, they had to start a life together. She didn't want to jump the gun and proclaim anything, but there was something special about her and Tom. Something that felt strong enough to think it might last.

Laura looked through the fridge and was about to take out the cheese when she heard a car outside, and then the front door opened. It was probably mum. Perhaps she had popped out to the shops for something. Maybe she had a takeaway as promised. She hoped she had something delicious. A pizza would be nice. It definitely wouldn't be her dad. The last time he went to the pub with work, he didn't get home until past eleven o'clock and was drunk, embarrassingly fumbling around with his key in the front door. Laura walked out of the kitchen and into the hallway, ready to see her mum.

'Where have you …' she started and then stopped. The front door was open and in walked her father, and behind him a policewoman. Her father didn't look like her father at all. All the blood from his face was gone. His eyes were lost, and he barely registered Laura. 'Dad, what's going on?'

'Are you Laura Burke?' said the policewoman with a soft, kind voice.

'Yes,' said Laura, panicking inside. What was going on and where was Mum? Was her father in some sort of trouble?

'We should sit down,' said the policewoman.

Laura looked at her father again, but he looked past her. He was in shock. He hadn't spoken. His face had an expression that Laura would never forget. Outside on their driveway sat a police squad car, and another officer was standing against it. Laura walked them through into the living room, and she sat down. Alexander sort of fell into his armchair. The policewoman remained standing.

'What's going on, Dad?' said Laura, a panic in her voice. Her heart fluttered anxiously, and she had a sudden sickness in her stomach. 'Dad?'

'Just look at me for a moment, Laura,' said the policewoman. 'My name is Constable Jenkins.' Laura looked at her. She was late thirties with dark hair and green eyes. She had a look on her face that made Laura uncomfortable. The look of someone about to deliver the worst news in the world. 'There's been an accident, Laura. A really bad accident.'

Laura suddenly realised.

'It's Mum, isn't it?' said Laura, already on the verge of tears. She felt a sudden terror.

'We don't know exactly what happened yet, but she was involved in a car accident earlier this evening.'

Constable Jenkins walked across and sat next to Laura on the sofa. Alexander was sitting in the armchair, still lost in his own world. Constable Jenkins sat close to Laura. She would need a hug. She was just a child.

'Is she …' said Laura, the tears already coming and running down her soft cheeks.

'It would have been quick,' said Constable Jenkins. 'I'm so sorry, Laura.'

At that point, Laura looked at her father. Tears were rolling down his face too, but his expression hadn't changed. He wasn't really crying, but just so sad and traumatised that the tears came without anything else happening. No noise. Nothing. Laura's body caved in, and Constable Jenkins took her, and let her cry against her. She had her own daughter at home who was near enough the same age, and it was the hardest thing she had ever had to do as a policewoman. Her own heart was breaking for that poor family. The worst thing, though, the horrible part was that it wasn't over. It was only just beginning.

Constable Jenkins's partner, Constable Briggs, was outside. He was getting updates from the station and was there if she needed him. Laura cried for a few minutes until Alexander finally got up, walked across, and held his daughter. The two of them locked together in the hell that had enveloped them. Constable Jenkins went into the kitchen to make them both a cup of tea, and to give them some space. Space to grieve and for the reality of what had happened to sink in. Although, of course, news like that never really sank in, did it? It would always be there. Etched permanently into their every waking hour. Embedded into their minds like a knife in a tree.

Laura couldn't believe it. From the best day of her life to suddenly the worst. How could her mum be dead? It didn't seem possible. It wasn't possible. There had to have been a mistake. She had spoken to her that morning. They were going on holiday to Mallorca that summer. Laura was going to order some new bikinis. Laura pulled away from her father and rubbed the tears from her eyes.

'Are they sure? Is she really dead?'

Alexander looked at his daughter. Tears were heavy in his bloodshot eyes. His pale face crumpled in agony and pain.

'They're sure. She's dead, baby girl. She's gone.'

Laura dived back into her father again. She wasn't sixteen at that moment, but a little girl. She wanted her father to hold her and make it all go away the way he did when she was young. She wanted to go back in time before this happened when she was happy. When she was with Tom and her mother was alive. She didn't understand how she was supposed to go on. How could she continue with her life? The pain inside of her was so strong she thought she might pass out.

Alexander held his daughter, and he couldn't get the images out of his mind. The image of his wife's body slumped, bloodied and mangled against that tree. The front of the car smashed; the windscreen broken where her body had been flung through it. It would have been quick. Poor young Charlotte on the road, her lifeless body broken. A leg at a strange angle, an arm over her head, and the pool of blood that surrounded her. It was so dark. All of that potential. All of that life. How were her parents ever going to get over that? She was an only child. Tim and Alice. Both the nicest, kindest people. They didn't deserve that sort of pain, and all of it had been his fault. His wife was dead because of him. Charlotte was dead because of him. Laura held him and needed him, and yet it was all of his doing. The choice he had made. The lie he had told. He held Laura, and they cried together, but he hated himself more than he had hated anyone his whole life.

Finally, Constable Jenkins came back in with two cups of tea and put them down on the coffee table. Alexander didn't know when they should tell Laura about Charlotte. She had just had the biggest shock of her life. He didn't know if she could handle more bad news. But when?

'What happened?' said Laura between big sobs.

Alexander looked at Constable Jenkins, and she looked

back at him. She knew what she had to do. She hated she was breaking that poor girl's heart, but it was her job. She would find out soon enough, and it was better that she was there when she did. She could offer them both support. They needed help. She could phone relatives and break the news or get them something to eat. She wanted to help, but first she had to tell Laura what had happened. She spoke slowly in a soft voice. Constable Jenkins was originally from Wales before she met her husband and moved to London, but she kept a strong Welsh accent. People had told her that her voice was good for things like that. For breaking bad news. It was lyrical and had a warmness to it. She explained to Laura that her mother had been driving, and for some unknown reason, hadn't seen a pedestrian. In her attempt to avoid the pedestrian, she swerved and hit a tree. She would have died quickly. It would have been over in a matter of seconds.

'And what happened to the other person?' said Laura between heavy sobs.

Constable Jenkins looked across at Alexander, and he looked back at her. He knew this was news he had to deliver himself. This might push her over the edge.

'Laura,' said Alexander, and she turned to face him. 'The person your mother hit was Charlotte.' He left a pause, his voice barely able to speak. He couldn't breathe. He didn't feel like he had enough air in his lungs to get the words out. The tightness in his chest got tighter still.

'She didn't make it either,' said Constable Jenkins. 'I'm so sorry, Laura.'

Laura's entire world came crashing down around her. Her mother was dead, and now her best friend. It was a cruel twist of fate. It had to be a joke. Surely, she couldn't have lost them both in the same accident. How was it even possible? Charlotte walked home by herself, but that was nowhere near their house or on the way to the shops. Why was her mother driving over there and why had Charlotte taken so long to get home? Laura didn't understand. She couldn't comprehend anything. She got up and ran upstairs to her bedroom, where she fell on the bed and cried. She buried herself as far into her duvet as she could and just cried and cried. It felt like her heart had been ripped from her body. The physical pain was almost unbearable. Her world was shattered, and she didn't know how she would ever come back from that sort of pain. It was impossible.

Downstairs, Constable Jenkins spoke to Alexander. They drank tea, and she explained all the help they could give them and then she gave him information about counsellors and advice phone numbers. There were people they should talk to. They needed help getting through it. Alexander heard every word, but not all of them infiltrated his mind, and instead drifted off into the room. She suggested Laura would need the most help. The sort of trauma she had been through wouldn't be easy to manage. She had seen other people go through similar things, and it had torn them apart. She would need her father more than ever. He had to be strong for Laura.

Alexander heard her speaking, but all he could think was that it was all his fault. His wife was dead, Charlotte was dead, and his daughter's life ruined, all because of a decision he had made. He didn't know if he could come back from that. If it was possible. The one thing he knew was that Laura could never know his part in all of it. She could never know what he had done because if she found out, he was sure he would lose her too, and that thought wasn't something he could comprehend. If he lost his daughter, then his life would be over. He might as well be dead himself.

32.

Minutes became hours and hours slipped into days, and the realisation of what had happened sank into their lives. The first day and neither Alexander nor Laura did or said much. The day went by in a haze. They barely ate or drank, and Laura spent most of the day in her bedroom. She lay in silence, occasionally breaking down into fits of tears, and then returning to a state of quietness. She stared at the ceiling and did her best to think of nothing. She listened to music, and Tom messaged her a few times, but she couldn't reply. What would she say? He probably already knew. News like that didn't stay hidden for long. She couldn't speak. She couldn't do much of anything. She thought of having sex with Tom and it made her sick to her stomach because at the same time her mother and best friend were dying. She had felt so happy when she left Tom's house. She remembered the feeling as she floated home on a wave of euphoria. Her life was perfect at that moment. She felt so lucky, had always felt lucky, and when she thought about the future, about sixth form and Oxford, she got goosebumps. She actually got goosebumps because she was overwhelmed with how magical life was and all the possibilities that existed.

But then.

Alexander sat in his armchair, got up and walked around the house, and then sat down again. He tried to think about what was next, the things he had to do, but he couldn't summon the energy or will-power to do them. He had to call Olivia's father. They didn't really get on, hadn't had a relationship in all the years he had known Olivia, but he had the right to know she had died. Died. He could barely think of the word without breaking down into yet more tears. He hated it. He hated himself. He just wanted Laura to be okay. But how could she be? How could either of them be okay?

He had to call his headmistress and tell her what had happened. She already knew, of course, but he had to ask for time off. He needed time to look after Laura and to grieve. He had to arrange the funeral, look into a life insurance claim because despite the horrific idea of Olivia's life equating to any sort of financial gain they would need it, and then on the Monday after it had happened, he had to speak with the police.

It was late morning, and Alexander was in the kitchen. He had made himself a cup of tea and was sitting staring out into the garden, the tea getting cold. He found he could end up staring into space and without realising it, thirty minutes could elapse. Laura had been in her bedroom all morning. He had tried to speak with her, but she said nothing. He wondered if she needed someone else to talk to. Perhaps they could see a counsellor together. The doorbell rang, and Alexander slowly got up and answered it. Outside was Constable Jenkins, the woman who had been so kind on Friday, and another policeman.

'Mr Burke,' said Constable Jenkins. 'Do you mind if we come in?'

'No,' he said quietly, his voice barely used for days felt distant.

It felt strange having people in the house. It was a reminder that life was still going on. That despite the cocoon of grief that he and Laura were living in, life was continuing for the rest of the world. As Alexander closed the front door, he got a glimpse outside. Of people walking past, cars driving, the noise and energy of life. Alexander offered them a cup of tea, and they declined. They just had a few questions.

'Why?' said Alexander as they settled into the living room.

'We're trying to ascertain exactly what happened,' said the policeman. His name was Constable Briggs. He was tall and young. He had only been on the force for just over a year and was eager to get ahead.

'It seems eyewitness reports say your wife was driving with undue speed and care,' said Constable Jenkins.

At that moment, the living room door opened, and Laura walked in. She had heard voices.

'What's going on? What's happened?'

She was still in pyjamas, her lank hair unwashed in a loose ponytail.

'It's nothing,' said Alexander.

'Then why are the police here?'

'We just have a few follow-up questions,' said Constable Jenkins, smiling warmly at Laura.

'I think it's best if you go back upstairs, love,' said Alexander.

'But I want to listen,' said Laura, who sat down on the sofa next to him.

She hadn't showered or brushed her teeth since Friday. Alexander was uncomfortable with Laura being in the room. He knew he couldn't answer questions honestly with her there. But he didn't want to cause a scene. Despite the overwhelming emotional grief that attacked him constantly, breaking him down piece by piece, there was also a small part of his brain that knew he had to be careful. He couldn't say too much, and he couldn't let Laura find out what had really happened on that awful day.

'Like I said, we have reports that your wife was driving recklessly on Friday,' said Constable Jenkins.

'What do you mean, recklessly?' said Laura.

'She was speeding,' said Constable Briggs. 'And driving without due care and attention.'

'That doesn't make sense,' said Laura, looking towards her father. 'Mum was always the slowest driver, wasn't she?'

'She was,' said Alexander uncomfortably.

'Do you know of any reason why she might have been driving like that?' said Constable Jenkins. 'Any reason at all?'

Alexander looked at his daughter, and he wanted to cry. He wanted to confess everything to her because it was eating him up inside. But he couldn't. He was a coward. A weak, pathetic, cheating coward. If she knew then she might never speak to him again, but not telling her was killing him too. It was a no-win situation.

'Could you give us some time alone, love?' Alexander said to Laura.

'But I want to stay—'

'Laura, please,' said Alexander, slightly louder than he had intended and with slightly more venom. His entire body was tense, and when he looked at Laura, she was shocked, and he could see that tears weren't far away. Alexander composed himself. 'I just need some time alone with the officers, that's all.'

Laura stood up and walked out. She didn't understand what was going on and why she couldn't stay in the room. Her father was being weird, and she didn't know why. She couldn't imagine. She would talk to him when they were gone. He was treating her like a kid, and she wasn't. She wanted to know what had happened to her mother and her best friend just as much as him. She still couldn't understand why they were in the same place and now why her mother would have been driving so fast and what had the policeman said? Without 'due care and attention'. That wasn't her mother. It was a family joke that she drove like an old lady. Always five miles an hour under the speed limit. The idea she was breaking the speed limit and driving recklessly made no sense at all to Laura. She wanted to know the truth. She wanted to understand what had happened.

'I'm sorry about that,' said Alexander when Laura had gone. He could barely look at the officers. 'The truth is that Olivia and I had an argument that night, and that's probably why she was driving like that.'

Alexander spoke slowly and steadily. He could barely contain the grief and guilt that threatened to spill out into the room. Every word felt heavy, almost as if each one pushed him further and further down.

'Can you tell us what the argument was about?' said Constable Briggs.

Constable Jenkins looked across at him for a moment. She wasn't sure they should be pushing him for more information. It wasn't a murder inquiry. They didn't need to know all the details. An argument was enough. But he had asked the question, and she was curious. She wondered how Mr Burke might respond. At first he cried, tears came, and she passed him the tissues that were on the coffee table. But then when he had calmed down, he spoke and told them everything. He explained that he had gone to meet a woman, and his wife had followed him. He said that he wouldn't have gone through with it. It was just a stupid mistake, but his wife had caught him, and she was so upset, and she drove off before he had the chance to stop her. She was emotional and angry, and that's why she was driving the way she was driving. It was his fault and his fault alone. He had killed his wife. He was responsible for her death and for Charlotte's too. If only he had stopped her. If only he had made a different decision.

Constable Jenkins couldn't believe what she had heard. When she met Alexander on Friday, they seemed like the happiest family in the world. A family full of love, and she was distraught all weekend thinking about them. Poor Alexander had lost the love of his life, and Laura had lost her mum and best friend. It was all Constable Jenkins could think about. That poor, perfect little family that lived in that lovely house. But it wasn't quite like that. Alexander had been cheating on his wife, and that's why she had died. That's why that poor girl died. He hadn't done anything wrong legally, but she knew Alexander would spend the rest of his life knowing what he had done, and it would tear him apart. He was guilty, and perhaps it was just one bad decision, but from her experience, sometimes that was enough.

'Thank you for your time,' said Constable Briggs at the front door.

'Sorry again for your loss,' said Constable Jenkins.

Alexander could barely muster a smile before he closed

the door on them and went back inside. Constable Jenkins opened her car door and got into the car next to Constable Briggs.

'Poor kid,' he said. 'Imagine losing your mum and best friend all at once, and then if she finds out why. Jesus. That's a lifetime of therapy right there.'

'It's going to take a long time to heal,' said Constable Jenkins.

'It makes you think though, doesn't it?' said Constable Briggs as he started the car. 'One minute you're here, and then the next you're gone. One decision. One wrong choice and it's lights out.'

They drove off, and inside Alexander sat in the kitchen and finished his tea. Telling the police what had happened was difficult, but it had felt like a release. He had needed to tell someone what he had done. He needed to confess his sins because they were sins. At that moment, he wished he was religious. He wished he could go to a church and confess what he had done. He needed to find some sort of relief from the pain that constantly attacked his heart. The pain that hit him again and again and again.

Upstairs, Laura lay on her bed, and the more she thought about it, the more confused she became and the more questions she had for her father. She had to know what had happened. Her mother and best friend were dead, and she would never be able to move on or get over it until she knew exactly what had happened. She would ask her father again, and if he wouldn't tell her, then she would find out for herself. She couldn't let it go. She needed answers. She had to know the truth; however awful it was.

33.

Laura stepped outside for the first time since Friday. The world seemed so much brighter than she remembered and so much louder. There seemed to be more cars on the roads, more people on the streets, and everything just felt different from she remembered. It felt strange to her that less than a week ago everything was normal. Her life was perfect. And yet here she was going outside, and she felt as though everyone in the world was looking at her. Everything was off, and just a walk along the high street felt like a marathon. She hated that it felt like that. She still hadn't spoken to poor Tom. He had messaged her and called so many times, but she couldn't face him. She couldn't speak to anyone. She could only imagine the gossip at school. The school she would eventually have to return to. She was trying to study at home, but her mind wasn't ready. It couldn't focus. The only thing she could think about was what had happened to her mother and best friend, and why her father was being so weird about it. After the police came on Monday, she asked him again and again what had happened, but he wouldn't tell her. He just said it was nothing, but she knew he was lying. That's why she was walking to the police station. She had to talk to Constable Jenkins. If her father wouldn't tell her what had happened, then maybe she would.

Laura had never been inside a police station before. She felt awkward as she walked inside. She didn't belong there. Luckily, it was quiet, and she walked straight up to the front where a policewoman sat.

'Can I help you?' said the policewoman.

Laura had no idea how it worked. Whether she could even see Constable Jenkins. Could she just walk up and ask to see her? And what exactly would she say if she did?

'I, umm, need to speak to Constable Jenkins,' said Laura,

nervously.

'Can I have your name, please?'

'Laura Burke.'

'Right, just give me a moment here, Laura,' said the woman with a smile, and then she picked up a telephone and rang someone. She spoke quietly on the phone for a moment, put it down, and then looked back at Laura with a smile. 'You're lucky. She was just about to head out. She'll be out in a moment.'

Laura sat down and waited, and then after a few minutes, a door opened and out walked Constable Jenkins. She smiled curiously at Laura.

'Laura, hello, can I help you with something?'

'Could we talk?' Laura said, somewhat nervously.

'Umm, yes, of course. Just give me a moment and I'll find us somewhere quieter.'

Laura waited while Constable Jenkins went off to find a suitable room. Laura looked around at the walls of the waiting room. Signs for missing children, and for witnesses to crimes. Photos of people who were wanted in relation to accidents. There was a whole world that Laura had never even considered before. A world of crime, of missing people, and of sadness. All of it, every sign she saw, involved some sort of pain. She had never really thought about it before because it hadn't been a part of her life. But now it was and would forever be a part of her. It was like a scar that would always be on her. A reminder of what had happened.

Eventually, Constable Jenkins came out and asked Laura to follow her. They walked through the station until they came to a small room. Laura wondered if it was an interview room like they had on television. It didn't look like it. It was just a small room with a table and two chairs. There was no large window or mirror, and no recording device as far as she could see. They both sat down. It was cold with no natural light.

'How can I help?' said Constable Jenkins.

Laura looked at her. She was kind, she knew that. She was wearing a wedding ring, and so she was married. Laura wondered if she had kids too. She seemed like the sort, thought Laura. She had the look of a mother. A nurturing, caring soul.

'What did my father tell you on Monday? I know he told you something and he won't talk to me about it, but something isn't right. Mum was the slowest, most careful driver in the world. I know she wouldn't have been driving recklessly. I know that something happened, and he won't tell me.'

Tears stung Laura's eyes. She was amazed she had any tears left.

'Laura, look, I understand, and I'm so sorry for everything, but I can't divulge any information your dad gave to me. You really need to talk to him.'

She looked genuinely sorry, and Laura knew she was just doing her job, but she couldn't let it go. If she didn't tell her something, then maybe she would never find out. She would always be left wondering and questioning herself. Perhaps her father would tell her one day, but what if he didn't? She had to get something from Constable Jenkins. Just a suggestion or a hint. Something.

'I tried, but he won't talk to me about it. My mother died. My best friend died, and none of it makes sense. I need to know what happened or I'll never be able to move on.'

'Laura, I'm sorry—'

'I just need to know,' said Laura desperately. She looked directly into Constable Jenkins's eyes. 'Something happened, didn't it? What's Dad hiding?'

'I really think you need to talk to your father, Laura.'

'But he told you something, didn't he?' said Laura. She knew she was getting more upset than she should and maybe she was coming across as crazy, but she didn't care. 'Please, just tell me something. Tell me I'm not wrong. Please.'

Laura watched Constable Jenkins' face and her

expression changed a little bit. She looked uncomfortable, and it was enough to make Laura believe she was holding something back from her. It was enough to convince Laura that she needed to press her father more.

'Laura, like I said, I can't tell you what he said to me, but …' Laura leaned forward ever so slightly. The tears pooled in her eyes. Her heart started beating slightly faster in her chest. 'But you should talk to your father. Talk to him, okay? Ask him again.'

'Okay. Thank you.'

Constable Jenkins smiled at Laura, and then after a moment, they both stood up. Laura hadn't got what she had come for, but she had something. Something solid and tangible to hold on to. There was clearly a message in Constable Jenkins's eyes when she had said to talk to her father. He was holding something back from her and she was going to find out what. She had no choice.

Alexander was at home. He was in his armchair in the living room attempting to read a history book. He was trying to distract his mind with stories from the English civil war, but he couldn't stop the horrible thoughts that ran like a plague through his mind. He couldn't stop thinking about the last moments of Olivia's life. The woman he loved. Her last moments were full of hatred and sadness that he had caused. He thought of his poor daughter. He so badly wanted to hug her and hold her and tell her it was going to be all right, but he couldn't. He couldn't because all he could think about was what he had done. The decision he had made that had ended two lives. Whenever he thought of Charlotte's parents and the pain they were going through, a huge, gaping hole opened in his own heart, and it was filled with a dark sadness. A huge void that used to be filled with love was now only full of hatred for what he had done.

Laura had gone out for a walk to clear her head. Alexander hadn't ventured out yet. He would need to go shopping soon, but the idea filled him with dread. He heard the front door open and then close. He heard Laura in the hallway, and then she walked into the living room.

'Good walk?' said Alexander hopefully.

He hoped it had helped. That it had given her a moment's peace.

'I went to the police station.'

'What? Why?'

Alexander tensed up. He closed his book.

'I hoped they might tell me what you said to them,' said Laura, and Alexander's heart fell in his chest. His body changed shape, and a nervousness prickled his skin. His mind drifted toward the horror of what he knew and the unthinkable pain of Laura finding out. 'Because I know there's something you aren't telling me. I spoke to the policewoman who was here the other day, and she said I should talk to you. I need you to tell me what happened, Dad. I have to know.'

Alexander felt his insides breaking up. His mind cracked, and he felt a hollowness that he had never felt before. It was like a complete absence of light and love. A black hole enveloped him, dragging him away from reality. He couldn't go on with this secret locked away in his mind. Perhaps the only way they could ever move forwards is if she knew what had happened. Maybe the truth would set him free, or at least start them both on the journey to some sort of redemption. Alexander knew he couldn't keep lying to her. He couldn't keep the secret for the rest of his life. It would slowly and gradually burn him up like a dying star until there was nothing left.

He looked at his daughter, and he cried. He couldn't help the tears. They came and ran down his face. Laura sat on the sofa opposite him.

'I'm sorry,' said Alexander. 'I'm so sorry, love.'

'Sorry for what, Dad?'

'I made a mistake. I made a decision, and your mother was angry with me, and that's why she was driving the way she was. It was all my fault. I'm so sorry.' Alexander spoke, and the words fell slowly out of his mouth.

'I don't understand, Dad. What decision?'

'It was just once, and nothing happened. I wasn't going to go through with it, I promise. I just made one bad decision, and your mother somehow found out—'

'What did you do, Dad?' said Laura, louder now. She didn't understand what he was saying. What he was talking about. What could he have done?

'I was,' said Alexander, and then he stopped and looked at his daughter. 'I'm sorry, baby.'

'What happened?'

'I was going to meet another woman.'

The air in the room changed. Laura immediately understood what he meant. He was going to cheat on her mother. That's why she was so angry with him. That's why they had an argument. That's why she was dead. That's why Charlotte was dead. He was meeting another woman. The words like gunshots exploded into the room. She understood everything all at once.

'I'm so sorry,' said Alexander again through a thick fog of tears.

Laura stood up, a sudden anger and rage at her father for what he had done.

'They're dead because you wanted to have sex with someone else! They're dead because of you!'

Tears were flooding down her face, and the anger inside of her threatened everything she knew in the world. How could he have done that? How selfish and cruel of a person he was. She hated him, and there was nothing he could ever say to her to change that.

'I hate you!' she shouted at him.

'I'm sorry,' he whimpered, broken and terrified of what would happen next.

'I was so happy, Dad. Our lives were perfect. Mum loved you so much. How could you do that to us? How could you destroy that?'

Alexander couldn't respond. He couldn't speak. He could only cry. The noise like high-pitched machine-gun fire.

'They died because of you, Dad. You killed them!'

Laura ran out of the room and upstairs to her bedroom. She fell on the bed and cried. Her life had been taken away from her. Everything she loved was gone, and to find out it was the fault of the one person who was supposed to love her the most. It was like a grotesque Greek tragedy. How could she ever get over knowing what she knew? The answer was that she couldn't. Not in that house. Not living with the man who had destroyed her life. She would have to move out somewhere. She would have to go on without him. It was the only way. She needed to cut the cord. A complete break. She wanted to jump into the abyss because it was better than staying where she was. It reminded her of those horrific photos she had seen of 9/11. Of people jumping to their deaths from skyscrapers because jumping was better than staying where they were. Jumping was a chance, no matter how slim. It was a sliver of hope.

Downstairs, Alexander fell onto the floor in tears. The truth was out and what he had done, the one decision he had made, the lie he had told, would define the rest of his life. It wasn't his choice. His choice had been then. When he had sat in his car outside school. When he had decided to drive to Sara's flat instead of home. That had been the choice. Now all choices were gone. Now it was only heartache and pain, and the faint hope that one day Laura might forgive him.

34.

It was the day of Olivia's funeral, and Alexander was in his bedroom getting dressed. He had been dreading the day, and without Laura for moral and physical support, he could barely contain his grief. He hadn't seen her since the day of the argument. The day he had told her what had happened, and she had packed up her stuff and left. She was staying with a friend. She wouldn't take his calls or return his messages. Alexander was completely and utterly alone. And now he had to attend Olivia's funeral, and he couldn't even imagine how he would survive the day. He felt like getting into bed and sleeping forever. He didn't want to exist at that moment. Death felt like it might be a wonderful release.

Olivia's father Gary had helped him arrange the funeral. When he had called Gary and broke the news, there had been a pause, a moment's silence, and then he had broken down. He knew he had been a terrible father to her, and like Alexander, the guilt had got the better of him. It was the guilt that was killing Alexander, and the same could be said of Gary. Alexander had offered for him to stay in the house, but he said he would feel more comfortable in a hotel. He had been in London for a few days helping with the arrangements. Alexander had done most of it himself. Olivia's friend, Jenny, had come over and offered to help too. She had organised the flowers, and the catering for the wake, which had been a tremendous help. He had reached out to all of Olivia's old university friends and made an announcement on Facebook. Hundreds of messages had come through to Alexander. People they hadn't seen or heard from in years were suddenly in touch and promising to come to the funeral. Alexander couldn't stand the idea of people coming to comfort him. To give him their best wishes. If only they knew. How could he face that many people without cracking? More importantly, how could he see Laura again without falling apart?

Gary was at Alexander's house, and they were waiting for the funeral car. It was coming at eleven o'clock. Alexander had sent Laura a message about coming in the car, but she hadn't responded. Gary had asked about Laura, but Alexander had blown him off with an excuse. She needed some time and space. Alexander couldn't tell him the truth. It was sad that the only people in the car would be Alexander and Olivia's estranged father. She had aunts, cousins, and a couple of uncles who would be at the church. Most of the church would comprise of Olivia's friends and colleagues. People from their past, shocked that one of them had died, and a numbing reminder of their own mortality.

'Ready?' said Gary, as the funeral car pulled up outside.

Alexander tried to stand up but found he could barely make it up before he was sitting down again. He couldn't hold his own weight. The world spun around, and he had to sit down.

'You all right?' said Gary.

Alexander tried again, and this time he managed to get up. His head felt light, and his body felt heavy. He felt like the smallest gust of wind, and he would be blown over. Gary walked outside and spoke with the driver before Alexander followed. Neighbours and people on the street stood outside, paying their last respects to Olivia. They all knew. Everyone knew. They had seen the newspaper articles like everyone else. They had heard the whispers as the news had gradually filtered through every one of their social groups that Olivia was gone, and in such awful circumstances. They all looked at Alexander and thought the same thing. Poor bugger.

The driver opened the door, Alexander and Gary got in, and they started the slow drive to the church. Olivia's body was in the coffin in the car ahead of them. Alexander couldn't bear to think of her body in there. The body he had touched on that Friday morning. She had been so alive that day. So full of life. They had almost had sex, and if they had it might have saved them. Saved her. They had their night away booked for The Langham hotel on Saturday. Alexander had only found out about that after Laura had told him. She was in on the surprise. Another grenade going off inside Alexander's heart. She had booked them a night away in a plush London hotel. It would have been so special. Alexander couldn't bear to think about it. Gary reached a hand across and gave Alexander's leg a gentle slap.

'Chin up, mate. We can do this.'

Alexander looked across at Gary. At the man he barely knew. At the man Olivia barely knew. He had been a cheater. His image and the memories of him had always clouded their marriage. If it wasn't for him, perhaps Olivia wouldn't have been so suspicious of Alexander. Maybe she wouldn't have followed him that day and she would still be alive. Alexander hated that Olivia's last thoughts of him were that he was no better than her father. Gary was a serial cheater. A man who had left his daughter and barely bothered to see her again. He had started a new family and abandoned his last. Alexander was nothing like that. He loved Laura more than life itself. He hadn't actually cheated on Olivia, and he was sure he wouldn't have gone through with it. He was a good man who had made one terrible decision and paid the ultimate price. Gary had made multiple bad decisions, and as far as Alexander could see, he hadn't paid any sort of price. He was happily living in Bristol with a new wife and three new kids. Olivia was just the last piece of an old life he had thrown out years before. Alexander wanted to hurt Gary. He wanted to punch him. He had ruined Olivia's life. He had destroyed any chance that she would fully trust someone again. Alexander sat in the car, and he wanted to hurt Gary, if only to make himself feel something.

It was a bright day without a cloud in the sky. The church was one of those incredible old English churches. Built over five hundred years ago, it had seen its fair share of pain. It was soaked into the walls and dug into the ground where hundreds of gravestones lay. Tears ran down Alexander's cheeks as they pulled up outside the church. He reached into his pocket and pulled out the small bag of tissues he had brought along. Gary waited for him to compose himself before he opened the door. A large group of people were milling around outside of the church. A sea of familiar looking faces. The same faces that might have been invited to a surprise fiftieth birthday party. A sea of pale, sombre faces on black bodies. A few smaller groups broke away from the main group. People that didn't know as many people but wanted to pay their respects. In one of those smaller groups was Laura. Alexander saw her, and he looked hopefully towards her, but she turned away and looked off into the distance.

'Ready when you are,' said the driver of the car.

Alexander, Gary, and a couple of the other family members were going to carry the coffin inside the church. Alexander didn't know if he could do it. If the weight of it would be too much.

'Can you do it?' said Gary.

'I, err, don't know,' said Alexander.

He felt an awful sickness in his stomach. A feeling he was going to vomit overtook him and he walked off towards a nearby tree. Gary asked around and got someone else to step in as a pallbearer. Jenny was in the crowd, and she saw Alexander walking away, and her heart sank. She couldn't believe that her friend was gone. They had only had lunch the other day. They would never get their spa day now. She wondered if Alexander had cheated on Olivia as she had suspected, or whether it was all in her mind. She guessed she would never know. She had to be there for Alexander either way. He looked awful, as if something had reached inside of him and pulled his soul out of his body. He looked as though he might drop dead at any moment himself. And poor Laura. God, poor little Laura. She couldn't imagine what she was going through. She had seen her but didn't know what to say to her. What could you say?

Everyone walked into the church, and the service began. A quiet, sombre affair punctuated with bouts of tears, and moments of quiet followed by hymns and a few speakers. Alexander had declined to speak because he knew he wouldn't be able to do it. Instead, he sat at the front of the church next to Gary, his head down for most of the ceremony, willing the minutes to elapse so he could go home. He was feeling anxious, and he wanted to get up and walk out. He just needed to breathe. He looked across and saw Laura. Dressed in a black dress, her hair tied back with flat black shoes. Alexander just wanted to hug her. He wanted to know that she was okay. At the end of the ceremony, they played Let It Be, Olivia's favourite Beatles song, and people gradually shuffled out under a gentle chorus of tears. Alexander stayed sitting down. Everyone left, and he just sat. He looked around the beautiful church, at its old stained-glass windows, and the stonework, and he thought about the history of it as The Beatles sang, Let It Be. Alexander thought to himself; how could he let it be? He couldn't. And so he sat by himself in that grand old church, and he wept. He wept for the life he'd had, the woman he'd loved, and would never see again.

Laura stood by herself outside of the church. None of what had happened there had meant anything to her. None of these people mattered. The only people who mattered were gone. Her mother and her best friend. She still had Charlotte's funeral to attend the next day. Laura was so sad that she could barely register it. She felt numb. She had seen Tom. He had tried to comfort her, but she didn't want it. She felt nothing towards him. They were over. At that moment, she didn't know what she wanted from her life. She had her exams, and then sixth form, but whereas before it had all seemed so important to her, now she didn't understand what was important and what wasn't. Charlotte and her mother were dead, and people were worried about whether they got an A or a B in their exams. How could she care? How could she care about anything?

'Hi, Laura,' said a man suddenly. 'You probably don't remember me, do you?'

She looked at him. He looked vaguely familiar, but she couldn't place him.

'No, I don't.'

'I'm Gary. Your grandad. Olivia's dad,' he said with a faint smile. He stank of cigarette smoke and aftershave.

She looked at his face for any signs of her mother. There was a slight resemblance, but that was all. Something in the eyes. Laura didn't know him. She had known that her mother didn't have a relationship with him. She had once heard her call him a 'shitting lowlife bastard'. She had seen a few photos of him when he was younger, and that was it.

'She hated you,' Laura said to him, and then she turned around and walked away.

She walked amongst the gravestones and read them. She read the names and looked at the dates. She had always loved doing that. She used to go there with her father when she was young. She remembered doing some gravestone rubbings for an art project at school. She didn't know any of the people. They were just names, and their lives were nothing more than dates. But her mother would be there now. She would have a gravestone with the dates of her life. The difference was that her dates meant something to Laura. She could trace all of those years. The same with Charlotte. They weren't just names and dates, but people who had lived.

The thing that Laura thought most about was that it was her dad who had changed the course of their lives. He was the one responsible for that end date, and she hated him with every fibre of her being. Everything channelled towards him. Her mother had hated her own father, and now Laura hers. It was something that drew them closer together. It made them the same, and she would cling to that. Anything to make her feel closer to her mother. To feel that bond. She let her hand drift across a gravestone, and she felt the roughness of the stone, and the subtle indentations of the engraving, and then she cried. It felt like she was crying for every poor dead soul in that graveyard, and yet she was only crying for one.

Part Five: The Present

35.

Louise rang the doorbell to Sam's flat, stood on the doorstep, and waited. She flattened down her dress and adjusted her hair quickly. She was so nervous. She was by herself, and she knew Josh wasn't there either. He was with Sam's ex-wife for the week. It would just be her and Sam in his lovely flat. She wasn't nervous because she thought that something might happen, but because of what she had to tell him. The truth about her life. She had lied to Jim and told him she was meeting up with an old friend for a drink. He had seemed curious because in all the years they had been together, she had never met up with anyone for a casual drink. So, after she put Ella to bed and gave Jim a quick kiss goodbye, she left the house and made her way to Sam's flat. She waited for a moment, and then the door opened, and he stood there.

'Hi, wow, you look ... incredible,' he said, and she could tell he really meant it.

'Thanks,' said Louise, slightly bashfully. 'You too.'

'Come in. I was just in the middle of something,' he said, and then he stood aside, and she walked into his flat. It smelled amazing. Whatever he was cooking had a strong Italian aroma. Lots of garlic, fresh basil, and tomatoes. Sam was making pasta from scratch, and had made his own tomato sauce, garlic bread, and put together a simple, rustic salad. There was red wine, and Louise felt the burden of what she had to tell him weighing her down. They hadn't said what tonight was about. She had said she wanted to talk. He had suggested dinner and there she was.

She walked through into the main living area with the kitchen and living room. Sam started stirring a sauce and fiddling with a block of cheese that needed to be unwrapped and then grated. He was dressed in a pair of black jeans and a slim grey shirt.

'Can I help?' she said.

'No, no, I'm all good. Please pour yourself a glass of wine. I hope you like it.'

There was a bottle of red wine on the island. Louise had a look at the label. It was an Italian wine she had never heard of before. Not that she had an extensive knowledge of European wines. Jim only drank cheap lager, and Louise barely drank these days. She poured herself a large glass of wine and took a sip. It was lovely. Fruity and not too heavy. She hadn't had a glass of red wine in a long time but found that she liked it. It was something that might be a part of her new life. She saw that Sam already had a glass and was drinking while he cooked. Laura sat down on one of the stools that was by the island. She looked around. It was such a beautiful flat, and she could imagine herself living there with him, Ella and Josh running around. She watched Sam cooking and admired the way he glided around the kitchen. It looked like he knew exactly what he was doing. The last time Jim had cooked for her, it had been overdone steak, soggy mushrooms, and undercooked chips, all flavoured in a sauce that had come from a packet. She had told Jim it was lovely, while wishing she was with someone who could really cook. Someone who appreciated all sorts of food, and not just cremated steak and greasy chips.

'It's almost ready,' said Sam.

'It smells wonderful.'

'The truth is in the tasting,' said Sam, who turned around and smiled at Louise. He took the homemade garlic bread out of the oven and placed it on a thick wooden chopping board. The pasta was served in a large bowl that Sam had picked up at a market in Italy. The salad was in another bowl he had got from Portobello Road Market, and all the food was brought over to the dining table. Louise walked over with her glass of wine.

'This looks incredible, Sam.'

'For an incredible woman,' he said, trying to look serious, before his face fell into an embarrassed smile. 'God, that was cheesy. Sorry.'

Louise laughed, slightly nervously. They looked at each other. Their eyes met, and they smiled. They hadn't spoken about 'the kiss' since it had blown both of their worlds apart. Louise had gone home afterwards, racked with a guilt, and she had decided that she needed to act. She needed to tell Sam the truth. Everything from The Incident forwards. If he still wanted to be with her after that, then they would lay the groundwork for their relationship, but he had to know the truth first. She was so tired of living a lie.

They sat down at the table. Sam had turned the lights on low, so the room had a soft glow to it. He had dotted a few candles about the room that gave off a pleasant aroma. It was the most romantic thing that had ever happened to her. Louise loved everything about Sam. Whereas Jim was salt of the earth, simple and physical, Sam was the opposite. He loved nice things, and he was soft and intelligent, creative, and thoughtful. He was everything that she craved. Dates with Jim had always felt slightly immature, like they were kids playing at being adults. With Sam, it felt sophisticated and grown up. She could imagine them going out to dinner in London at nice restaurants and watching plays together.

'A toast,' said Sam, raising his wineglass in the air.

'To?'

'To the future?'

Louise slowly lowered her glass and put it down on the table. Sam did the same, a confused, worried look on his face. Before there could be a future, she had to revisit the past.

'I have to tell you something,' she said.

'Okay.'

He was sure that whatever she said, they could get over it. He wanted her just as much as she wanted him. He had no idea what it was she wanted to say, but he didn't care. It wouldn't matter. He was sure of that.

'I haven't told you exactly who I am,' said Louise, and then she began at the beginning. She felt like she was dropping a bomb into the middle of her life, and she hoped that after the main explosion had gone off and all the shrapnel had landed, she would still have a life left. 'My name isn't Louise Bailey, it's Laura Burke.'

She watched as his face changed as she explained exactly who she was and what had happened. She talked about her life growing up, about her dreams of going to Oxford and becoming a barrister, and how it had all fallen apart on that day. That awful, fateful day ten years before. About the years that followed where she made one terrible choice after another and then changed her name because she thought if she could erase her old self and become someone new, then maybe she could somehow rid herself of the pain inside of her. That if she could change, then maybe she could forget, but then she realised that change didn't wipe the pain from her memories or her nightmares. That having a child and living with Jim had happened with no real thought, and it wasn't until she met Sam that she began to believe in herself again. That she could see a future where she could be happy.

'I just want you to know that despite everything,' said Laura with tears in her eyes. 'I really like you, and if after this you still want me, then I still want you too.'

She was silent and looked at Sam. What was he thinking? He hadn't said a word since she had started talking. She felt the tears in her eyes, and they seemed to take on all the pain she had felt since that day. All the anger, sadness, regret, and pain shot through her, and she felt all of it so intensely. Sam stood up in silence. He walked towards her and held out a hand. Crying, she took his hand in hers. She stood up until she was facing him. She could barely stand; such were the emotions she felt at that moment. The pain of her mother's loss and her best friend's death that had never really gone away but were just hidden in days and in the turning of time.

'Laura Burke,' he said softly.

'Yes.'

'I love you.'

Three simple words.

It was all she needed to hear. The tears came stronger, and he held her against his body. She had told him everything, and he loved her, and nothing else in that moment mattered except the feeling of his body against hers and the words that stayed in her mind and would stay there forever. *I love you.* She was no longer Louise Bailey. She was a ghost that had stalked a part of her life that was over now. She was Laura Burke again, and as such she needed to face not only the future but also the past. But now she wasn't alone. She had Sam by her side. She had Ella. They would be a proper family. The family that she had craved on all of those long, lonely nights when she had cried herself to sleep. When happiness felt impossible.

'Are you sure?' she finally said when the tears subsided.

'I wasn't before tonight, but as soon as you were done telling me everything, the only feeling I had left was love.'

'Me too,' said Laura.

And then they kissed, and it was even better than the first time because she really, truly felt like she was kissing him, and not the person she used to be. Sam felt a relief because she had been honest with him, and he had seen how difficult it had been for her, and yet she had done it. She had trusted him, and he knew that was something solid they could build their relationship on. Trust and love were all they needed to build their life together, and that's what he wanted. It's what they both wanted, and neither of them wanted to wait a moment because they had both felt such sadness in their life that just the thought of finally being happy couldn't wait another second. Laura just needed to go home and break the news to Jim that they were over.

36.

Alexander was sitting at the dining room table while Belinda cleared the plates away. It was a wet Wednesday evening, and Belinda had some news she wanted to share with Alexander. He had been unusually quiet the last few days and clearly had something on his mind. Ever since Belinda had found out what had happened to his wife, she had been trying to think of a way she could talk to him about it. He obviously hadn't got over it, and maybe having her there to talk to might help. But how could she bring it up? How could she tell him without telling him how she had found out? She didn't want to upset him. She couldn't risk their friendship unless he was ready. They had settled into a nice, steady rhythm. Their lives fit together well, and she didn't want to disrupt that.

'Tea?' she said.

'Please.'

Belinda turned the kettle on and put tea bags in mugs before she sat down again.

'It's getting lighter in the evening,' said Alexander.

'I love this time of year. Coming out of the darkness of winter and into the light of spring. It feels like everything is renewed.'

'Hope,' said Alexander, but his face had a look of complete hopelessness.

Belinda wanted to share her good news with Alexander. She had got a job, and she was starting in the morning. She had been out for a walk that afternoon and had walked past a cafe and they had a sign on the door that said they were looking for staff. Belinda had never worked in a cafe before, but thought it was time she did something. She had kept herself busy cleaning Alexander's house and working on the garden, but she needed to earn some money. It was a simple waitressing job, nothing extraordinary, but it was a start. It was hope.

'I got a job today,' said Belinda suddenly.

Alexander looked across at her.

'Congratulations,' he said with a smile. 'What is it?'

'It's at a cafe on the high street. I start tomorrow. It's not what I want to do long term, but it's something. I can start earning money, and then eventually I can move out. Get out of your hair.'

Belinda laughed slightly nervously because they hadn't discussed how long she would be there. She just assumed that at some point she would move out. She was so thankful for him taking her in, for saving her life, but he wouldn't want her living there forever. Living with Alexander felt like she was in a sort of limbo. Caught between the life she had and the one she would have in the future.

'There's no rush. I like having you here.'

'I know, it's just, eventually I'll have to move out.'

'Eventually.'

Belinda enjoyed staying with Alexander. Their relationship and friendship had grown over the time they had been together, but there were still so many moments when she felt uncomfortable. When so much wasn't said. The deafening pauses. When she felt like if only he would tell her what had happened, then maybe they could move on and be better for it. He was holding so much back. She finished making the tea before she returned to the table.

'I've been thinking about going back to Ireland to visit my ma. I think I might be ready to face my past.'

'That's fantastic, you should. I'd be happy to help with flights.'

Another long pause. She wanted to say it so much. To say the words out loud. She knew. She knew all about Olivia. She had seen the newspaper clippings. She had gone online and googled her, and all sorts of articles had come up. Local and national newspaper articles. She had read all of them and knew everything. How horrific the crash had been. How devastated the family of the poor girl she had hit were.

How they would never get over it. How they didn't understand what had happened. She had read the few quotes there had been from Alexander at the time. She had seen his daughter's name come up. Laura Burke. The one thing that Belinda didn't know was what had happened to her. Where had she gone and why did he never talk about her? Belinda had questions, and maybe the answers would fill that gap that still existed between them. Those moments of silence when she knew he was thinking about it.

'I think I'm going to read for a bit,' said Alexander, getting up.

Belinda couldn't hold back anymore. He had said it himself. It was the time for hope.

'Where do you go every Saturday morning?' said Belinda suddenly.

She felt her cheeks redden slightly. Alexander stopped. He turned slowly.

'Sorry?'

'Every Saturday morning you leave, and you're gone for about two or three hours, and then you come back, and I was just wondering where you go,' said Belinda. Her accent got a little stronger, and she spoke faster when she was nervous. An old habit that had never left her. She remembered when she had to speak at school, her teachers would always tell her, 'Slow down, Belinda, no-one can hear you when you speak like that'.

She didn't know what Alexander would do or what he would say. Would he be angry with her? Tell her to mind her own business? She felt that they had become closer, and maybe he was ready to talk to her. After a moment, Alexander looked at her with a solemn expression.

'I go to see my daughter and granddaughter at the park,' said Alexander, taking her by surprise. She had assumed that for some reason they were no longer in contact. She had never been to the house, and he never spoke about her.

'Oh, right, I just thought—'

'What did you think?'

'I don't know … I think I assumed that because you haven't really spoken about her that maybe she had moved away or something,' said Belinda. She didn't know whether she should say something about his wife. That she knew.

'She lives not too far away, and we meet up every Saturday morning for a few hours,' said Alexander with a gentle smile. 'She's so busy during the week with work, and so Saturday is all the time we get, unfortunately.'

Belinda looked at him, and he smiled at her. She had obviously got it all wrong.

'I'm sorry,' said Belinda.

'For what? For caring about me. I don't think that's a crime.'

'But if you ever need to talk or want someone—'

'Then I'd come to you,' said Alexander. His face looked lighter. The darkness was gone, and he looked almost cheerful. Belinda had misread the situation with his daughter. Everything was fine between them. She was busy with work. It all made sense. 'I'm going to read now.'

'Okay,' she said with a smile.

'And Belinda.'

'Yes?'

'Well done on the job. I really am proud of you.'

'Thanks,' she said, and it meant the world to her.

She was starting something new in the morning. It was just a cafe, but it was a start. She wanted to get her life back together again. She wanted to visit Ireland and see it with fresh eyes. She didn't want to see the grey concrete she had grown up with, but the beautiful, green, wild Ireland she had dreamt about as a child. She wanted to visit Dublin and see the city her brother had known. She needed to reconnect with that part of her. Her Irish heritage. She felt it deep within her.

Alexander walked into the living room and sat in his armchair. He had some reading he wanted to get done, but he couldn't stop thinking about the lies he had told Belinda. The thing was, he couldn't tell her the truth. It was too awful. He didn't want her to know what a terrible human being he was. So terrible that his own daughter wanted nothing to do with him. It had been nearly ten years since he'd last seen her, and then it had been her shouting at him, telling him to leave her alone, and that she hated him. Those were the last words she had said to him. *I hate you!* Then she had walked away, and he hadn't spoken to her since. Now he just had those Saturday mornings at the park where he would watch her from afar. He would watch her and his beautiful granddaughter, and he would dream about the day when he would have a relationship with them. He didn't know when it would be, and how it would happen, but one day he hoped. He couldn't tell Belinda any of that because he couldn't bear the thought that she would think about him the same way his daughter did. A weak man who had caused the deaths of two people, and for what? He had destroyed his life, and he deserved to pay the price for what he had done. Yet he still hoped that maybe one day there would be some sort of redemption for him. Some hope. It was that time of year again. Spring. The time for renewal. And maybe for Alexander Burke, a chance to begin again. To reclaim something. He hadn't realised it, but as he sat and thought about all of that, a tear had fallen from his face and landed on the book he had in his lap.

37.

They were going on an adventure! That's what she had told Ella that morning over a breakfast of soft-boiled eggs and soldiers. *Get ready, baby girl, we're going on the train somewhere new!* Ella got very excited. She loved going on the train. The train meant fun, and perhaps the chance for a hot chocolate with whipped cream on top. She loved to scoop the cream up with her finger and eat it. Ella adored the train. She loved to watch the world fly by the window and the feeling of going so fast. You didn't get that feeling in a car. Cars were boring, but trains were very exciting indeed. If it were up to Ella, they would go everywhere on the train.

Ever since her night with Sam, Laura had been on edge. She knew she had so much to do. Things to organise and plan. Jim knew that something was going on. He had detected a change in her, but whenever he asked her if she was all right, she said she was and smiled. Inside she was breaking apart with a mixture of desperate sadness that she had to leave Jim and the damage that would cause to both him and Ella. On the other hand, she was excited to start a new life with Sam and all the possibilities that presented. They had spoken at length, and he had said that she could move into his flat. She had asked him again and again if he was sure, maybe it was too soon, but he said he was. He wanted them to be together. He wanted to help her get ready for her university course, and he wanted them to have a life together. He loved her, and she loved him. The adventure she was taking Ella on, though, wasn't about Sam or Jim. The adventure was about her father.

Laura hadn't forgotten the last time she had seen him. Ten years before and about six months after The Incident. It was long after the funeral, when life had fallen back into some sort of normality. Laura was at sixth form college, trying to focus on her studies and rebuild her life. Unlike at secondary school, not everyone at college knew her and what had happened. She wasn't the topic of every conversation. People had moved on. She was still living with her friend then. They had a spare room, and her parents had kindly said she could stay with them for as long as she needed. She had a part-time job so she could help financially, and she was desperate to move on and forget what had happened. One evening, she was at her friend's house when her dad turned up out of the blue. He wanted to talk. He needed her to come home. He couldn't cope without her. She was all he had left. He was a mess. They had argued in the garden. She had told him she wasn't coming home. That she could never forgive him and that she hated him. She had said it with such spite and venom that she had taken herself by surprise. But she did hate him. She didn't care how he felt or how much pain he was in. She hated him for what he had done. The horrors he had created. The deaths he had been responsible for.

Laura and Ella got on the train and found two seats by the window. Ella loved the window seats the best. They had a table too, and they put their drinks down. Laura had a flat white coffee and Ella had hot chocolate. She dipped her finger in and took some of the whipped cream on the tip of her finger and sunk it into her mouth with an eager smile. After the train pulled away from the station, Ella stared out of the window with a face of pure wonder, and Laura just watched her. Ella had never been to where they were going before. It was impossible to imagine. How could she have not? But then Laura hadn't been back there in years either. The last time she had seen her house, the house she had grown up in, was during that summer before sixth form. Once she moved away, she stayed away. The memories were too painful.

'Look, Mummy,' said Ella, pointing out of the window. 'So fast.'

'We are going very fast,' said Laura with a smile.

She was so nervous. She knew she wouldn't see him. It

was a Friday, and he would be at school. She just wanted to go back and see the house again. Prepare herself. She thought if she was starting a new life with Sam, perhaps it was time to reconnect. The anger she had then had slowly been losing its momentum. To be honest, she wasn't sure how she felt about him anymore. After about ten minutes of looking out of the window, Ella turned to her mum.

'Where are we going, Mummy?'

'We're going to see the house where I grew up.'

Even hearing herself say the words out loud almost brought tears to her eyes, and she had to compose herself and keep herself together in front of her daughter. The last thing she wanted to do was fall apart on the train.

'Is there a playground?' said Ella, which made Laura laugh.

'Yes, there's a park nearby, baby girl.'

Ella smiled, then she took a sip of her hot chocolate and kept looking out of the window.

The train pulled into the station, and Laura and Ella got off the train and started the short walk to her father's house. It felt surreal to be back amongst the streets she had grown up on. The streets that until that fateful day had been nothing but kind to her. She had so many wonderful memories of her life there it was impossible just to feel sadness at being back. As soon as they walked out of the train station, she saw all the shops that looked just the same as they always had. Some of them had changed, but the quaint buildings looked the same, and there were so many trees. It all looked so much smarter than she remembered, and it was so peaceful. Perhaps it was because of where she lived with Jim that was so much less salubrious. It was as if she was seeing it with fresh eyes. She imagined bringing Ella up there, and how much nicer it would be. The sky seemed bluer somehow and the air cleaner.

Laura and Ella walked away from the train station and towards her father's house. She had the awful fear that she might meet someone she knew, or worse, her father. There was always the chance he might be off for some reason. She had checked the school's website, and it still listed him as a history teacher there. She felt strange stalking her own father online, but that's what she had to do to make sure it was safe to go back.

The walk from the train station to his house was only about fifteen minutes. The same walk she had done countless times growing up. They strolled down the streets she remembered from her own childhood. It felt so different from the part of London where she lived that was so densely populated, so urban, and dirty. Where she lived with Jim, they had rows and rows of cheap fast-food takeaways, and grotty looking pubs, and newsagents. The houses were crammed together as if to form one long house, and the roads were packed full of cars so you could barely fit between them. But there the roads were wide and the houses much larger and so pretty. Most were semi-detached and had driveways. The shops were small artisanal delicatessens and upmarket cafes. People sat outside and sipped lattes and ate freshly made pastries. There were so many trees she had forgotten how it felt almost semi-rural. Kew Gardens and Richmond Park gave the area a real greenery and the river Thames snaked around it, where they had gone every year and excitedly watched The Boat Race. They finally got to the street where her father's house sat. It was on a corner and was bigger and grander than she remembered. She was relieved to see that her father's car wasn't in the driveway.

'There it is, baby girl,' said Laura, as they stood opposite the house. 'The house that Mummy grew up in.'

'It's really big.'

'Yes, it is,' said Laura, struggling to hold back the tears.

She put her hand to her mouth so Ella wouldn't hear her crying. She couldn't help herself. Just being there again brought back so many memories of her mother and Charlotte. There were so many good memories. She remembered learning to ride her bike outside with her father when she was about seven. She remembered so many moments growing up in that house and being so happy. Her first day at secondary school when she had left in her brand new, and slightly too large school uniform, with Dad while her mum cried and kept saying how she couldn't believe it. Memories like confetti blew through her mind, cascading down and drowning her in all of their wonderful colours. And then the last memory. The memory that would never leave her. The day she had come home from Tom's house, the day she had lost her virginity and her life felt perfect, and then her dad had come home with the policewoman and her entire world changed. The memory that would be stuck forever, pinned to her like the most important tweet. This is your life.

As Laura and Ella stood across the road from her father's house, the front door of the house unexpectedly opened and out walked a woman. Laura saw her immediately and didn't know what to think. Who was this woman leaving her father's house? A cleaner perhaps, but she didn't have any equipment or cleaning supplies. And surely she would have a car and there wasn't one parked outside his house. She was about the same age as her, so she thought that hopefully ruled out a girlfriend. She had long, red hair, was pale and slim, and wore a pair of black trousers and a white shirt. Laura watched her for a moment. She seemed comfortable there. She made sure the door was locked, and then she strolled casually out of the drive and onto the pavement opposite her. Laura and Ella were standing next to a Land Rover, and so Laura used that as cover. She watched the woman through the windows, and Laura was confused. Had her father taken in a lodger, perhaps? He couldn't be struggling financially. Maybe he was just lonely. It made her realise that in all the years she hadn't seen him that he had been living, and his life would have changed dramatically. He would have aged. It was silly, but when she thought of her father he was exactly the same as if she hadn't been gone at all. As if all the years she had been gone would vanish when she returned home. She would be sixteen again and him forty-three. But time hadn't stood still, and he, like her, would have changed so much.

'Come on, I have something to show you,' said Laura when the woman was out of sight.

'Is it the playground?' said Ella, who was getting a bit bored just looking at a house.

'Not quite, but I think you'll like it.'

She took Ella's hand, and they crossed over the road. They walked down another road and then turned down the small lane that went behind her father's house. Growing up, Laura had been forbidden to play or go outside of their garden. Her father had put a lock on the gate at the bottom of the garden so she couldn't get out. The lane ran behind all the houses on the street and provided access to the gardens. There were always motorbikes and bicycles parked on the lane, and a few of the houses had large enough garages at the back that they would drive their cars in. It had been a somewhat mysterious place to Laura as a child. A forbidden place and one of intrigue and danger. She held Ella's hand until they finally got to the gate at the bottom of her father's garden.

'Where are we?' said Ella as they stood at the gate and peered into the garden.

'That's my old garden,' said Laura, as nostalgia ripped through her body, tearing at her heart, pulling it one way and then the next.

It hadn't changed a bit. Her mother's old office stood like a relic from the past, still standing where it always had. Beyond that the garden was a little more overgrown than she remembered, and there in the middle of the garden was her tree. Laura loved that tree. She used to climb it when she was a child, and then her father had added the swing, and Laura and her mother had painted it blue and yellow. She remembered it like it was yesterday. She remembered how the wooden seat felt on her bare legs. The coarseness of it. The joy of swinging as high as she could with her parents telling her not to go too high or she might go all the way over and flip inside out. She could almost feel the sunshine on her face as she looked up at the sky, laughing with joy. She thought of her mother walking down to her office, where she would talk to people. Laura never understood when she was younger. Why would Mummy get paid just to talk to people at the bottom of their garden? It felt like such a silly job. It wasn't until Laura was much older that she truly understood.

'Can we go to the park now?' said Ella.

'Yes, of course, baby girl. It isn't far away.'

'Good, because I really want to play at the park.'

Laura looked down at her daughter, and a few tears gathered in her eyes, but she quickly brushed them away. She wanted the very best for Ella. She wondered what memories she would have of her childhood and how many more were still to come. She promised herself there and then that she would do whatever she could to make sure that she would have so many wonderful, beautiful memories. That she would make every choice in her life with her daughter first in her mind because she was the most important thing. Out of the chaos and horror of what had happened on that awful day, and the years of suffering that followed, the one and only good thing to have come out of it was Ella, and so she had to be perfect, and at that moment she was. Laura just had to make sure she stayed that way.

38.

Alexander was ten years old when he first left Scotland. He remembered it vividly. They crossed the border into England, and he felt like he'd flown on a plane to a faraway country. England. He had heard so much about it, but actually going there felt like the greatest adventure in the world. It was the first time he'd heard voices that weren't Scottish. It felt exotic to a small boy from Glasgow, who had only been to Edinburgh once. A week in Whitby by the beach. It had been a gloriously sunny week full of sandcastles, ice cream, and for the first time in his life, Alexander had seen a lighter side to his father. Up until that point, his father had been largely absent. Either at work or at the pub. He barely saw him, and when he did, it was never a pleasant experience. He was a man of a different era. A man moulded in the harsh, working-class tenements of Glasgow. He drank heavily to deal with the disappointments of his life. With the disappointment of Alexander. At least that's what Alexander thought. But in England during that week, something happened to him. A lightness came over him.

Alexander had a memory of him laughing on the beach. They were building a sandcastle. Alexander, his father, and Alexander's sister. It had taken them nearly all day, and it was quite impressive by the time it was done. People came by and commented on it and said how incredible it was. Other children looked at it with a heady mixture of admiration and jealousy. Alexander looked up at his father, who was standing and looking down at them, a cigarette hanging from his mouth, and he looked genuinely happy and proud of them. He smiled. At that moment, Alexander felt loved by his father. Properly loved the way a child should feel. They took a photo by the sandcastle, and Alexander remembered that when they got their photos developed back in Glasgow, how it made them all smile with nostalgia. They had fish and chips on the beach that night, and Alexander thought it was the happiest he had ever been. He wondered if that's how other children felt all the time, but more importantly, he didn't want it to stop.

Alexander was thinking about that moment as he sat in his car outside school. It was a Friday, and he was about to drive home. The feelings inside of him had been building for the past few months. The ten-year anniversary, if you could call it that, of that day was approaching. The day he sat in his car outside of school and made a decision. The decision that would alter the course of his life. The decision that had him sitting in his car on that Friday thinking about his father. Why his father? He had died many years before. Alexander hated his father for most of his life. He hadn't achieved anything, and he resented Alexander for the success he had. All Alexander had wanted in life was not to be him. Not to be bitter and cruel, sad and alone. Once upon a time, Alexander had everything he ever wanted. He had the life he had set out to achieve, and then he had ruined it. He had blown it up with one decision. One lie. He had been cruel to Olivia, and now as he sat in his car, he was sad and alone. Perhaps children are destined to repeat the mistakes of their parents. Did he really believe that? He hoped it wasn't true. And yet he didn't know because he didn't know his own daughter. She hated him. Her last words to him. A flash of anger on her face that had scared him. *I hate you!* Alexander had never yelled at his father that he hated him. He had never said the words out loud, but he had thought them almost daily.

Alexander had made the decision that tomorrow he was going to see his daughter again. Instead of watching her from afar, he was going to walk over and say hello. He had thought about it a great deal after he had lied to Belinda. He wondered what it would feel like to have a daughter again. He wanted it so much. Perhaps it had been having Belinda around. She had somehow jarred his memory. Before she had entered his life, he had been living in a bit of a fog. A daze of self-hatred and loathing. But she had given him hope in the same way that he had given her hope. Hope that there was a way back for him and Laura. That she might have some good memories of him, the way he had fond memories of his own father. Alexander's last thought as he sat in the car was that despite hating his father, he would have given him a second chance. If he had come to him and said sorry and that he loved him, Alexander would have let him back into his life in a heartbeat. He hoped Laura felt the same.

Alexander started his car and drove home. Belinda would be home already, and he was going to get fish and chips on the way, and then he was going to tell her the truth. It was the start of the rebuilding process. If he wanted Laura back in his life, then she would meet Belinda, and he wanted no more secrets. It was time to come clean.

'It smells wonderful,' said Belinda when Alexander took the fish out of the paper, and then piled the chips on two plates. The salt and vinegar hit her nose and took her back to a place in her own life. The smell of fish and chips. The treat that happened every few months when her father was actually working. He would come home, usually on a Friday, if he hadn't gone to the pub, with a big bag of fish and chips doused heavily in salt and vinegar. The hot steam from the chips hit her nose, and she felt like a child again. 'It's been so long since I've had fish and chips.'

'Me too,' said Alexander with a wistful smile.

There was something wonderfully nostalgic about it for the both of them. He laid the food out on the dining room table. He opened a bottle of wine, and Belinda had lemonade because she never drank alcohol. Still. They ate in silence, and when they were done, he asked her about her day, and she told him about working at the cafe. She enjoyed it, and it had given her the desire to go out and find something else. She wanted to work. She enjoyed the routine of it. She spoke about wanting to do something meaningful. Something that made a difference because there were other people who might fall down the cracks like her. People who through no fault of their own could end up on the streets, and she wanted to help them the same way that he had helped her. Alexander listened, and he was proud of her. The same way he would be proud of a daughter.

After they were finished, their stomachs full, Alexander cleared everything away and then they sat down. Alexander looked across at Belinda, and then he said.

'Ten years ago, almost to the week, my wife died. She was driving home and was involved in a car accident. A teenage girl died too. It changed my life.' Alexander stopped for a moment, choked on his own words. A few tears settled in his eyes. Belinda looked at him across the table, and then she reached across and put a hand over his. 'I lied to you when I said I met my daughter every week. I go and see her. I watch her playing with her daughter in the park, but we haven't had a relationship since my wife died. She blames me for what happened, and she's right, it was my fault. I killed them, and I've had to live with that guilt ever since.'

Alexander wiped the tears from his face. Belinda wouldn't tell him she already knew about his wife. She was surprised about his daughter, although now he had said it, it made sense. The sadness that sat in him like a physical object. The fact he never spoke about her or that she never came to visit. Belinda's heart broke for Alexander. She didn't know why he blamed himself for what happened, but she didn't care. All she cared about was the man she knew. The man full of empathy and love, who had taken her in and given her a new life. The man she would think of as the father she had always wanted. Alexander Burke was a good man, and no matter what had happened in his past, in her mind at least, he had redeemed himself.

It was fathers, Alexander thought to himself later. After they had talked, Belinda and Alexander had settled in to watch television together. Alexander wasn't really paying attention. He was thinking about tomorrow and about fathers. Belinda had been traumatised by hers, Alexander by his, and now Laura by him. Fathers and daughters. Why did they cause so much damage to each other? He hoped that tomorrow he could start fixing things. That he could begin gluing the cracks together again.

He thought of his father on that beach in Whitby. Why couldn't he have kept that going? Why when they got home, did he have to revert to his old self? Why couldn't he just love Alexander like that all the time? Maybe if he had, then his life would have been so different. Perhaps Olivia would still be alive. Maybe Laura would still love him. All of it was connected. Every relationship was like a brushstroke on a much larger painting. Each adding something and taking something away. He hoped that tomorrow was the beginning of a new painting. A fresh canvas that might somehow replace the old one and be even brighter and more vibrant.

39.

Laura had Ella in her arms as she frantically rang the doorbell, trying her best to stop the tears that had been streaming down her face since she had left their house. Their house. Now Jim's house. Luckily, it was late, and Ella was tired, so wasn't awake enough to know what was going on. She just knew that Mummy and Daddy had an argument. They had shouted a lot, especially Daddy, and then they had left and taken a taxi to Sam and Josh's flat. They were going to have a sleepover. It was almost dark, and Laura just wanted to get inside. She wanted to feel Sam's arms around her. She wanted him to tell her it was going to be all right. She had been running for the last ten years, and she was tired of it. She wanted to feel at home. She wanted to feel like she did before the day her mother had died.

Finally, the door opened, and Sam stood there, and when he saw her and the tears that were now cascading down her face, he immediately put his arms around them and ushered them inside his flat. Josh was already asleep, and so they quietly walked past his bedroom and through into the living area. Laura placed Ella down on the sofa, and she immediately fell asleep, her limp body sinking into the sofa. Sam went to get a blanket, and they placed it over her. They would transfer her into Josh's bedroom later. When they were done, they went into the kitchen, and Sam looked at her. He held her face in his hands.

'What happened?' he said quietly.

'It didn't go well. I broke Jim's heart, and I don't think he'll ever forgive me.'

Sam put his arms around her and pulled him into her. She cried into his shirt, her body shuddering against his. She knew telling Jim the truth would be hard, but she hadn't realised just how hard it would be, and how much it would take out of her.

Laura had put Ella to bed early. She was tired after their adventure, and she fell asleep quickly. She couldn't be there when she told Jim the truth. When she ripped his life apart. No child should have to watch that. Laura didn't want to do it, but knew she had no choice. The wheels had already been set in motion. She was leaving Jim and taking Ella with her. It was a choice that had already been made, and now she had to break the news to Jim.

She was cooking them dinner while he took a shower. She hadn't known what to cook for such an evening, but it had felt important. She ended up cooking Jim's favourite. Steak and kidney pie, chips, and baked beans. It did in so many ways sum up Jim. Plain, solid, and working class. Comfort food. A part of her would always love that about Jim. She knew all he wanted was to be loved, to provide, and to have a family. She admired that about him, and she felt rotten that she couldn't be the one to give him that. But being honest and ending things before they progressed, she felt was the honourable thing to do. Let him down gently while he still had enough time to build the life he wanted with someone else.

'Something smells good,' said Jim, walking into the kitchen.

His short hair was still slightly wet, and he smelled of his deodorant. He was in jeans and a tight, white t-shirt that sat flat against his hard body. Laura looked at him for a moment and felt a pang of pity. The poor bastard had no idea. Like a dog about to be put down.

'I made your favourite.'

'Lovely jubbly,' said Jim, always a fan of Only Fools and Horses.

'I'll bring it through in a minute.'

'Perfect,' said Jim, who grabbed a cold can of lager from the fridge before he went into the living room. They always ate in the living room in front of the television. They only used the dining room table if they had guests. Laura didn't particularly like it, but it was Jim's way. He said that growing up they always ate in front of the television. The dining room table was only for special occasions. Laura served up two plates of food and brought them through into their small living room. Jim was scrolling through the television for something to watch.

'Do you think we could talk rather than watch television?' said Laura, putting the plates down on the coffee table.

'Umm, yeah, sure, why not,' said Jim, who took a sip of his beer. 'Is something going on?'

'What do you mean?'

'You're being all weird, and Ella was in bed super early. It just feels like something's going on,' said Jim, before he took a sip of his beer.

He took his plate and started eating the pie first. Laura had always been fascinated by how Jim ate. When they first started going out, she would ask him questions about it all the time. If he had four things on a plate, he would eat them one at a time. Tonight, he was going to eat the pie first, then the beans, and finally the chips. Laura wasn't that hungry and casually picked at a couple of chips, dunking them in the small puddle of tomato ketchup on her plate.

'There is something I want to talk about,' said Laura finally.

She felt her heart racing. Her hands wouldn't settle.

'Oh yeah?'

He was oblivious. He hadn't seen the look on her face or detected the atmosphere in the room. Jim knew she wasn't entirely happy, but he also never imagined for a moment that she might be leaving him. In his mind, they were together for life. Like swans, he had joked once.

'I'm leaving you, Jim.'

He looked at her. Had he heard her properly? It had been a long day.

'What?'

'I'm sorry, Jim, but I'm leaving you. I'm not happy, and I haven't been for a long time. I think we both need a fresh start.'

She hadn't known how she was going to do it, but in the end, it had just come out. Blurted out quickly with very little care or thought. She just had to get it out there. Jim stopped eating, put his plate down on the coffee table along with his beer. He wiped his mouth with the side of his hand.

'Sorry, I don't understand. You're leaving me?' he said, looking at her for any signs of a smile in case she was joking. He didn't always get her humour. 'Is this a joke?'

'Jim,' she said, looking at him. 'You know I'm not happy.'

'Yeah, I know, but I thought with the holiday coming up, and Ella starting school—'

'It's more than that,' she said, cutting him off.

He looked at her. She could almost hear the thoughts running through his mind. He was trying to understand what was going on. Piecing it together brick by brick.

'Is there someone else?'

'Sorry?'

'You heard me. Is there someone else?' he said, slightly more aggressively than before.

She tensed up. She hadn't prepared herself for this question. It was a perfectly logical question, and she should have been ready for it, but she wasn't. So, when he asked her, and in the way he asked her, she replied without thinking. Straightforward. No more lies.

'Well, yes, sort of.'

'I knew it,' said Jim, who stood up suddenly and started pacing around the room like a caged animal. Jim had gone from this poor, injured creature she wanted to hug and make feel better to an aggressive and angry one rather fast. She recoiled against the sofa.

'Who is it?' said Jim, his voice full of spite.

'No one you know. I think you should calm down, Jim. Ella's asleep.'

'Don't tell me to calm down. I can't believe this.'

He paced around, rubbing his head. She had never seen him like that before. Not with her, anyway. There was that one time a few years ago, before they'd had Ella, when they were in the pub and a couple of men started causing trouble. One of them had tried chatting Laura up at the bar, and Jim had seen it. Jim approached the man, and without even asking what he was doing, he just punched him square in the face. The other man came across, but Jim was like a wild animal, and he went after him too. Laura hadn't liked the look on his face then, and she didn't like it again in their living room. There was something barbaric and uncivilised about him. Something primal.

'I'll kill him,' said Jim, almost to himself.

'Jim, please stop, you're scaring me.'

'What do you expect?' he said, turning to her. 'You shag another man and expect me to be all right with it? What's the matter with you, Louise? Huh?'

He was standing over her and shouting, and for a moment, a split second, the thought crossed her mind that he might hit her. He had never been physical with her before, but there was always a first time. She had this thought when she saw the anger in his eyes, and the vein that throbbed in his neck, and that's when the door opened and in walked Ella. She was holding Floyd the teddy loosely in her hand. Jim stopped and turned away so his daughter couldn't see his face.

'What's going on?' said a very sleepy Ella. 'Why is Daddy shouting?'

'Oh, it's nothing, baby girl,' said Laura, getting up from the sofa.

The conversation with Jim hadn't gone well, and Laura realised it was her chance to escape. She hadn't even told him about her name, and that she wasn't who she said she was. She needed to get out of the house and talk to Jim again when he had calmed down. She picked up Ella, who immediately snuggled into her neck, and faced Jim. He had his back to her.

'I think it's best we go,' said Laura, which caused Jim to turn around.

'Go where?' He had tears in his eyes.

'Just go. I'll pack a small bag for the both of us.'

She passed Ella to Jim while she went upstairs and packed a few days' worth of clothes for each of them. The night hadn't gone well. It wasn't what she had wanted. She wasn't entirely sure what she had expected, but not that. Not the shouting match and the anger. Not the fear that he might hurt her. She found herself visibly shaking when she was folding up some of Ella's clothes. When she got downstairs, she put their bags at the bottom of the stairs, got out her phone and ordered a taxi before she walked back into the front room. Jim was holding Ella on the sofa, rocking gently backwards and forwards.

'Don't do this, babe,' said Jim, who was crying more now. 'I can't lose you both.'

'You'll never lose Ella. She's yours, Jim. She'll always be yours, and I'd never do anything to get in the way of that. I promise,' said Laura, sitting down next to him.

He turned and looked at her. He was the poor injured animal again. It broke her heart.

'But without you, I'm nothing. I'll just die.'

'You won't, Jim. You don't need me. You'll find someone better than me. I'm not who you think I am at all.'

'What's that supposed to mean?'

She took a moment. A deep breath.

'My name's not Louise Bailey, it's Laura Burke. I've never been who you thought I was. When I'm gone, google my mother, Olivia Burke, and maybe you'll understand.'

When she finished speaking, her phone buzzed that her taxi was waiting outside.

'Time to go,' said Laura.

Jim could barely speak or comprehend everything that had just happened. Her name wasn't Louise. She wasn't who he thought she was. Had their entire relationship been a lie?

He handed Ella over to Laura because he couldn't face another fight. He was broken at that point. His mind pulled him away in too many different directions.

'I'm sorry, Jim. I never wanted to hurt you.'

Jim looked at her, his face red with tears and pain. She looked down at him and knew that she had hurt him so much that perhaps he might never fully recover. She knew that sort of pain. She still had the scars all of those years later. She couldn't help the tears that came as she walked out of the house. She left Jim a mess. He didn't get up and say anything before she left. She hoped he would be all right. She knew the fallout had only just begun. She got in the back of the taxi, and they pulled away. As they drove to Sam's flat, the awfulness of what had happened, of what she had done settled in her mind, and she cried. She tried so hard not to with Ella's body slumped against hers, but she couldn't help it. She had never wanted to hurt Jim. Perhaps she knew it was inevitable, but now it had happened, it was more painful than she thought possible. She was happy to finally be moving on with Sam, but to have broken someone's heart like that had its price, and it's a price she knew she would be paying for a long time.

40.

Alexander sat in his car across the road from the park. He took a couple of deep breaths, trying to compose himself. His hands were shaking nervously in his lap and a sickness sat in the pit of his stomach. The day had finally arrived. The day he had thought about constantly for the past ten years. He was going to see his daughter. She didn't know it yet, and maybe it wouldn't go as he hoped, but he knew he had to try. His life had reached a tipping point. Belinda had made him see that. He couldn't go on just watching her from afar, seeing his granddaughter and her not knowing he existed. It was time to come out and live in the world again. There was only so much pain and suffering a human heart could endure before it was too much, and they needed a release, or they would just give up. He didn't want to give up. He wanted to fight for his life. Olivia's death couldn't be for nothing. He took one last deep breath, and then he opened the car door and got out.

Charcoal clouds floated overhead with the promise of rain, and a gentle wind whipped around his ankles. He hoped she would be there. Perhaps with the weather she might have stayed at home, and his hopes, and all the bravery it took to get there would be dashed. Alexander had dressed slightly smarter than usual for his weekly trip to the park. Usually, he wore jeans and a casual top. Today he wore trousers, a shirt, and a new jacket he'd bought at Marks and Spencer. He wanted to look his best to see Laura and to meet his granddaughter for the first time.

Alexander walked slowly past the crowd of parents watching their children play football. Some parents screamed and shouted while others sipped quietly on their takeaway coffees. Flat white and skinny latte parents stood in their Barbour jackets gossiping about the latest school gate scandal. Alexander walked past them and on towards the playground where he could hear the shrieks of children playing and running around. The clouds moved overhead, getting darker and darker in the gun-metal sky. Alexander finally reached the edge of the playground. He was slightly hidden behind a small cluster of trees, but he could see the playground and all the parents. He scanned the playground, and no Laura. He looked down at his watch. It was almost ten-thirty. She was usually there by ten. His heart sank in his chest. He looked around the playground again, just in case he had missed her, but he hadn't. He stood behind the trees and looked down at his watch. He'd give it fifteen more minutes or until the heavens opened and it started pouring with rain.

Alexander waited anxiously. There would be other weekends. He also knew where she lived and he could go there, knock on the door, and say hello. He thought the park would be a better place for a meeting. It was neutral territory. If she really didn't want to see him, she could easily walk away. He would walk away too if it was too difficult for her. But that morning when he woke up, he was excited for the first time in a long time. He couldn't wait to speak to her again. He was equally terrified, but perhaps it would be the start of something new. He thought of the day when he had taken Belinda home for the first time, and how difficult it had been, but how their relationship had evolved and where they were now. Surely the same was possible with Laura.

He looked down at his watch. Fifteen minutes had almost passed, and the clouds were still just as dark and menacing. She wasn't coming. He was about to turn around and walk back to his car when he saw her. She was walking with Ella by her side. Ella was clutching a teddy in her hand and stomping her Wellington boots on the ground. But then next to her was a man he had never seen before. A man who wasn't her boyfriend. A man with a son about the same age as his granddaughter. They were talking and looked for all the world like one happy, lovely little family.

Alexander stood behind the trees and watched them. There was something different in Laura's face. The way she walked and the way she talked to the man. He was handsome, and just the sort of man Alexander would have picked for her. Smartly dressed, he was clearly someone successful, or at the very least a professional of some sort. They looked happy and were clearly together. As soon as they reached the playground, the children ran off, while Laura and the man sat on a bench together. He put his arm around her, and she rested her head on his shoulder. Alexander was confused. When he had found Laura, he had seen her with another man. The man he assumed was her boyfriend or husband, and the father of his granddaughter. But now she was clearly with this new man. Alexander wanted to know. He wanted to be a part of her life, her decisions, and to help. That was it. He wanted to help her. He had more than enough money from Olivia's life insurance that he had never been able to share with Laura. It remained in the bank, mostly untouched. A quarter of a million pounds that was just sitting in an account, waiting for Laura and his granddaughter. He wanted to help her, even if it was just financially.

A few spots of rain fell as Alexander stepped out from behind the trees. It was now or never. It had taken all of his courage, and all of his strength to be there at that moment. Regardless of the man she was with, Alexander knew he had to walk into that park and speak to his daughter. Another moment in his life and another decision. He walked towards the playground, and as he did, the rain got heavier. Umbrellas were shooting up all over the park. Parents were pulling up hoods, and the ones on the playground were gathering up their children. The clouds opened, and it started to pour. Alexander walked faster. He was nearer the playground than he was the trees that might have given him some cover. Laura and the man she was with quickly gathered up their children and hurried out of the park.

'Come on, baby girl,' said Laura, grabbing her quickly by

the hand, and they started walking away from Alexander. Ella had a little yellow raincoat, and Laura pulled the hood up for her. The man with Laura had a large, black umbrella, and he put that up so he could cover himself and Laura, while his son had a blue raincoat and Wellington boots. The kids laughed and giggled as they made their way out of the park and towards the road. Alexander followed them as quickly as he could. He wanted to see where they were going. Maybe he could see Laura somewhere else. Perhaps they could still talk. He didn't want to lose that day. The rain came down even harder. Across the park, the game of football had been abandoned, and parents and children ran for cover.

Laura and her little family were crossing the road towards a street that ran away from the park. Rain ran down Alexander's face as he followed them. He was maybe twenty feet behind them. He continued on quickly. He was almost at the road when he saw it. His granddaughter's teddy bear in the middle of the road. She must have dropped it. The brown lump lay in the road, sodden wet from all the rain. It looked sad. But she must love it, thought Alexander. He would retrieve it and give it to her. A hero before she even knew who he was. But then he saw her. His granddaughter peeking out from between two cars opposite. She had spotted her teddy in the road. She was going to get him. He was her favourite. Laura's sudden realisation that her daughter had stopped and was behind them.

'Ella!' called out Laura. 'Ella!'

Alexander didn't stop for a second. He saw what was about to happen. The possibility of Ella running into the road, and he started to run first. Ella. God, she was beautiful. Ella either hadn't heard her mother or she cared more for her teddy because she stepped out into the road. The rain was coming down in sheets. Alexander ran as fast as he could. He got to the road, and to teddy first. Ella had stopped a few feet in front of him. She saw the man getting her teddy. The kind man had saved Floyd. Alexander picked up teddy as the car came around the corner. Their windscreen wipers were on full, but there was barely any visibility, and they didn't expect a man to be stopped in the middle of the road. Alexander looked at Ella and he smiled. His beautiful granddaughter. God, she was perfect. He threw Floyd towards her just as the car hit him. The force of the car hitting him made Alexander's body fly through the air and land in the middle of the road ahead of them. The car skidded to a halt, half in the other lane. There was a sudden silence, and all they could hear was the rain smacking against the pavement.

'Ella!' Laura shouted in a panic and ran to pick up her daughter. 'Oh my god, baby girl.'

She grabbed her and held her close to her body.

The driver of the car got out. A young woman, early twenties, in complete shock.

'Oh no,' she said, her hand clasped to her mouth. 'I, I, didn't see him.'

It was then that Laura looked along the road and saw the man in the street. Sam immediately rang for an ambulance. Laura looked at the man, and even through the rain, he looked familiar. But it couldn't be. It was impossible. She passed Ella to Sam and then walked towards the man lying in the road. He hadn't moved. He wasn't moving. As she got nearer, the realisation crystallised in her mind. It was him. But what was he doing there? Had he saved her daughter's life. Was he alive?

'I rang for an ambulance,' said Sam from behind her.

'I can't believe this. I didn't see him, and then it was too late,' said the driver of the car. She began crying. Laura looked towards Sam for a moment, who had Josh and Ella at his feet, both holding his hand. They were all sodden wet. She walked over and knelt down beside her father.

'Dad?'

His eyes were barely open.

'Laura,' he said with a faint smile. His Scottish voice was soft and quiet.

'Oh my god,' said Laura, her hand over her mouth. 'Dad, what were you—'

'I was coming to see you, to tell you ....'

He reached out one of his hands to Laura. She saw and held it. Alexander looked up at his daughter. He felt pain all over his body. His head felt light and faraway. He could barely see, but he didn't know if it was just the rain.

'Tell me what?'

Alexander felt a strange sensation in his body.

'That I love you,' he said, barely getting the words out. 'And that I'm sorry.'

Her heart cracked. Alexander lay on the road, his daughter's hand tightly in his. He looked at her face. It was so beautiful. She hadn't aged a minute since the last time he'd seen her. Alexander felt the air leaving his body, and he knew what was going to happen. There on that street in the rain, he knew that was it. But he had seen his granddaughter. He had told Laura that he loved her. She smiled down at him. Her face was like an angel. Alexander Burke knew he was about to die.

41.

The tears on Laura's face joined the rain, so she couldn't tell which was which. It was all just water, different, but the same. She sat next to her father, holding his hand. She squeezed it tightly to let him know she was there. He seemed to be drifting in and out of consciousness. Laura barely felt the rain or thought about anything else but that moment.

'What's going on?' said Sam from behind her.

He had both kids next to him, looking on with a mixture of confusion and concern. They knew that something bad was happening, but they didn't know what. Laura could barely speak.

'It's my father,' she finally said.

'What? I don't understand,' said Sam incredulously.

Laura looked down at Alexander. He was barely conscious. His breathing was getting shallower. In the distance, Laura heard the sirens of an ambulance. They were on their way.

'They're coming, Dad. Hold on. Please hold on. I was thinking about coming to see you again. I was ready, Dad. I'm sorry it took so long, but I just needed some time.'

Alexander looked up at her. He smiled and then tried to breathe, but it felt impossible. His lungs were full of blood. That's what was going to kill him. He could feel a heaviness in his body. It wouldn't be long now. He could hear the sirens, but they wouldn't be there in time. He looked at his daughter. He wanted to speak. He wanted to say so much that he had been building up inside of him, but he couldn't. The words wouldn't come.

'You have a granddaughter. Her name's Ella,' said Laura between tears. 'She's four going on fourteen. You'd love her. She's so funny and smart. Smarter than me. I'm going to university next year to study law. Better late than never.'

Laura wanted him to know everything. She wanted him

to know that she still loved him. He was barely there. His eyes closed, and his breathing got slower and slower.

'I'm sorry,' said Laura, her tears getting stronger as the rain eased off. 'I love you, Dad.'

She squeezed his hand, and then he opened his eyes for one last time. The sirens were almost there.

'Love you too, baby girl.'

The last actual thought that Alexander Burke had before he died was more of a photo. It was a photo of them together. Olivia had loved it, and so she had framed it and put it on the stairs. It was the photo of Olivia, Alexander, and Laura at Seven Sisters Country Park in Sussex. They were standing by the cottages they had there, and in the background you could see the white cliffs and a wide flat beach. They all looked so happy. It had been one of those days. Warm, beautiful, and they had all been so happy. They didn't know it then, of course, but it was the last day they would ever have like that. It was about a month before Olivia died. Alexander remembered that photo. He thought of the image, and he remembered how he felt then. He remembered how happy they all were, and his heart filled with love. For a moment, and maybe it was just the endorphins rushing to his brain, but he felt euphoric. He felt so happy that he wanted to cry. He wanted to laugh. It was the last feeling he had. The last image he remembered. They were so happy. And then there, on that road in the rain, he died.

'Dad?' said Laura. 'Dad? Dad?'

She knew he was gone. She fell on his chest, resting her head against it, and she cried. All the tears she had left. Sam took the children away so they wouldn't have to see it. Laura sat with her father until the ambulance came. The paramedics rushed across but soon realised that they were too late. Sam walked across and took Laura in his arms. He held her and let her cry. The children came and hugged her too as the rain finally stopped, and then a police car arrived. Laura needed to sit down. She would have to talk to them, and the poor girl who had hit her father was distraught. Laura sat on a small wall outside someone's house, and as she did, a ray of sunshine poked through the clouds and shone on her. The sunlight hit her face and covered her in warmth, and for a moment, she closed her eyes and felt the sun on her. She felt happy to be alive. To have the chance to redeem herself. To put the past behind her. To move forwards. She didn't understand why her father had died. What the point of it was. Perhaps it was some sort of price for the death of her mother. Cosmic karma. Or perhaps it was just a random act of bad luck. Perhaps that's what all of life was. She thought about how she had tried to control everything, to put structure and meaning into her life, but when it came down to it, she was just at the mercy of luck, timing, and the consequences of her own decisions.

Both children were finally asleep. Sam had made up a temporary bed on Josh's floor for Ella, but they would need to sort out something more permanent soon. Laura had sat with them until they were both fast asleep. She enjoyed the darkness of the room. The feeling of two children falling asleep and feeling safe because she was in the room. She was there to protect them, and that's what she would do. She wandered into the living room. Sam was on the sofa, and there were two large glasses of wine on the coffee table. Laura walked over, sat down, and pulled her feet up next to Sam. She looked at him and smiled.

'You all right?' he said.

'Not really, but I will be.'

She reached across and took her glass of wine. She took a long sip. She enjoyed the feeling of it. The warmth of it. She enjoyed drinking it with Sam. She had finally found someone she wanted to spend the rest of her life with. Someone her father would have approved of.

'He would have liked you,' said Laura. 'My father. I think he was always a bit of a snob.'

'What does that say about me?'

'It says that you're the sort of man he wishes he was. Educated, a bit posh, and successful. He came from a working-class family from Glasgow, but he always wanted more. He was never happy just settling for something.'

'Is that where you get it from?'

'What?'

'Your dogged determination, strength, and drive to be better.'

'Probably. Although Mum was driven too, and brilliantly clever.'

'It seems like you got some good genes.'

'It's just a pity they both died too soon,' said Laura, and a wave of sadness gripped her again and she cried. She put her wine down and cuddled into Sam on the sofa. It had been an awful day. She still had to deal with Jim and sort her life out. She had so much to do, and everything felt very up in the air, and sort of translucent, but she had Sam. He was the one thing that would keep her from falling apart. She loved him with every ounce of her being.

Later that night, as Laura and Sam walked to bed, they poked their heads around the door and checked on the kids. They were both sleeping snug in their beds. Josh was sleeping with his bum in the air, in the most uncomfortable position imaginable, and Ella was on her back, arms overhead, and snoring away. For such a small human being, she couldn't half make a noise. Laura and Sam looked at each other, realising how lucky they were to have two such incredible little people under their roof, before they smiled at each other and then went to bed.

One Year Later

42.

Belinda looked out of the plane window at Dublin below. It felt surreal that after all of these years, she was finally going home. Home had always been such a difficult word for her. She didn't know what it really meant. Growing up, she had hated home. She loathed the awful drabness of it, and her father, who had cast a horrible shadow over everything. It had always felt intensely claustrophobic. It was a home she had grown up in but was never happy in. In London, she moved around from place to place, but none of them ever truly felt like home. They were just arbitrary buildings. Probably the place she felt most at home was with Alexander. She thought about him a lot on that short flight from London. She remembered the day when the woman had come to the door and explained that she was his daughter. Belinda didn't need her to say it because she knew as soon as she saw her. She could see Alexander in her and had seen enough photos of her as a teenager. She hadn't changed that much. She had come in and told Belinda what had happened. That Alexander had been killed. It had knocked the wind out of her. She had lost her own dad and now the man she thought of as her second father. She was crushed, and the home she had grown to love suddenly changed. Although she had stayed living there when Laura, Ella, Sam, and Josh had moved in, it slowly began to feel like their home and not hers.

The plane started the descent towards the runway, and Belinda felt a pang of nerves. Her mother was meeting her at the airport. She had seen her once when she had come over to London and stayed with Belinda's aunt. A meeting that had been both emotional and difficult. It was hard for Belinda to see her, to talk to her, and be around her without thinking of her father. He was gone, but the memories remained. The grip he had on them was still present. Her mother had aged, but she seemed happier than she had before. Without the constant threat of her father, she had changed. She had a job, and she was talking about moving out of that house. Too many memories, she had said. She wanted a small flat nearer to Dublin. Somewhere she could call home. Home. A difficult word for them both.

The plane touched down; the wheels landing heavily against the runway, and Belinda was back on Irish soil. She was returning for a new job. In London, after the cafe, she had found a position at a non-profit charity that worked to help the homeless. Her position was mainly clerical, but she enjoyed it. She liked knowing she was doing a job that meant something. That helped get people off the street. She worked there for six months, and when she heard of a similar charity in Dublin doing the same work, and they were hiring, she applied. She didn't think she'd get it, but she did, and a few weeks later she was landing at Dublin airport.

She got up with everyone else as the seatbelt sign went off with a ping. She heard a mixture of English and Irish voices, and they gradually all walked slowly off the plane. It was only the second time she'd been on a plane and in Dublin airport. The last time was when she left to go to London all of those years ago. When she had run away with the help of her darling brother. It felt like a different lifetime now. She was such a different person. She had come close to losing everything, but Alexander had saved her. She collected her suitcase, which Laura had kindly given her, and which contained all of her worldly possessions, and started the walk towards arrivals where her mother was waiting for her. Belinda was staying in her new flat until she could find herself somewhere to live. Laura had also very kindly given her some money to help her get started. She said it's what Alexander would have wanted.

Belinda walked with everyone else from the plane until she was out of arrivals. The small part of the airport was filled with people all waiting for someone. Husbands, wives, and friends. Belinda searched the crowd until she saw her mother, who was waving, and already had tears in her eyes. Belinda walked towards her, wheeling her suitcase behind her. She thought for a moment about the second when she had been standing on that railway bridge. Bare footed, afraid, and dirty. She stood there for a moment and contemplated the end. She had almost lost everything. She thought about Liam and the babies she had lost. The lives that could have been. She thought briefly of her brother, who had died so young. The boy who had so often put himself in front of her and took a beating from their father to save her. Her entire life, when she thought about it, she had needed saving. Now it was her turn to save others. That's what she wanted to do. And then she was in her mother's arms, tears falling down both of their cheeks, their bodies tightly squeezed together as one.

'Belinda, love, you're home,' said her mother between heavy sobs. 'I can't believe it.'

'I am,' said Belinda. 'I really am.'

Laura was in her mother's old office. She had opened the doors and let the sunshine in. It was a beautiful day outside. One of those gloriously sunny days when London came alive. It was still the morning, and they had talked about heading into London later. They might take a walk along the Southbank, have a stroll around The Tate gallery with the kids, and then have dinner at one of the pubs along the water. Life couldn't be more different now for Laura.

She was cleaning the office because they were turning it into a workspace for them both. Sam was going to use it for his writing, and Laura somewhere to study when she started university in the autumn. She had gained a place studying law at Kingston University. She was excited to finally be continuing on the journey she had started as a teenager. Life had taken her away from that journey for a while, but she was finally back on it. It wouldn't be the same, of course.

She was with Sam, and they had two children between them, but she would be a barrister. She would fulfil that goal and connect the dots between her old self and who she had become.

The office needed a good clean, and they were putting in two new desks. Sam would move his Mac out there, and Laura had a desk with another computer that she would use for her studies. They kept her mother's old sofa, and pushed it against the back wall, along with a coffee table to make a sort of mini living room between the two desks.

'How's it going?' said Sam, leaning against the office door.

'Good. Fancy a coffee?' said Laura. 'Mum's old machine is still here, and it still works. I think I have some pods inside.'

'Sure, why not,' said Sam with a gorgeous smile.

Josh and Ella were both running around the garden, enjoying the sunshine.

'Can you push us on the swing?' shouted Ella from the garden.

'My work is never done,' said Sam.

'That's a good thing, though, right?'

'Of course,' said Sam with a smile.

He walked across quickly and gave her a kiss. She felt the softness of his lips and the slight bristle of the beard he had grown. She liked it. It suited him.

'Love you,' she said, as he walked out.

'Love you too,' he replied, and then he disappeared into the garden.

Laura stood at the door for a moment and watched them. Ella went first, and Sam pushed her as high as he could, despite her protests to push her even higher. Josh watched on, waiting patiently for his turn. Laura remembered swinging on that swing as a child. It had just been her then. She had always longed for a sibling. A brother or sister to play with. She had never had one, but Josh and Ella had each other, and who knows, maybe they would have another one someday.

When Laura had arrived home that day, she would never have imagined the next year of her life. The story Belinda had told her about her own life, and how Alexander had saved her. It was incredible, and she had cried through the whole thing. She had liked Belinda very much. She had such an incredible energy and spirit, and despite what she had been through, she had such an enormous amount of empathy and love inside of her. You would think that someone who had been through what she had been through might lack both of those things. Surely the human heart could only feel so much pain, lose so much, before it stopped working. But Belinda had proved that not to be the case at all.

Luckily, things with Jim had worked out too. Once he had calmed down, and they had the chance to sit down and really talk, and he knew about her past, they had moved on. He was dating something new, and he had Ella every other weekend. Ella still loved her daddy, but she also loved Sam. Laura told Ella how lucky she was because she had two dads who loved her so much. 'Double love,' Ella had said in response. She was right. Ella had all the love in the world.

Laura watched the kids on the swing for a minute, and then she walked across to the corner of the room where she had put her mother's old record player. She had kept the record player, and her mother's stack of vinyl. Laura had a memory of dancing around the office with her mum, laughing and giggling, while they danced barefoot to one of her records. Laura looked through the pile of records: Wham, Duran Duran, Queen, The Smiths, Culture Club, UB40, Spandau Ballet. Laura looked through until she found the one she was looking for. She plugged the record player in and then pulled the record out of its sleeve. She put the record over the spindle, pushed the start button, and then put the tonearm down on the edge of the record. It crackled for a moment as it started to go around, and then it started. Dead or Alive, You Spin Me Around (Like A

274

Record). Laura turned up the volume. It took her back to that day she danced around the office with her mother. Barefoot and carefree. Laura started dancing, and then after a moment, Ella, Josh, and Sam walked in.

'What's going on here?' said Sam.

'A dance party,' said Laura.

Ella loved dancing and was soon dancing around the office with her mum, and Josh and Sam joined in too. Laura spun Ella around, and she laughed, and Laura smiled, and couldn't help but remember doing the same thing with her mother, her father in the garden, putting the finishing touches to the swing. Life had come full circle. If her life really was like a tree, as she had thought, she wondered where she was at that point. If childhood and adolescence were the trunk, and then she had been lost for a while on the wrong branch, where was she now? She supposed she had found a sturdy branch. A steady branch with a route right to the top. A branch that would hold and sustain her. She felt strong and stable for the first time in her adult life. She felt as though the tree was taking shape and blossoming. She had lost a lot, but it had made her more determined and better equipped to face any harsh winters that lurked around the corner.

'Another one,' said Ella when they had finished dancing. Laura walked across and looked through her mother's record collection again. She looked through the pile until she found the one she knew her mother loved.

'This was your grandmother's favourite,' said Laura.

She took off Dead or Alive and replaced it with the new record. She put the tonearm down, and then after a second it started.

'Although this time, I get to dance with Daddy.'

The beginning of Ever Fallen in Love (With Someone You Shouldn't've) by the Buzzcocks came on, and Laura grabbed Sam, and they started dancing around the room together. Ella and Josh danced together next to them.

'Well?' said Sam.

'Well, what?'

'Have you ever fallen in love with someone you shouldn't have?'

Laura smiled at him, and then she kissed him.

'Only you,' she said when she pulled away.

Laura and Sam danced together, and she thought of her parents. They loved that song. It was the first song they had danced together to at university. She remembered the story being told once after a few drinks. It was the first dance song at their wedding. Her parents. She was sad when she thought of them. A heaviness sat on her heart whenever she caught herself nostalgically remembering moments from her past, but now she had Sam and the kids, and a future to look forward to. She thought about something that Belinda had said to her once. They had been talking about her dad, and Belinda had looked at her and said in her lovely Irish accent,

'Death is never the end of the story, Laura. It's just the beginning of another one.'

That had stayed with her, and she thought about it often. Death wasn't the end of the story, just the beginning of another one.

43.

Before

Olivia had woken up first. For a moment, she wasn't sure where she was, and the beginnings of a hangover had just started to take hold. She looked across at the boy sleeping next to her. She was in his room in the shared house he lived in with three other boys. She couldn't believe that she had only met him last night. His long dark hair was splayed out on the pillow, and he had his pale, white arms over his head. She watched him sleeping for a moment. She didn't do one-night stands at all. He had been her first. Fragments of memories of the night before played through her mind. It had been the sort of night she had envisaged at university.

She had a quick look around the room. It was a small box, like most of the other student rooms she had been in. It was similar in size to her own, but while her room was decorated with photos, had a lovely rug on the floor, a potted plant, and a nice, warm duvet, his room was rather bland. A small desk with history books in a neat pile, a wardrobe, and that was it. Even the duvet was plain black. She thought his room funny because the boy she remembered from last night was anything but bland. He was funny, honest, and he excited her.

He slowly opened his eyes and looked at her. He looked equally as groggy as her. They hadn't been that drunk, but obviously drunk enough. She looked at him and smiled.

'Becky?' he said slowly.

'What?' she said, shocked that he hadn't remembered her name. He definitely didn't seem like the sort to play the field, and they'd had a magical night. He looked at her and then his face broke into a broad smile.

'I'm joking, Olivia. I wouldn't forget the name of my future wife.'

'Future wife?' she said, curiously.

He was either full of it or full of himself. That was quite a statement to make after only one night, no matter how good it was.

'Definitely.'

He got up onto his elbows, and then he leaned across and gave her a kiss. A long, slow kiss with morning breath. But neither of them cared. There was something special about that kiss.

'It's colder in your room than mine,' she said.

'Then you'd better get closer to me under the duvet. Body warmth.'

'Oh, that's the reason.'

'Amongst others.'

Olivia snuggled into Alexander under the duvet. Her legs rested against his, and his hand seemed to go straight to her hip. He ran a hand along the soft curves of her body. They were both naked except for their underwear, but it didn't feel remotely strange or uncomfortable for either of them. They both felt for the first time in their young lives completely comfortable with someone. Olivia and Alexander were just meant to be. Under the duvet, they looked at each other through the early morning light. Despite not going to sleep until nearly three o'clock in the morning, it was early. Both early risers. Old habits.

'Do you want to get breakfast soon? I'm starving,' said Olivia.

'Me too. I have a lecture at nine-thirty.'

'Me too.'

Alexander ducked out from underneath the duvet for a moment before he returned.

'It's almost eight o'clock,' he said.

'So?'

'So we have time.'

'For?'

Alexander leaned across and kissed Olivia, but this time he didn't stop. His hands moved from her hips to her breasts, and she leant back, and Alexander leaned across until he was on top of her. He looked down at her and smiled.

'What?' she said.

'I was just thinking about the future.'

'And what exactly were you thinking about the future, Alexander Burke?'

Alexander looked down at Olivia. She was the most beautiful girl he had ever met, and by far the most beautiful girl he had ever been in bed with. When Alexander said he was thinking about the future, he really meant he was thinking about the past. He was thinking about his childhood in Scotland, and how he had got to where he was now from there. There were moments during his childhood when he worried he'd get nowhere in life. That he would end up like his own father and his father before him. But there he was in bed with the most beautiful girl in the world at university in Bristol. He was studying history, and from that exact moment on, anything was possible. He was excited, and how could he not be? He wasn't his father. He was Alexander Burke, and this girl beneath him, Olivia Holmes, was going to be his wife, and one day they would have everything they ever wanted. He had never been surer of anything in his entire life.

Be sure to follow Jon on Twitter *@JRance75,* on Facebook *@JonRanceauthor,* and check out his website *www.jonrance.co.uk* for all the updates on his latest work.

Thank you for reading. I hope you enjoyed *One Lie.* Do leave a review if so on all your preferred platforms to help spread
the word!

Thank you!

Printed in Great Britain
by Amazon